Jaylin's World: Dare to Live in It

Jaylin's World: Dare to Live in It

Brenda Hampton

www.urbanbooks.net

Urban Books, LLC
78 East Industry Court
Deer Park, NY 11729

ISBN 13: 978-1-60162-335-5
ISBN 10: 1-60162-335-6

First Trade Paperback Printing February 2012
Printed in the United States of America

10 9 8 7 6 5 4 3 2 1

This is a work of fiction. Any references or similarities to actual events, real people, living, or dead, or to real locales are intended to give the novel a sense of reality. Any similarity in other names, characters, places, and incidents is entirely coincidental.

Distributed by Kensington Publishing Corp.
Submit Wholesale Orders to:
Kensington Publishing Corp.
C/O Penguin Group (USA) Inc.
Attention: Order Processing
405 Murray Hill Parkway
East Rutherford, NJ 07073-2316
Phone: 1-800-526-0275
Fax: 1-800-227-9604

ACKNOWLEDGMENTS

Thanks to all of my readers for continuing to take this *Naughty* journey with me. I know the ride has been long, laughable at times and shocking at others. While this is the last book in the series, I still view it as the beginning of something much bigger to come! Wait and we shall see!

To Jaylin Jerome Rogers, thanks for giving me your life, love, honesty, and most of all, your story. I couldn't have pulled this off without you, or without the support from my publisher, Urban Books. Thank you all!

Without further ado, *Naughty* is, as *Naughty* does. . . .

SCORPIO

Almost three weeks ago, my husband, Bruce, the kids and I were riding in our SUV and the unthinkable happened. As I sat in the hospital, still in shock, my mind drifted back to the powerful punch I had landed on the side of Bruce's face.

"You son of a bitch!" I yelled, with venom in my eyes. I had just looked at his cell phone, where his ex-girlfriend Mercedes had sent him a text message, telling him how spectacular his sex was the night before. I knew she wasn't lying about the two of them spending time together, because Bruce had crawled into our bed at two in the morning, smelling like sex.

"What in the hell are you talking about?" he shouted. "You always bitching about something, and that's why this marriage is so fucked up!"

"No, it's fucked up because you're a liar and I'm not going to keep being faithful to a man who cheats and who is unemployed!"

I held up his phone to show him the text message from Mercedes. He turned his head, snatching his phone from my hand. In an instant, our lives quickly changed. He swerved to avoid a Ford pickup truck in front of us that was carrying loads of plywood. The tires from the SUV screeched so loudly that I could still hear the sound in my ears. Smoke clouded the air, burned rubber filled my nostrils and our SUV flipped over numerous times. Our bodies were jerked around, and glass shattered every-where. The mangled metal squashed us all, and my neck was hurting so bad that I could barely turn around to see about my children. All I heard was Mackenzie crying, but Bruce Jr. was silent. Somehow, I managed to crawl out of the broken window, cutting my legs and arms even more. By that time, Bruce had, in his arms, what looked to be our lifeless son's body. Blood covered his entire body and his eyes were closed. Bruce kept shaking Bruce Jr., but got no response.

"Oh, my God!" I screamed, with tears pouring down my face. "Pluu . . . please tell me my baby isn't dead!"

Bruce looked at me with tears, hurt and pain in his eyes. "I—I don't know. . . ."

Mackenzie's cries snapped me out of my trance, as I couldn't believe what had happened. I rushed to help remove her from the wreckage. After Bruce carefully laid our son on the wet grass, he came over to help as well. We both pulled Mackenzie from what was left of the SUV; and once she was out, I tightly embraced her. She could barely stand up.

"It hurts, Mommie," she cried. "I'm hurting all over!"

I kissed her forehead to calm her. "It's going to be okay, honey. Help is on the way."

Bruce picked up Mackenzie, moving her away from the smoking SUV. He then used his cell phone to dial 911. I stumbled over to Bruce Jr., who was lying in the grass and looking helpless as ever. He wasn't breathing. At that moment, all I could do was secure him in my shaking arms and scream out at the top of my lungs, *"Noooooooooo!"*

Minutes later, I heard sirens; my head was spinning. I watched the paramedics work on both of my children, and I prayed for God to save them. When all was said and done, the paramedics told me that we were lucky and the seat belts had saved us.

Ever since that day, I'd been at the hospital, either in Mackenzie's room or in Bruce Jr.'s. Mackenzie had already had one surgery to repair her fractured arm and leg. Her body was badly bruised and she was in so much pain. The doctors said she was getting better by the day, but she couldn't catch a break from the pain. Her pretty face, which resembled mine, was covered with bandages, and her arm and her leg were in casts now. Her midsection was wrapped tight too. When she joked with me about how she looked like a mummy, I knew she'd be okay. I stood, placing soft kisses on her forehead.

"I love you," I said. "And you don't look like a mummy. You look like my little princess."

The Princess and the Frog." She smiled, referring to the black princess from Disney.

"Yes, baby. Just like her."

The doctors had given Mackenzie some medication for her pain, and the focus in her eyes was slowly fading. I rubbed her soft hair as the tears continued to fall from my eyes; then I kissed my nine-year-old child, and left to go see about my son.

As I walked down the hallway, my arms were folded in front of me. I felt so alone. Bruce Jr. was alive, but he had lost so much blood that he had to have a blood transfusion. I was skeptical about contaminated blood, particularly because of HIV, going into his body, but the doctor said the blood transfusion was necessary. Sure, with Bruce and me donating our own blood, I would feel safe, but according to the doctor, we really didn't have to do it. Our conversations with the doctor about blood types led from one thing to another. Bruce had said before that Bruce Jr. didn't look nothing at all like him; and when the doctor informed us that their blood types didn't even match, I could have died.

"Are you telling me this kid ain't mine? I knew it!" he shouted as the fury in his eyes cut me like a knife.

I was so embarrassed that this conversation was happening in front of the doctor, but what could I say or do, but come clean. I lowered my head, refusing to look at him. "No, he's not yours. He's someone else's."

Bruce let out a deep sigh and pounded his fist on the doctor's desk. I jumped, fearing that his fist would land somewhere on me. "You mean to tell me that you let me take care of another man's child for almost two fucking years, knowing that he wasn't mine! How low can you go, bitch? I guess I don't have to ask who his damn father is, do I?"

I wanted to defend my actions, but even I knew I'd been wrong for trying to keep this a secret. I looked Bruce straight in his eyes, knowing that our marriage was now over. "His father is Jay . . . Jaylin Rogers. I'm sorry for lying to you, but let's discuss this at home. Please do not disrespect me in front—"

"Disrespect? Really? Woman, you don't want to talk about disrespect, do you?" His face scrunched up, causing him to look like a raging monster.

Before I could answer, the doctor stood up, trying to calm the situation. Bruce didn't care what the doctor had to say, and there was no need for him to await a response from me. He left, but not before making it clear to me that he wanted a divorce. Yes, I'd known it all along, and from where else could Bruce Jr. have gotten his gray eyes and curly coal black hair? The secret I had planned to take with me to my grave was now revealed.

Bruce left the hospital that day, and ever since then, he had not returned. He was furious with me, but I didn't have time to entertain another argument with him. To me, it was the door he had been looking for, for months. We had been arguing about every little thing. After he'd lost his job at the bank, he'd gotten lazy and refused to look for another job. Everything was on me. Even though I didn't mind, I saw that Bruce hadn't put forth any effort to help me with our kids or with the bills. He had been running the streets and coming in when he felt like it. I hadn't had sex with him in months, only because I knew he'd been seeing Mercedes again. He denied my accusations, but the text message said it all. There was no doubt in my mind that he was with her now, instead of being at the hospital with me. That, in itself, was hard for me to swallow, but I just couldn't muster up enough energy to deal with him, when I was dealing with my kids.

I walked into the hospital room, slightly smiling at the wonderful nurse who had truly been there for me and for my children. Her name was Ann, and she stood next to Bruce Jr., checking his vitals. She pulled the sheets over him for comfort.

"How's Mackenzie doing this evening?" she whispered, trying not to wake Bruce Jr.

"She's okay. She just went to sleep too. How long has Bruce been asleep?"

"Not long. Why don't you go outside and get some fresh air. Or, go get something to eat. I know you haven't eaten anything today, have you?"

I shook my head, replying no. I hadn't eaten much at all, and I could tell I was down at least five to ten pounds since I'd been here. I used the bathrooms at the hospital to wash up, and my sister, Leslie, had brought me a few pieces of clothing to change into.

"I'll be okay, Ann. I'll get something to eat later."

Ann told me she'd bring me back a salad, and she left Bruce Jr. and me in peace. I sat next to his bed, looking at the tubes in his nose. His lungs had been punctured and he had IVs poking him in two different places. *My poor, poor baby,* I kept thinking. I hated to sit there and watch him suffer, but at this point, it was a waiting game. The doctors diagnosed that both of my children would get better, and I was grateful for that.

I scooted back in the chair next to Bruce's bed. The room was a bit chilly, so I tightened the pink fuzzy sweater I wore. I dabbed my red sore eyes with a tissue and blew my nose that wouldn't stop running. Trying to relax, I turned on the TV. Instead of watching it, though, I closed my eyes, thinking about how I'd gotten to this point in my life. My mind traveled back to the night Jaylin came to my house several years ago, suggesting that we would be *Naughty No More*. I told myself that I had to forget about what had happened that night. However, looking at Bruce Jr. every single day of his life, I couldn't forget. Even while I was pregnant, the thought of Jaylin being the father had crossed my mind numerous times. What he had put on me during his last visit to my condo was like magic. And according to him, a dream that he'd had brought him to my front door that day.

"Jaylin, I do love my fiancé, Bruce," I confirmed. "But I will never, ever love a man as much as I love you. So, if that's what you came here to hear, then I have no shame in saying it. Yes, I still love you, but there isn't a darn thing I can do about it. Who in the hell could blame me, after what you did for Mackenzie and me? You changed my entire life around. At the time we met, my life was headed for destruction. We endured a lot in our relationship, but overall, you were a blessing to me. Therefore, losing you was tough. I—I can't forget what we shared, and I will never forget. Call me stupid or whatever you want, but my love for you can never be replaced."

Jaylin was speechless and he continued to stare at me. He was so damn sexy, and his heart-piercing

*gray eyes, along with the Alicia Keys song "Like You'll
Never See Me Again" playing in the background, had
me so caught up. As we held each other closely, I felt
him rise down below. He slightly backed up, clearing
his throat.*

*"Listen, I gotta jet. I hope everything works out for
you and Bruce, and, uh, I appreciate you sharing with
me how you feel." He loosened our embrace and made
his way to the door. When he reached for the doorknob, I covered his hand with mine, halting his steps.*

*"I'm getting married soon. This might be our last
chance," I said. "Please stay with me for a while."*

*He turned to face me, locking his eyes with mine.
"Our last chance for what?"*

*I got on the tips of my toes and whispered in his ear,
"Last chance for us to be naughty. I will never interfere with your marriage to Nokea again. I wish you
and her nothing but future happiness. I hope you feel
the same way about me and Bruce, but please allow us
to have this one last time together."*

*He stood for a moment, seriously debating with
himself. I could tell he was so weak when it came to
me. I stepped forward and when my lips touched
his, he held my face in his hands, sucking my lips in
like kissing was going out of style. "Call Bruce," he
ordered, barely taking a breath between our kisses.
"Tell him to come much later. I—I gotta tell you about
a dream I had, but you gotta promise me that we will
be Naughty No More."*

*Rushing, I reached for his belt buckle before he
changed his mind. "After tonight," I said. "You go your
way and I'll go mine. I promise you there will be no
phone calls, no questions and no attachments. Let's
just get this over with and do something that we both
have been dying to do."*

Jaylin didn't say another word. He followed me to my bedroom. After I removed my clothes, his eyes scanned down my jaw-droppingly curvaceous naked body. Jaylin seemed hesitant, so I stepped up close to him, removing his clothes for him. As he stood naked, I dropped to my knees, inserting into my mouth the dick of a man I craved for. As the slurping sounds from my juicy wet mouth filled the room, his hands roamed in my long hair. He pumped my mouth, stroking it from every angle that he could. My hands massaged his tight, muscular ass, and not wanting his come to go to waste in my mouth, I backed up to the bed. My legs fell apart, and my index finger went into action. I slid it into my wetness, finger fucking myself as Jaylin observed. He loved to watch me perform on myself, but he could never watch for long. He dropped to the floor in front of me, pushing my legs close to my chest. The view for him was breathtaking. When I felt his tongue slide into me, I gasped, sucking in as much air as I could. My head dropped back, and I squeezed my watery eyes tightly together.

"Is it really you?" I cried out. "Baby, please confirm that it's really you doing this to me. It's been so long since I felt like this."

"It's me," he confirmed. "When I put this dick inside you, you'll know for sure that it's me."

Only Jaylin could suck my pussy this well, and his tongue was fiercely working my furrows from top to bottom. He circled my swollen sensitive clit and I was seconds away from popping an oozing cherry into his mouth.

"Hold on, baby," he said, feeling my legs tremble. "It has been a long time and I want to enjoy this for a little while longer."

My hands clawed the silk sheets and I took deep breaths, trying to calm the explosion sparking be-

tween my legs. It was so hard to do, and as my legs started to shake more, I felt Jaylin's tongue slither out of me.

"Turn on your stomach and get on your hands and knees," he ordered.

I rolled over, hiking my apple-bottom ass in the air while on my knees. My face dropped to a plush pillow as Jaylin's tongue went back into action. He pulled my butt cheeks apart, exposing my dripping wet slit from behind. Seconds later, he rimmed my anal hole by placing delicate licks on it, making his tongue flutter. I was losing my mind, and his tongue was feeling so good that more tears welled in my eyes. I couldn't believe how much love I still had for this man. And as his tongue traveled back and forth from each hole, I couldn't take it any longer. I was defeated and my nails scratched the sheets.

"What are you doing to me?" I cried out again. "Why are you doing this?"

Jaylin ignored me. He stood up straight, displaying every bulging muscle on his naked body. I did my best to calm myself. When his dick entered me, I felt as if my world was standing still. My insides expanded, and with every pleasurable thrust, we both let out satisfying moans that echoed loudly in the room.

"Mmph, mmph, mmph," he uttered as I kept throwing my pussy back to him. He held on tight to my hips while he swayed his hands against my soft curves. I turned my head to the side, anxious to see the look in his lustful eyes. The words that he spewed confirmed that he was enjoying himself, but I wanted to see how much. Jaylin's eyes were closed, and he kept wetting his lips with his tongue. His strokes inside me were so on point, and there was no doubt that we had one hell of a connection. I loved doing it doggy style with him, but I also wanted to feel his body on top of mine.

I wanted to slide my hands down his chiseled body and grip his ass, while forcing him into me. More than anything, I wanted him to come, so I reached my hands back to grab my cheeks. Every time he went in, I forced my cheeks together. When he pulled out, I opened them up wide. Jaylin, no doubt, was ecstatic. He replaced my hands with his. As he carefully observed his insertions, he had to let loose.

"Daaamn, Scorpio," he moaned tense as ever. He squeezed my ass, and that's when I felt a flood of his juices coat my walls. I inched forward, and his goods slipped from my insides. We were never known for wrapping it up after just one explosion. So when I lay on my back, Jaylin crawled between my legs. He held himself up over me, and I wrapped one of my legs around his waist. Like I had envisioned, I rubbed his body; then I slid my hands down to grip his butt. For a moment, we stared into each other's eyes.

"You never answered my question," I whispered. "Why are you doing this to me?"

He pecked my nose, continuing to stare at me again before saying anything.

"Just say it, Jaylin. Why are you here, and what made you want to do this with me?"

"I had a dream. I'll tell you about it later, but I'm here because I think I'm still in love with you."

Something went through me, and my body tingled all over. After all this time, I couldn't believe he had said those words to me. His words encouraged me to find out more, but he placed his finger on my lips to shush me.

"Not right now," he said. "We'll talk after we're finished."

Jaylin lowered his head to my breasts. As his tongue turned circles on my nipples, he inserted himself again. The skillful rhythms of his strokes were tearing up my insides—in a good way, of course. After intense fucking for at least an hour, we both cut loose together. Sweat ran from our bodies. We were breathless, taking in more juicy kisses and sharing just how much we had missed each other.

"Would you please tell me what's going on?" I said embracing him while I straddled his lap. "Are you and Nokea over?"

Jaylin comfortably held his head against my chest. His arms were around me and I softly rubbed through his sweaty curly hair. He began to tell me about a dream he'd had. Still, when all was said and done, according to him, he was still happily married to Nokea. Damn was all I could say, but after a performance like that, I could tell he wasn't happily married at all.

"I—I just had to do this, Scorpio. I needed this, and I missed you so damn much." He looked up at me and rubbed back my hair with his gentle hands. "That dream fucked me up, and I couldn't stop thinking about you. Understand, though, that no matter what I'm feeling right now, I can't . . . I just can't leave my wife. I love her a lot and that's not going to change."

It was no surprise to me how Jaylin felt about Nokea, but there was no guilt in me whatsoever. I just had to deal with his marriage, and since I was getting married in a few weeks, what the hell? We agreed to go our separate ways, but it felt good as hell for us to go out like we did. I promised him that I wouldn't hold on to something that would never be. I even cried in his arms that night, sharing with him how much it pained me to let him go—again.

Jaylin understood my frustrations, and on his drive to the hotel, he called to put me at ease. He again told me he loved me, and expressed his regrets that we could never seem to get our relationship to work out. We both agreed that things happened for a reason.

When I ended my call with Jaylin that night, he wished me well. Other than a letter his lawyer had sent, relinquishing Jaylin's parental rights to Mackenzie, this phone conversation was the last I'd heard from him. The letter was something that I requested. Even though I had the letter in my possession, I never, ever did anything with it. Something inside me didn't trust Bruce to do right by me, and I was right.

Now I had to focus on getting my kids better, and the thought of losing them made me think about Jaylin even more. Did he even deserve to know about his son? What about Mackenzie? He would kill me if something happened to her, and I didn't call to tell him. Besides, I didn't want to go through all of this alone. I needed Jaylin so bad, but I wasn't sure about telling him about his son. That would bring about so much trouble for me, and for his marriage. I was torn with my decision, but deep down, I knew that Jaylin had to know the truth.

NOKEA

I almost hated to say it, but life with Jaylin was so perfect. My husband was truly the best, and waking up with him every single morning made me the happiest woman in the world. He had a better attitude about life in general, and things really took a turn for the better when Shane moved to Miami Beach, Florida, with us. He and Jaylin had been doing well with their business ventures. Now, with two ambitious men working together, the sky was the limit. They'd made so much money in the housing/property market. Even though housing was in the negative, rich folks still had money to buy property. Just last week, Jaylin and Shane had closed a deal they'd been working on for months. It was an investment of $2.5 million that had turned into a payout of $9 million. I didn't know which one of them was the happiest, but a celebration was well in order.

Nanny B put together a dinner party for us that night, and we celebrated with our neighbors, and with Shane's girlfriend, Tiffanie. He'd met Tiffanie during a visit with us a while back. At the time, he was dating Scorpio and didn't want to complicate his relationship with her. Tiffanie was patient, though. When I told her that Shane was moving to Florida, she wasted no time getting to know him. They went on a few dates, and it wasn't long before he started spending a lot of time at her house. Her family owned several exquisite restaurants, Leylah's Kitchen, named after her mother, and Tiffanie had a lot to bring to the table. Even so, Shane seemed to hold back a little. He talked to other women on occasion, and he had gone out on a few dates with other women. I hadn't said anything to Tiffanie about this.

Tiffanie wanted him to move in with her, but for now, he continued to stay with Jaylin and me. Of course, Jaylin didn't mind, and I think they wouldn't have had it any other way. Most of their business was handled at home, but a few months ago, they rented an office space, which was less than five miles away. Jaylin made it clear that he didn't want to do any heavy work, but to be honest, he and Shane were starting to spend a lot of time away from home. That was okay with me—as long as Jaylin was happy, I was happy.

I guess the only thing in the world that troubled me was the fact that I still hadn't conceived another child. I mean, the doctors said my chances were slim, but I had hoped that they were wrong. Jaylin and I often made love, but both of us were over the age of thirty-six; we weren't getting any younger. Jaylin hadn't said anything about another baby, but I knew he hadn't said anything because he didn't want to hurt my feelings. For the time being, LJ and Jaylene were truly enough. We loved them with every fiber of our beings, and they made our lives feel so complete. I wouldn't trade my life for anything in the world, and I was so blessed to have a family that loved me so much.

On Saturday, Jaylin, Shane, Tiffanie and I were on the beach playing volleyball. The weather was perfect. At ninety degrees, no one was complaining. I wore a nude-colored bikini that meshed well with my caramel-colored skin. Jaylin and Shane were in swimming trunks, and Tiffanie had on a white bikini. She and Shane were winning the game, simply because Jaylin couldn't seem to concentrate. He was too busy standing behind me, complimenting my backside and watching me do all of the work. Shane served the ball over the net, and when Jaylin hit it back over, he ran up from behind and grabbed my waist. Tiffanie hit it back over, but Jaylin let the ball fall in the sand. He pecked down the side of my neck.

"Are y'all going to play ball or what?" Shane asked.

Jaylin ignored Shane, then squatted down. "Get on my shoulders," he said, holding the ball in his hand. "We will win this game."

I straddled Jaylin's strong shoulders and he stood up, balancing me with no problem.

"What's up now?" he said to Shane and Tiffanie.

Tiffanie put her hand on her hip. "That is so unfair. You guys . . ."

Before she said another word, Shane lifted her, placing her on his shoulders. She laughed and held on tight. As slim as she was, I didn't think Shane would have a problem balancing her either. When I served the ball over the net, she did her best to hit it. She wobbled on Shane's shoulder, but he kept telling her that he wouldn't let her fall.

"Are you sure?" she said, purposely waving her hands in the air. She put Shane's strength to the test. Since she kept wobbling around, they both fell to the sand. Jaylin called the game after that; with me still on his shoulders, he jogged back to our house. I was laughing and bouncing all around, knowing that there wasn't a chance in hell he'd let me fall. When we got to our house, Jaylin carefully lowered me to the ground. We entered the house through the sliding glass doors and made our way into the oversized kitchen. Nanny B had an apple pie baking in the oven; it filled my nose with pure sweetness. Shane and Tiffanie came in, sniffing at the aroma as well.

"What else is for dinner tonight?" Jaylin asked, opening the refrigerator. "I'm surprised all Nanny B has in the oven is a pie."

"I told her not to cook dinner," I said. "I thought we could all go out to dinner."

Shane and Jaylin eyeballed each other.

"You and Jaylin can go," Shane said. "I gotta catch up on some work."

A tiny frown covered Tiffanie's face. "But, honey," she whined, "it's the weekend. I want to go to dinner, and can't you put off what you have to do until tomorrow?"

Shane glanced at Jaylin again. "Not tonight," Shane said. "If I could, I would."

He took Tiffanie's hand and left the kitchen. They headed to the lower level, where his living quarters were. I didn't want to pry, but I had to.

"What's up with that?" I asked.

Jaylin bit into an apple, doing his best to play it off. "What's up with what?"

"The two of you eyeballing each other."

Jaylin shrugged; then he walked off to our bedroom. I followed behind, still waiting for an answer.

"Out with it, Jaylin," I said, following him into his spacious walk-in closet. "Come on and tell me. What's up with Shane and Tiffanie?"

Jaylin removed his shorts and grabbed a pair of stonewashed jeans from a hanger. He tossed the jeans over his shoulder and stood naked. "Whatever is going on, it's not our business. All you need to be concerned about is me, not them."

I stepped forward and eased my arms around his perfectly cut waistline. "I am always concerned about you, but I know how much Tiffanie likes Shane. Is he not feeling her anymore? If not, he should be honest with her about how he feels."

"Oh, he's definitely feeling her, but he may be feeling other people too. Tiffanie needs to stop forcing him to be with her, and the worst thing a woman can do is force herself on a man. If she backs off a bit, he'll come around."

"Back off," I said, surprised. Tiffanie had in no way been pressuring Shane about anything, and what Jaylin said made no sense to me. "Jaylin, she's not pressuring him. She gives Shane all of the space he needs! Like I said, if he's falling for someone else, then he needs to be honest."

Jaylin stared at me, then sighed. "Please, please don't get yourself involved in this. I know you like Tiffanie, but their relationship is none of your business. Back off, Nokea. I can see it in your eyes that you really want the two of them together, but they have to want that too."

"I do. They make a beautiful couple, and Shane has waited almost a lifetime to find happiness. A good woman is staring him in the face, and I hope he realizes it."

"He will," Jaylin said, reaching for the closet door and slamming it shut. He hit the light switch, leaving us in complete darkness. I waited for him to say something, but he didn't. I felt around for him, but he wasn't there.

"*Jaaaylin,*" I sang out. "Where *arrre* you?"

He said not a word in return. Just as I was getting ready to move over to the light switch, I felt my bikini bottoms coming down. I stepped out of them, and knelt on the floor in front of him. We embraced, and his hands slid down over my curvy backside.

"So, is this how we're doing it now, huh?" I asked.

"Yep. 'Cause every time I put you in that bed out there, our kids come running in here, trying to be nosy.

It's worked out for us in the closet before, and since I was in the mood to dip into that pussy, what the hell?"

I laughed, knowing Jaylin was so right. Lately it seemed as if Jaylene, who was four years old now, and LJ, who was almost seven, weren't giving us any breathing room at all. Nanny B kept them as busy as she could, and on Saturdays, Jaylin and I always tried to set aside that day for ourselves. It didn't matter one bit to me where we made love. We had done it all over this house, and just last week we found ourselves getting a quickie in the garage.

I lay back on the floor, and as soon as Jaylin cracked his code, someone knocked on the closet door. I couldn't help but laugh, for I had a feeling who it was.

Jaylin put his lips to my ear. "Shh," he whispered. "Stop laughing and do not respond."

"Mommie . . . Daddy," LJ said, knocking. "Are you in there?"

Jaylin must have known that I was getting ready to open my mouth, so he placed his hand over it. I chuckled a bit, knowing that LJ was not going away. Moments later, Jaylene's voice sounded off.

"Daddy," she said in her sweet, timid voice. "Please open the door."

Jaylin dropped his head on my chest. "Damn," he whispered. "I can't believe this shit. How in the hell did they know we were in here? This is so fucked up."

He slowly pulled out of me, then crawled his way to the door. He cracked it a bit and looked at them on the other side. "Yes," he said. "What is it?"

"We want some ice cream and cake," LJ said. "Nanna told us to ask you if we could have some before dinner and she said we should wait until the apple pie—"

"Yes. Please eat as much cake, pie . . . ice cream as you'd like."

I heard them run away from the door, and Jaylin crawled his way back over to me. He circled his thick head against my slit, making sure I was still wet. . . . I was. Trying to rush, he quickly cracked my code again. This time, he was able to get off more strokes. He whispered that he loved me, and just as I switched to a doggy-style position, another knock interrupted us. Jaylin slowly eased in and out of me, yelling out, "What?"

"Nanna said—"

"To hell with what Nanna said," Jaylin shouted. "Go get your ice cream and cake! Do not knock on this door again, and I will be out in a few minutes!"

"Mommie too?" LJ added.

We couldn't help but laugh. I gave up and moved myself forward. Jaylin pulled my hips back to him. "Hell nah," he whispered. "We ain't finished yet." He paused his strokes. "LJ, your mother is not in here. She's outside."

"Uh-uh. You're lying to me, Daddy. I saw her. . . ."

I would have given anything to see Jaylin's face. "Did his ass just call me a liar? Fuck naw." Jaylin backed up a bit, but I quickly grabbed his hand.

"LJ, I'll be out in a minute," I said. "I'm looking for something to wear tonight, okay?"

"Okay," he said. I heard him walk away again.

I backed up to Jaylin, and we hurried to finish up. It didn't come without a fuss, though, and Jaylin couldn't seem to get what LJ had said to him off his mind.

"Well, you did lie to him," I said, putting on Jaylin's long white pressed shirt to cover up.

He was zipping his jeans, and couldn't believe I had defended LJ. "I don't care what you say, he was out of line. He don't say no shit like that, and I'm going out there to see what's up with him."

Jaylin left the closet, but I wasn't worried about anything. When it came to his kids, he was a big ole wuss.

They had him wrapped around their fingers, and he hadn't disciplined either of them a day in their lives. Now, he would scare them when he raised his voice, but that was it. I, however, had no room to talk about Jaylin. My parents taught me never to put my hands on my children. They were given timeouts and stuff like that, but there was no denying that Jaylene and LJ were two very spoiled children.

When I stepped into the kitchen, Nanny B was standing near the refrigerator, shaking her head. Jaylin stood behind LJ, looking at him like he was crazy. LJ and Jaylene had two big bowls full of ice cream and thick slices of chocolate cake. LJ's jaws were too fat for him to swallow, and Jaylene had chocolate all on her face and hands.

"Mommie," she said, holding out her hands to me, "this is de-delicious!"

LJ nodded, and Jaylin playfully slapped the back of his head. "You are a bad example for your sister. I can't believe Nanna let y'all do this."

Nanny B pursed her lips. "You told them to have at it, so I did. I let them get whatever they wanted, and don't blame me because you told them to eat as much as they wanted."

Somebody had to get order in this place, so I removed their bowls and made both of them get up from the table. Jaylene had the nerve to cry, and LJ pouted. They both ran to Jaylin for comfort. Like always, he was the sucker.

"Leave their bowls alone, Nokea. I'm the one who told them to get it. I'll clean up the mess."

"No," I said, dumping their bowls in the trash. "Eating this much cake and ice cream will make them sick." Jaylene threw a fit, but I ignored her. She wailed out loudly and Jaylin went to the rescue. He put her in his arms and started to tickle her belly. LJ was hanging on to his leg; he was so jealous that Jaylin hadn't picked him up. Nanny B made it all better when she suggested they go watch *The Princess and the Frog*. LJ was in love with the princess, and Jaylene wanted to be her. They rushed out of the kitchen with Nanny B, leaving me there to clean up their mess.

"I thought you were going to clean this up," I said to Jaylin, wiping down the table with a wet rag.

"I was, but then I thought about your horny ass in the closet. You should have let me leave, but you kept backing that ass up to me and wouldn't let me go. If you would have come out of the closet like your kids asked you to, then you wouldn't be in this predicament."

I pointed to my chest. "Me horny? No, I don't think so. That was your horny self, and you were the one who . . ."

I paused when I saw Tiffanie come up the steps. Her eyes were red, and it looked as if she'd been crying.

"Are you okay?" I asked.

She sniffled and combed back her straight black hair with her fingers. To me, she could have been Zoe Saldana's twin. I couldn't believe that as pretty as she was, Shane was causing her grief. He definitely had to be out of his mind, because Tiffanie probably had many, many options.

"I'm fine, Nokea. I'm on my way home. I'll see you sometime tomorrow."

Jaylin didn't say a word. Obviously, he knew what was going on, but didn't want to tell me. I walked Tiffanie to the door. After I let her out, I went back into the kitchen to find Jaylin. He wasn't there. I suspected that he'd gone to the lower level to talk to Shane. I didn't like being kept in the dark, but truthfully, it wasn't any of my business. I figured I'd talk to Tiffanie later. After I cleaned up the kitchen, I went to my bedroom to shower and change into something casual for dinner.

***

Dinner was cozy and delicious. Jaylin and I walked to a sushi bar close by. On the way back, I hugged his waist, while he had his arm around my shoulder. Life had been so good to us, and I was a bit disappointed that Tiffanie and Shane couldn't get their act together.

"I'm staying out of it, Jaylin, but I hope Shane knows what he's doing. Tiffanie is a jewel, and he's always talked about meeting a woman who has her head on straight."

"Truth is, Nokea, Shane just ain't ready to settle down. He's talking to a few other chicks, and Tiffanie is having a hard time accepting that. He already told her that he wasn't ready for the kind of relationship she wants. When he suggested that they take it slow and just be friends, she got upset. If you ask me, he's being too damn nice to her. He needs to cut her off, until she's willing to abide by the rules."

I slowed my pace, easing my arms from around Jaylin's waist. "That's not nice. I knew Shane was talking to other people, but I didn't think it was serious. Maybe Tiffanie should just back off, because no woman needs to keep pursuing a man who doesn't want her."

Jaylin pulled me back into his arms. "It's not that he doesn't like her, and believe me when I say he does. Shane is just . . . He's funny-acting about relationships. Since he's been burned so many times, it's hard for him to keep putting his heart into relationships. Whatever he decides, I got his back. He'll know when the time is right, and only the man himself knows when that time really is."

Jaylin and I went into the house, but everyone was asleep. Shane was gone, and Jaylin said he was at a friend's house. It was after midnight, so I changed into my short peach nightgown and got into bed. Like

always, Jaylin stripped naked and climbed into bed behind me. He cradled my backside and kissed my cheek.

"Good night," I said, turning my cheek up to him. "I
love you."

"I love you too, but you'd better remove that nightgown so we can finish what we started in the closet
earlier. I had to rush, and now I can take my time, since
the kids are asleep."

I swear, as soon as those words left his mouth, the
double doors to our bedroom squeaked open. Jaylene
stood in a soft pink nightgown, while holding a white
teddy bear in her hand. Her thick, long pigtails were
braided past her shoulders, and she had on a game
face for her daddy. She held the teddy bear against
her chest, and her big, round gray eyes stared right at
Jaylin.

"Daddy, can I sleep in bed with you?" she said, sway-
ing from side to side.

Jaylin dropped his head back on the plush pillow,
letting out a deep sigh. "When . . . Why in the hell did
these kids learn how to walk? We didn't have this problem when they couldn't walk. We have got to get a lock
on those doors."

Before Jaylin could say anything else, Jaylene had
run into the room and got into bed with us. She was
all smiles, and Jaylin couldn't do nothing but cover his
bottom half with the covers. He put his arms around
Jaylene, and she laid her head on his shoulder. Within
minutes, she was out.

"Psst," he whispered over to me. "Are you asleep
too?"

I yawned and chuckled underneath my breath. "I'm
on my way."

"You think this shit funny, don't you?"

"It is funny. And that's what you get for spoiling her
so much. She's going to keep doing that every single

night. Until you start telling her no, then you can forget about getting some nooky."

Jaylin looked at Jaylene and kissed her forehead. She moved around; then she tightened her arms around his neck. I couldn't help but laugh and turn my back.

"Psst," he whispered again. "What you doing?"

"I'm going to sleep."

"Damn, that's fucked up. I thought you'd play with my dick or something. You can bring some kind of excitement to a brotha, can't you?"

I reached over and rubbed my hand on top of the cover; I felt his hardness. After I slapped my hand around a few times, I turned my back and smiled.

"Dang, you wrong for that." He pinched my butt really hard.

"Ouch," I yelled, and then moved over. "That hurt!"

"Good. And whenever I make my way into it again, I'm gonna kill it! I can promise you that."

"I look forward to it. Now go to sleep. Thanks to your precious little child, you don't have anything coming tonight."

He agreed, and within the hour, we had all fallen asleep. I was knocked out, until I heard the phone ring. It was on the nightstand next to Jaylin, and he reached over to answer it.

"Hello," he said in a groggy, soft tone. "Who?" He paused for a while. Figuring that it was Shane, I barely tuned in. I glanced at the alarm clock and it showed 3:45. My eyes were too tired to stay open, but I heard Jaylin say, "All right, tomorrow." He hung up the phone.

When I asked who it was, he confirmed that it was Shane. I glanced over at LJ, who was now in the bed with us too. I dropped my head on the pillow so I could go back to sleep.

JAYLIN

The phone call I'd gotten last night shocked the hell out of me. All I could hear was Scorpio crying over the phone, telling me that she needed to talk to me as soon as possible. I had no idea what was going on. Even though I wanted to elaborate on her purpose for the call, I couldn't. Nokea was awake, and there was no way I was going to tell her Scorpio was on the phone.

Yes, I was a bit nervous about the call, and it had been at least two years . . . more than that, since I'd last seen her. I'd be lying if I said I hadn't thought about her from time to time, but it wasn't like my thoughts of her were interfering with my marriage. I figured she was pretty happy with Bruce. Also, since I'd given up my parental rights to Mackenzie, everything, to me, was a done deal. That was something I never, ever wanted to do, but Scorpio made me feel so guilty for trying to hold her back. She had agreed to keep what had happened between us a secret, and the least I could do was give her something she had asked me for in return. The decision I'd made about Mackenzie didn't come easy. As a matter of fact, that shit hurt me like hell. I wasn't quite right after doing that. To this day, it disturbed me that Mackenzie was not a part of my life. She was the person who'd shown me how to love somebody, and giving up my parental rights to her was like giving up on the love of my life.

On Sunday, I told Nokea that Shane and I were going to the office to catch up on some work. She knew

I'd been spending some time at our new office, but she also knew that this was something I didn't want to do on a regular basis. I told her I'd be back soon. Even though I wanted to tell Shane about the phone call from Scorpio, I didn't. I wasn't sure how he would feel about it. After all, the two of them used to be lovers.

As soon as we got to our building, Shane went into his office and got on his computer. I went into my office and closed the door. I sat back in the leather swivel chair; then I picked up the phone. I called Scorpio's cell phone number as I kept taking peeks at Shane through the tall glass windows. He seemed occupied, so I didn't expect any interruptions. Scorpio answered her phone, causing my stomach to feel queasy.

"It's Jaylin. What was up with your call in the middle of the night?"

"I'm sorry about calling so early in the morning, but I figured everyone would be asleep. I—I need you, Jaylin," she said as her voice cracked. "I don't mean to burden you with this, but I need you so bad."

I laid my index finger on the side of my face, almost afraid to ask her why she needed me. "What's going on, Scorpio?"

"My babies were in a car accident. They almost lost their lives, and I'm so—"

"Who? Mackenzie? Mackenzie was in a car accident?" My brows went up.

"Yes. She was badly hurt, Jaylin, and I can't do this alone."

"Why you . . . When did this happen?"

"Almost three weeks ago. She's been in the hospital since then, and she broke—"

"Why you just now calling me? It's been three fucking weeks and you just now calling? How serious is it?" My face was scrunched, and I could feel my frustrations building.

"She broke her leg and arm. Her whole body is messed up. She's covered with bruises, but the doctors said she'll pull through this. My son is messed up pretty bad too, and—"

"Where are you?" I was mad as hell at Scorpio for just now calling me. And even though Mackenzie was my adopted child, that I had given up my parental rights to, I still cared about her well being. I figured Scorpio was probably going through, so I did my best not to upset her—for now.

"I'm at Cardinal Glennon Hospital. I've been here since the accident happened, and I—I feel as if I'm losing my mind. I want to take my babies home, but the hospital—"

"If they need care, then you gotta let the doctors do what they have to do." I glanced at my watch. It was one-fifteen. "Calm down, all right? I'll get a flight out of here as soon as I can."

"Thank you," she rushed to say. "You have no idea what this means to me."

"You know how I feel about Mackenzie, Scorpio. A piece of paper will never diminish what we have. Let her know I'm on my way."

I hung up. Even though I knew this shit was not going to sit right with Nokea, there was no way for me not to go to St. Louis. I wasn't even sure how I was going to break the news to Shane either. Before I went into his office, I came up with something.

I sat on the leather sofa in his office and placed my hands behind my head. "Check this out. . . . I just got off the phone with this brotha I met a while back. He's from Chicago, and he wants me to fly in tonight to check out some property he got for sale. I'm gon' shoot there, stay the night, then come back this way tomorrow."

"Do you need me to go with you? I'm not doing anything else, and I can let you know if I think the investment will be worth it."

"Nah, just chill. If it turns out to be something worthy, you and I will go back together later."

Shane nodded; then he looked down at his vibrating cell phone. He sighed, so I knew it was Tiffanie.

"Yeah, baby," he said, then paused. He rolled his eyes, then massaged his temples. "Yes, I'm working right now. I'm at the office with Jaylin and we're in the middle of a meeting." He paused and looked over at me, shaking his head. "Okay. Dinner sounds good. I'll see you around eight or nine o'clock tonight." He paused for a long while; then he ended his call.

"Look, man. If you don't want to be bothered with her, then tell her. Why you stressing like that over a woman you don't seem to care much for?"

"I am digging the hell out of Tiffanie, but like I said, she always trying to plan my life out for me. I gotta be on her schedule. When I got plans to do something else, her feelings get hurt. She's always getting emotional, and I don't like that shit, man. I like a strong woman, and Tiffanie ain't really representing that."

"I know what you mean, but ease up on her. She is a nice woman. If or when you get too tired of the shit, back out of it."

I looked at my watch again; then I told Shane I had to go book my flight. Before I did, I called Nokea to tell her my plans. I didn't like lying to her, but for now, I had to do what was necessary.

"Are you at least coming home to say good-bye? I can't believe it's that urgent where you have to rush out right now," she said.

"The faster I get out of here, the quicker I'll get back. I'll be back tomorrow, and it shouldn't really take that long."

I could always hear the disappointment in Nokea's voice. She didn't like being away from me, and I didn't like being away from her either.

"Okay, baby. Be careful and call me when you get to Chicago."

"Will do," I said, and then I extended my love to her.

Shane dropped me off at the airport, and almost four hours later, my plane had landed in St. Louis. I got a rental car, and then I drove to Cardinal Glennon Hospital. During my ride, I couldn't help but think about Mackenzie. I was mad at myself for giving up on her, and it was not a good feeling. Thinking so much about Mackenzie caused me to think about my long-lost daughter, Jasmine. I hadn't seen her since she was a year old, and it was like she and her mother, Simone, had disappeared. They had to be living in another country or something. I'd put out so much money for private detectives; but with no success, I gave up. I didn't want to, but I felt as if I had to accept my blessings, LJ and Jaylene, and move on. I even thought about the son Scorpio had mentioned. I didn't even know she'd had a baby, and I hoped that my visit wouldn't interfere with her marriage to Bruce. I prepared myself to see him at the hospital, and I wondered what he'd think about me coming to see Mackenzie, who was his biological daughter. I thought about the kind of relationship he had with her. Had she forgotten about me? If I were Bruce, I wouldn't be too happy about my visit, but my concern was only about Mackenzie's condition. I had to see for myself that she would be okay. From what Scorpio had said, I could tell my little girl was probably going through hell. I was regretting even more that my attorney, Frick, gave Scorpio that letter terminating my rights. If I could take it back, I sure in hell would.

Before finding Mackenzie's room, I had to stop off at the restroom. I took a leak; then I went to the sink to wash my hands. I checked myself in the mirror. . . . My trimmed goatee was going strong; my face and body were tanned as ever; my healthy curly hair was lined to perfection. I was casually dressed in a tan military shirt and heavy starched jeans. A yellow gold Movado watch was on my wrist, and I couldn't help but look at the platinum gold wedding band on my finger. I immediately thought of Nokea, but my mind quickly switched to the reason I was there. That was, of course, to see Mackenzie.

I left the restroom and went to the information desk to find out what room she was in. The two receptionists sat behind the counter, looking as if they had been shocked by electricity.

"Her name is Mackenzie Rogers," I said, repeating myself again. "Can you tell me what room she's in?"

One lady turned to the computer, but the other lady held her stare. "She's on the third floor." The woman paused; then she gave me the room number.

"Thank you," I said, walking away with my hands in my pockets.

Like always, heads were turning; women were whispering; I could spot a gay man a mile away. Sometimes the looks didn't even faze me, but I would be lying if I said the attention didn't make me feel good. I got on an elevator, full of women. I smiled and they smiled back. When the elevator stopped at the second floor, one woman, in particular, brushed herself up against me. I kept a blank expression on my face. When she excused herself, I responded, "No problem." She wiggled her fingers, waving good-bye. The elevator closed;

then it opened on the third floor. As I was getting off, I bumped into a nurse, who stumbled right into my arms. She seemed shaken up as she inquisitively looked into my eyes.

"I am so, so sorry," she said, holding on to my arms. "I must have tripped or something."

"Are you okay?" I asked, helping her keep her balance.

"Yes, I am. Can—can I help you find someone?" she asked.

"I'm sure I can find my way, but, uh, are you one of the nurses on this floor?"

She held out her hand so I could shake it. "Yes, my name is Ann. Who are you looking for?"

"Mackenzie Rogers."

Ann smiled and smacked her forehead. "I should have known right away. You're Mackenzie and Bruce's father, aren't you? They look just like you, especially your son. He is so adorable! Trust me, the both of them will be fine. Come with me."

I followed behind Ann, anxious to see Mackenzie. I knew that a lot of people felt as if she was my biological daughter—and no matter what, I was claiming it. Ann knocked on a door, and when she entered the room, I went in behind her. Scorpio was standing by the window, biting her nails. She had on a fuzzy pink sweater, some hip-hugging jeans and a pair of white tennis shoes. Her face was pale as ever and her long coal black hair was pulled back into a ponytail that was in no way sleek. No matter what, she still looked pretty, but I could see the stress on her face. She hurried up to me, putting her arms around my waist and laying her head against my chest. I embraced her back.

"I'm so glad you're here," she said, full of emotions. "Thank God you're here."

"You knew I would come, didn't you?"

She nodded. Ann left the room, closing the door behind her. Scorpio backed away from our embrace and I walked behind the curtain so I could see Mackenzie. She was resting peacefully, but seeing the bruises and swelling on her face damn near made me want to cry. I couldn't believe how tall she'd gotten; time surely had gotten away from me.

"Her face was a lot worse than that. They removed the bandages earlier, but the casts on her leg and arm will be there for a while. She will need therapy, and she keeps complaining about her side hurting. I know it's from her ribs."

I stepped closer to the bed and leaned down to kiss Mackenzie's cheek. My thumb touched the soft baby hair on her forehead, and I knew right then and there that I would never, ever part ways with her again. Maybe this wouldn't have happened if I had done all along what I wanted to do, and that was allow Mackenzie to live with me. As I gazed at her, Scorpio touched my back.

"I'm going to Bruce's room. I'll be back in about thirty minutes."

I nodded. When she had left the room, I sat in a chair beside Mackenzie's bed. I held her hand in mine, smiling at her perfectly polished pink nails. I kept kissing her hand. When her fingers wiggled, I looked up at her. Her eyes fluttered and she slowly opened them. At first, she just stared with a blank expression on her face. I wasn't sure if she recognized me or not. Water rushed to the brim of her eyes, and then poured over. I stood up, leaning over her.

"What you crying for?" I asked.

She cracked a tiny smile and threw one of her arms around my neck. "I thought I had died and gone to heaven, Daddy," she said, choked up.

Her words pierced my heart. I swallowed the lump in my throat, trying to hold back my emotions. "No, baby. You didn't die, and you won't die. I'm here, and I'm always going to be here for you."

Mackenzie was so emotional, and she wouldn't let me go. She kept kissing my cheeks, and I was kissing hers too. I did my best to calm her, and I reached for the tissues to dab her watery eyes.

"There," I said as she started to calm down. We smiled at each other, and I sat back in the chair next to the bed. I kept her hand in mine, squeezing it.

"Are you in any pain?" I asked.

"A little."

"What hurts?"

She pointed to her side. "It hurts a little, but not as much as it did when the accident happened."

"So it's getting better?"

She nodded.

"Good. And according to your nurse, Ann, she said you should be feeling a whole lot better real soon."

"Well enough to go home? I want to go home with you, Daddy."

Just hearing her say that pleased my heart, but I knew it wouldn't be easy. "We'll see about that, okay? I'll talk to the doctors today and see what's up."

Mackenzie was quiet. She turned her head and looked out the window.

"Where's your dog, Barbie? I know you miss her, don't you?"

Mackenzie turned to me. "I miss her a lot. A few months ago, Bruce made Mommie and me get rid of her. He said she was a bad dog, and she kept messing up the house. She was my best friend, and I cried for three whole weeks."

Now, hearing that really pissed me off. I'd bought that dog for Mackenzie, and how dare Scorpio let this motherfucker tell her what to do. She knew how attached Mackenzie was to Barbie, so I didn't understand why Scorpio would even allow it.

"Where's Bruce at now? Have you seen him?"

Mackenzie shrugged a little. "No, I haven't seen him since I've been in the hospital. Mommie's been here every single day, but I think she's with my little brother right now. Did you meet my little brother yet? He's handsome, just like you are, Daddy."

"No, I haven't seen him yet, and my concern is for you. I wanted to make sure you were okay, and I feel so much better being here with you."

The door opened, and when I turned, it was the nurse Ann coming back into the room. She stood at the end of Mackenzie's bed, tickling Mackenzie's toes.

"Oh my," she said to Mackenzie. "Somebody has a big ole smile today. I wonder why? Is it because your daddy is here?"

Mackenzie smiled, holding the biggest grin ever. Ann kept teasing Mackenzie, and she told Mackenzie that a late-night snack was coming soon. Before leaving the room, Ann asked if I would step out in the hall for a minute.

"Sure," I said, following her into the hallway. She stood with her arms folded and had a look of concern on her face.

"I'm glad you're here, Mr. Rogers, but I really need for you to do me a favor."

"Of course. Anything."

"Please get Scorpio out of this hospital. The children will be just fine, and I, along with the staff here, are taking very good care of them. I'm noticing her going into a depressive state, and I'm severely worried about her. She has not left this hospital for one second. If she could go somewhere, get something to eat and rest, I would feel so much better."

"No problem," I said. "If you don't mind, I'm going to sit with Mackenzie for about another hour or two, and then we'll go. Thank you so much for everything, and I appreciate your kindness."

"Anytime."

I moved toward the door, but Ann reached for my arm. "I forgot to tell you that the doctors may be releasing Mackenzie soon. I know she's anxious to get home, and Scorpio talked to the doctors as well. As for your son, it may be a while before he's able to go home. Possibly another week."

"For the record, he's not my son. Mackenzie is my daughter, but Bruce is not my son."

Ann's eyes widened. "For real?" She chuckled. "I'm sorry. I thought he looked just like you. You know how they say, 'We all look alike,' but please forgive me for being incorrect."

"No problem," I said, returning to Mackenzie's room.

I sat with Mackenzie for the next few hours, and Scorpio had come in at least three or four times. She looked worn, and I felt so bad for her. I suggested that she leave the hospital and go home to get some rest.

"No," she said, gazing out the window. "I'm fine right here."

"Have you eaten anything today?"

"A little."

"A little what?"

"Some . . . some chips, I think."

I stood up and walked over to her by the window. I rubbed my hands up and down her arms. "Listen, you won't be any good to your kids if you don't get some rest and take care of yourself. Go home and I'll stay here with Mackenzie. You can come back in the morning, but not until you've had something to eat and have gotten some rest."

"No," she said again. "I don't want to go home. There's nothing there for me, and I'm not going home to an empty house, which has too many bad memories."

I could already tell that some drama was going on with her and Bruce. I didn't want to throw that "I told you so" bullshit up in her face right now, but I had a feeling that Scorpio's marriage would fail. "I'm going to get a room at the Four Seasons. Let's go get something to eat. After you get a nap, you can come back in the morning. Ann said the kids will be fine, and you know she's got them all taken care of."

Scorpio hesitated; then she looked up at me. "Can I stay in the room with you? I don't want to be alone, Jaylin, just . . . just not right now."

I couldn't believe the feelings I still had for this woman. I knew that staying the night with Scorpio wasn't a good thing, but I couldn't help but agree to it. "Let's go," I said. "Go say good night to your son, and I'll say good night to Mackenzie."

Mackenzie had already shut it down for the night, so I kissed her cheek and whispered that I'd see her tomorrow. I left the room and waited by the elevators for Scorpio. Moments later, she came out of the room and we left the hospital together. We went through the drive-through at McDonald's, and all Scorpio ate was a Double Cheeseburger. When we got to the Four Seasons, I got the Presidential Suite and we made our way to the room. It came with one king-sized bed, a couch, two chairs and a table. My thoughts were all over the place, and I couldn't help but think about the last time Scorpio and I were together. It was a night to remember, and sex between us was off the chain. While in the car, she said she hadn't showered in days; so it was no surprise when she went into the bathroom to handle her business. I sat on the bed, massaging my forehead and thinking about my wife and kids at home. I hadn't called Nokea since I'd left Miami, and I knew she was wondering where I was. She'd called my cell phone twice, so I dialed out to call her.

"It's about time," she said in a playful tone.

"I apologize, baby. I got so wrapped up with seeing the property, and as of yet, I still haven't seen it. My friend Curtis couldn't find the keys to let me inside and we have to wait until tomorrow. I'm at his house right now, and I'm about to shut it down for the night."

"What time are you coming back tomorrow?"

"It depends on what time I can get inside to see the property. It's a thirty-two-thousand-square-foot building, and from the outside, it looks as if it may have some potential. He got some other property he wants to show me too. If Shane and I can get some designers to fix it up, it may very well be worth it."

"I thought Shane was going with you. He came to the house, but I think he's still at Tiffanie's house. They had dinner tonight. Hopefully, they're patching things up."

"Maybe so, but, uh, I told him I was coming to Chicago by myself. Curtis be acting kind of funny, and he don't like dealing with a lot of people."

"I know how that is. Get some rest and I'll see you tomorrow."

"You too, baby. Tell the kids I'll see them soon."

We ended our call, and I sat back on the bed, feeling like crap. Everything with Nokea and me was going so smoothly. I didn't like lying to her at all. To clear my conscience, as soon as I got back home, I was going to tell her about Mackenzie. Especially since she was definitely going to be a huge part of my life again.

Still sitting back on the bed, I removed my shirt and turned on the plasma TV. I could hear the shower running, and I started letting my imagination run wild. I knew exactly what Scorpio looked liked in the shower, and the thought of her lathered naked body was fresh in my mind. Yeah, I wanted to get up and join her, but I knew I couldn't go there. As a matter of fact, I wouldn't go there. The way I felt after betraying Nokea the last time Scorpio and I had sex was enough. I couldn't even look Nokea in her eyes, and it took me months to recover from what I'd done. Lying to Nokea was one thing, but sticking my dick where it didn't belong was another.

I heard the shower turn off, and as I was flipping through the channels, Scorpio came out of the bathroom. A towel was wrapped around her curvaceous body, and she had another towel on her head, shaking her wet hair dry.

"I needed that so bad," she said, "you just don't know. . . . I feel like a million dollars right now."

I glanced at her, but shifted my eyes back to the TV. "You'll feel like a million more dollars after you get some rest."

She removed the towel from her head and laid it on a chair. With the other towel still covering her, she got into the bed next to me.

"Can you scoot down and hold me?" she asked.

I scooted down, allowing Scorpio to get close and rest her head on my bare chest. Things were pretty quiet for a while, until she lifted her head to look up at me.

"You smell so good. Are you comfortable?" she asked.

"I'm okay. Just get some rest."

She laid her head back on my chest and crossed her leg over mine. I was glad that my jeans were still on, and that was a good thing.

"Are you mad at me?" she blurted out.

"Why do you think that?"

"I don't know. You've been real quiet, and I figured Mackenzie must have told you about the accident."

"No, she didn't get into any details. Was she supposed to?"

"I guess not. But Bruce and I were arguing right before the accident happened. It was all my fault, Jaylin, and I caused him to take his eyes off the road."

Yes, I was irritated. "What's going on with you and Bruce? Mackenzie told me he made her get rid of Barbie, and I can't believe you agreed to it. You know how much that dog meant to her, and to me."

"I know, but for some reason, Barbie got really, really mean. She didn't like Bruce, and now I understand why. I got rid of her to keep down confusion. She started peeing all over the house, and I can't tell you how many times I stepped in dog poop. She bit Bruce and tried to bite me too. Mackenzie was very upset, and I promised her that I would get her another dog. Bruce and I have been having problems for months, and he's seeing Mercedes again. I stopped having sex with him and everything. We were arguing all of the time. When I asked him for a divorce, he slapped the living daylights out of me. We got into a huge fight, and the police were called to our house that night. At this point, I just want out of my marriage, Jaylin. All I care about is my babies, and he can do whatever."

"I'm sorry to hear that it didn't work out. And you're right. . . . At the end of the day, the kids are what truly matter."

Scorpio stretched her arm around my waist, holding me tight. She spoke softly. "Do you ever think about me? About that night we shared together? I know how much you love Nokea, but is there an ounce of love in your body still left for me?"

I cleared my throat, for her questions deserved an honest answer. "Yes, I've thought about you a lot, and

I still think about you. All of the time, I wonder what you're doing, how things are coming along, and I often think about what if you and I were still together. I told you before that I still had love for you, but this thing between us is too, too complicated. Complicated because I am with my soul mate, and I intend to be with her for the rest of my life. I love Nokea too much, Scorpio, to settle for anything less."

"Trust me, you would be just as happy with me, as you are with her. I would love you so much more, and that is the sole reason why I can't get ahead with any other man in my life. I'm not going to talk about this anymore, but I wanted you to know how much you mean to me and my family too."

Scorpio lay for a while, without talking. It wasn't long before I heard her lightly snoring. She was resting well, but I couldn't get a lick of sleep. It was obvious that she was never going to turn me loose, and I couldn't quite understand how we kept finding ourselves right back in each other's arms.

She turned in her sleep. When the towel slid away from her naked body, I couldn't help but admire it. I wanted to wake her up so badly, just so I could slide my dick into her. Instead of lying in bed with a hard-on and crazy thoughts, I got up and went downstairs to the casino. I stayed there for at least three hours, putting hundreds and hundreds of dollars into a Lucky 7 machine that was going up and down. The jackpot was over $4,000, and a black older lady sitting next to me kept telling me the machine was going to hit.

"That machine has been hot all day. How much money have you put in there?" she asked.

"It ain't been too hot. I've probably already put at least a thousand dollars in it."

She laughed and kept playing her machine. I already had put so much money into mine, but I reached over and started playing hers. She said she had lost about $300, and it was obvious that the old woman may have been playing with her Social Security check. The jackpot on her machine was over $8,000. When I fed in another $100, she thanked me.

"See what you can do with that," I said.

She pulled the handle twice, and to both of our surprise, the Lucky 7s fell on the payline. She screamed out loudly, covering her mouth.

"We won!" she shouted. "Thank you! Thank you, thank you, Jesus, we won!"

Everybody started crowding around, and the flashing lights were going off. The lady kept hugging me. When she asked me if I was going to offer her some of the money, all I could do was laugh.

"That's not my money, that's your money," I said.

"But . . . but you gave it to me. You put that money in there and the jackpot belongs to you. Plus you have to get back all of the money you put into the other machine."

The lady reminded me of Nanny B, chubby and adorable. I leaned in and kissed her cheek. "Enjoy your money, ma'am. Have a good day."

Her eyes watered and she watched me walk away.

When I returned to the suite, it was almost three o'clock in the morning. I quietly made my way into the room, only to see Scorpio lying on her back with her legs partially opened. My eyes dropped between her legs, and my dick started throbbing. Her breasts were so plump and pretty. Like always, her pussy looked good enough to eat. My mouth had gotten moist. I had to wipe the wetness from my lips.

Then I asked myself, *Why in the hell am I standing here depriving myself?* Hell, I'd gotten away with the shit before. Once a man gets away with it one time, we are always gaming to creep again. What Nokea didn't know wouldn't hurt her, would it? There was no way in hell she'd find out, and I knew Scorpio wouldn't say a word. She'd kept our secret for this long, so what did I have to lose?

I slowly removed my shirt, but then I thought again about how guilty I felt the last time I'd gone there with Scorpio. I could barely look Nokea in the eyes, and it took me a while to forgive myself for what I'd done. Not wanting to feel that way again, I sighed and walked toward the door. I thought about getting another room for the night, just so I wouldn't put myself in a messed-up situation as I had done before. But no sooner than my hand touched the doorknob, my selfish way of thinking wouldn't allow me to walk away. It wasn't nothing but sex, and since I lived many miles away from Scorpio, the chances of her interfering would be slim to none. With that in mind, I removed all of my clothes and made my way onto the bed, easing between Scorpio's legs. I wrapped them around my back. When I felt her legs tighten, I knew she was awake. I turned my tongue in circles around her hard nipples. As the arch in her back formed, she reached down and navigated my nine-plus inside her.

"Ooh, Jaylin," she painfully let out. "Make love to me this time. I still love you so much. And this dick . . . you know how much I love you inside me."

I kept dipping into her soaking wet tunnel, without a thought or care in the world. She and I having sex together, we could star in a porn movie and make millions. Sex between us was that damn sexy, and the connection we had was addictive. I flipped her on top of me, and Scorpio rode me at a slow, tranquilizing pace. We stared into each other's eyes, and that alone was powerful. I felt heavily sedated by her slow movements. Before I left the hotel room, I intended to give her my all.

"Don't leave us," she said, grinding down on me. "Please don't leave us again."

While massaging her curvaceous ass, and tightening up my eyes from the feel of her gushy, warm pussy, all I could say was "I won't leave you. Never again." My dick was probably speaking for me right now, but my heart was in it too.

SCORPIO

Okay, so I was feeling much better since Jay Baby was here. I wasn't sure how long he would stay, but it was already Tuesday and he hadn't gone anywhere. Mackenzie was coming home today, but the hospital didn't want to release Bruce until Friday. I had not a clue where this thing between Jaylin and me was headed, but I didn't have the guts to tell him about Bruce Jr. being his son. He was so into making sure that Mackenzie was well, and so was I. I hadn't even gone back to the hotel to be with him, and for the past two nights, I stayed at the hospital. I didn't want Jaylin to think all I wanted from him was sex, because that was simply not the case. I truly loved him with everything I had, and I wanted nothing more than for my kids and me to be a part of his life. I didn't even know if that was possible, but I was sure Jaylin would someway or somehow work all of this out.

Mackenzie had left the hospital with Jaylin and me. We went back to my house, and even though I dreaded going home, I knew Bruce wouldn't be there. As a matter of fact, he'd already packed up his belongings and left. He hadn't called to check on the kids or me. At the end of the day, Mackenzie was still his daughter. What a deadbeat sperm donor he was, and for him not to even care about her well-being showed me what kind of man he really was.

Jaylin carried Mackenzie to her bedroom, and he spent at least an hour talking and playing around with her. I returned the numerous phone calls I'd gotten, most of them from the stylists at Jay's, trying to find out how everything was going. My sister, Leslie, called to check on us too, and I returned her call, just to let her know we were doing okay. The nurse who was hired to assist Mackenzie had beeped in to say she was on her way. I was so glad about that. I wanted to get back to the hospital to check on Bruce Jr., so I went upstairs to Mackenzie's room to see what she and Jaylin were up to. He was sitting on Mackenzie's bed, listening to her read a book to him. I stood in the doorway, so happy to see them together again.

"The nurse is on her way to see about Mackenzie," I said. "When she gets here, I'm going back to the hospital to see about my son. Will you be here when I get back?"

Jaylin stood up and stretched. He walked toward the door, and then stepped out in the hallway to talk to me. He stroked his goatee, so I knew his response was going to be slightly disappointing.

"I'm leaving tonight. I'll be back, though, and I already told Mackenzie that she and I will be spending more time together."

I swallowed the lump in my throat. "I don't know how that's possible. Please don't hurt us again, okay? We just can't handle—"

He put his finger on my lips to shush me. "I'm going to work this out. Just give me a minute, okay?"

I nodded, and trusting every word that he said, I reached out to embrace him, and we kissed. After the nurse got there, I said good-bye to Jaylin and told Mackenzie I would see her later. I wasn't sure how soon it would be before I saw him again, but my gut assured me that it would be soon, just like he'd said.

JAYLIN

The nurse was there to see about Mackenzie. I could already tell she was in good hands, but no hands were better than my own. Not even Scorpio's hands, and what I was feeling inside was in no way personal. Nokea had to deal with it, and so did Scorpio. As soon as Mackenzie got well, she was coming to live with me. No ifs, ands or buts about it. I would talk Scorpio into taking some time for herself and letting Mackenzie stay with me. As for Nokea, I intended to tell her the truth about Mackenzie's accident, and let Nokea know that I wasn't willing to walk away from Mackenzie again. More than anything, I wanted all of my children together, and having them grow up together would make me the happiest man in the world.

For the last few days, I'd been in touch with Nokea. I told her that my trip was taking more time than expected. As much as I wanted to be home, I just couldn't get there. I missed my family like hell, and three long days away from them was enough.

Later that day, I said my good-byes to Mackenzie, but again, made her a promise that I intended to keep. I would see her soon and we would once again live together as a family. She seemed so happy, but definitely not as happy as I was. I was on my way out the front door, and just as I stepped onto the porch, a gray Lincoln MKT truck pulled into the driveway. I wasn't sure who was inside it, because the windows were tinted. The door opened, and I swore it was Boris Kodjoe himself getting out of the truck. The brotha resembled Mackenzie, so I suspected that I had finally come face-to-face with Bruce.

"Who the fuck are you?" he asked, closing the door to his truck.

I walked up to him, holding out my hand. "Let me formally introduce myself to you. I'm Mackenzie's father, Jaylin. Jaylin Rogers. You must be the mutha-fucka who abandoned your kids, right?"

He turned up his lips. "This is one hell of a surprise. I assume you were just inside fucking my wife, but that's cool with me. Have at it, bro. Since you're here, maybe she'll stop talking about you all of the time. Maybe I can stop being compared to a muthafucka I do not know, or have never met. Maybe you can be a father to her son that damn sure looks nothing like me. As far as Mackenzie is concerned, good luck with that. She's spoiled as hell, and the shit just drives me crazy."

He walked away and went into the house. I wanted to say something, or even go after him, but I was stopped dead in my tracks. That brotha had some issues, and I could tell that he and Scorpio had a tumultuous marriage.

I got in the rental car, and as I was driving, my mind started to wander. I played back everything Bruce had said to me, and did he suggest that his son, Bruce Jr., looked nothing like him? The words that Ann, the nurse, said came to mind: *"You're Mackenzie and Bruce's father, aren't you? They look just like you, especially your son."* Then my mind traveled back to what Mackenzie had said: *"He's handsome, just like you are, Daddy."* I didn't even know how old Bruce Jr. was, but I quickly thought back to that night with Scorpio. I was so caught up with the thoughts of my dream on that day, I pumped all kinds of juices into her. Years ago, we'd tried hard for her to get pregnant, but nothing ever happened. I know damn well she didn't get pregnant that night, and if she had, she would have been anxious to tell me. Even within the last few days, she would have said something. *Wouldn't she?* I thought about how many times Scorpio played around with lying to me about my child she claimed to be pregnant with, but wasn't. Actually, it was someone else's baby. About her lying to Shane about being pregnant by him, and now, obviously, Bruce had some concerns too. Maybe he was just bitter about their marriage not working out, but the harsh look in his eyes said there was more to it. I made a quick U-turn in the middle of the street, making my way to Cardinal Glennon Hospital.

It was already going on six o'clock, so I knew I'd miss my flight back to Florida. Maybe I could catch a later one, but for now, I had to see what was up.

Very impatient, I tapped my foot on the floor of the elevator, while stroking my goatee. My thoughts were all over the place, and when the elevator opened at the third floor, I got off and went straight to Bruce Jr.'s room. I was surprised not to see Scorpio in there. When I looked at the bed, there he was. His head was turned to the side—beautiful curly hair lay on his head—and I watched as his chest slowly heaved up and down. I could see a few bruises on his face too. Wanting him to open his eyes, I stepped forward. I rubbed his hair, already stunned that he looked like a lighter-skinned LJ. As I continued to touch his hair, he slowly switched his head to the other side. That's when I whispered his name, and, I admit, even that pained me. Because even with his eyes closed, I had known the truth.

Moments later, he sucked his tongue, then swallowed. His eyes shot wide open and stared right into mine. I took a double look, seeing that they were gray just like mine. Almost losing my balance, I stumbled backward, dropping into the seat behind me. All kinds of shit was going through my head, but at the top of the list was . . . Nokea. What in the hell was I going to tell her? My heartbeat had picked up and my hands had a slight tremble. The wrinkled lines on my forehead were laced with beads of sweat. I was nervous, because at that very moment, I knew that the perfect life I'd had with Nokea was about to change. A few seconds later, I could hear Scorpio outside the door talking to someone. Bruce Jr. started moving around a bit, and all I could do was sit there like a mannequin. When Scorpio came into the room, I remained in the chair. I gazed down at the floor, shielding my face and unable to look up at her.

"Tell me something," I said, clearing mucus from my throat. "Why in the fuck do you keep on doing this shit to me? Please, please tell me why, so I can understand the kind of woman you really and truly are."

I finally looked up and she stood dead in her tracks, speechless. She had a soda can in her hand, which she carefully laid on the serving table.

"Do what?" she softly said, rubbing back her long hair. "What are you talking about?"

My blood pressure was rising by the second. I just knew she wasn't going to lie to me, was she? My face scrunched up and I stroked my goatee—hard. I nudged my head toward Bruce Jr. "Who—who in the hell is his father?"

"It's Bruce," she said, lying her ass off. I couldn't believe it.

"Do you think I'm that fucking stupid? I don't need you to validate a gotdamn thing for me. Just by looking at him, it's obvious. How could you keep something like this from me?" My voice rose even higher and my fist swung out to hit the air. "Gotdamn you, Scorpio, how could you!"

She clenched her hands together to stop them from trembling. "I—I just found out when he came to the hospital and needed a blood—"

I jumped to my feet. "You're a fucking liar!" I pointed to my son. "There ain't no way you lived with him every damn day of his life and you didn't see me! Do you really want me to believe that?"

She jumped from my loud voice; then she lowered her head. When she lifted it, tears rushed to her eyes. "I'm sorry. I did it for you. I—I didn't want to break up your marriage. I knew that finding out about him would devastate you, and I couldn't hurt you anymore."

"You expect me to believe that bullshit? For real? You kept quiet because you didn't want your marriage to end. You know damn well you wasn't thinking about me or my marriage."

"It's the truth!" she shouted. "I swear to God that I did it for you, and I would do anything . . . anything in the world for you. I knew Bruce Jr. looked like you, but I kept telling Bruce that he looked more like my father than anyone. I tried, Jaylin. I really did try not to hurt anyone."

I was so damn distraught. I couldn't believe that Scorpio had pulled this shit on me again, and just like every single child that I had, with the exception of Jaylene, the women in my life were playing games. This was yet another child that I didn't get a chance to see come into this world, and one that had been kept from me. I was beyond pissed, and being in front of Scorpio down right disgusted me. I could have smacked her ass—I was so angry, but instead, I bumped her shoulder on my way to the door.

"Please don't be mad at me," she cried. "Think about what I just said. You know darn well I would have been proud to tell the world this baby was yours. I did it to protect you, and no other reason even makes sense.

The same goes for Mackenzie. I never moved forward with relinquishing your parental rights. I never saw a lawyer because I knew how much Mackenzie meant to you. Every thing that I've done, I've done it all for you."

I kept moving out the door and didn't dare to look back. So much anger was inside me, and I had no idea what the hell I was going to do. I drove back to the hotel, deciding to stay there for one more night. I couldn't let Nokea see me like this, and she, of all people, would know something was wrong. I didn't know what to think—and never, ever did I think I would be faced with some shit like this. After nearly four years of having a flawless marriage, now this. I'd dreamed of having another son, but little did I know, he had already been born. So much for that peaceful-ass life I wanted, huh? My shit had caught up with me, and the truth had made its way to the light!

I didn't get much sleep last night, and after thinking about what I should do, I had come to a conclusion. I got dressed, checked out of the hotel and made my way back to the hospital. When I got to my son's room, Scorpio was lying sideways in the bed next to him. She heard the door open, and she turned to see who it was. I walked up to the bed, and then I leaned down to kiss my son, who was awake and playing with a toy in his hand.

"I'm on my way back home," I said dryly to Scorpio. "In one week, you need to prepare yourself for some changes. I have a house up for sale in Miami, and you and my kids are moving there. Shut it down in St. Louis, and switch ownership of Jay's to someone else. Put your house up for sale or let your sister, Leslie, move in. I will have a friend of mine help you with this transition. Once you're settled into your new place, I'll

be there to discuss our future. Until then, do not call
my cell phone, and don't call my house. This may be a
very difficult time for Nokea and me, and I need for you
to show her some respect. She didn't ask for none of
this, Scorpio, and I was the one who fucked up. I gotta
make shit right for myself, and this is the only way I
know how."

Scorpio moved her head from side to side. "There's
no way I can move—"

"You can, and you will," I interrupted. "You've caused
me enough heartache, and there ain't no way in hell my
kids are going to live without me. If you prefer that we
take this shit to court, then let's. I don't think you want
to go that route. Besides, you want to spend the rest of
your life with me, don't you? Here's your chance, so let's
roll with it."

I kissed my son again. Before I left the room, though,
I stopped at the door.

"Stop calling him Bruce. And when I see you again,
have a different name for him. Find out the process of
what it takes to change his name and make arrangements to do it."

I turned my head, looking at Scorpio from the corner
of my eye. She didn't say anything. As far as I was concerned, my issues with her were a done deal.

NOKEA

At last, Jaylin was home. He made it in late Wednesday night, and for a second there, I had gotten kind of worried. He kept calling with one explanation after another, telling me why he wasn't going to make it home that night. When he got home, though, his conversation put me at ease. He seemed excited about the numerous properties he'd seen, and said that he was considering purchasing two of them. It was good to see him throw himself back into work. He said that at the end of the day, there was nothing wrong with making more money. I wholeheartedly agreed. I wanted to make sure Jaylene and LJ didn't want for anything when they got older, and the money Jaylin had been making was very much starting to be large enough for generations to come. I started paying much more attention to our bank statements. Every time Jaylin cut a new deal, he kept me posted. I did have a bank account of my own, and every time I looked up, Jaylin was throwing all kinds of money in it, just to make sure I had enough to do whatever I wanted. He had me spoiled. Maybe not as much as he had the kids, but I appreciated him always looking out for me.

On Thursday afternoon, Jaylin and Shane came in, talking loud about an issue with work. The kids were in their study room, being homeschooled by their teacher, Mrs. Mahoney. Nanny B was resting, and I was in the kitchen being nosy, listening to Jaylin and Shane's conversation.

"I told you he was wasting our time," Jaylin said, opening the refrigerator. "I could tell he didn't have any money by looking at his shoes."

Shane laughed and slapped his hand against Jaylin's. "Next time, I'll know better. If a brotha's shoes ain't right, that says a lot about him."

Jaylin pulled out two bottles of water, tossing one to Shane. They gulped it down; then Jaylin cleared his throat. "Movie night is tonight," he said. "Are you and Tiffanie going to join us?"

"I'm going to join y'all, but Tiffanie isn't. I invited Joy to come over—that's if the two of you don't mind."

Jaylin looked at me, waiting for me to say something. We had movie night in our theater room on Thursdays, and Shane always invited Tiffanie. I shrugged, having nothing to say.

Jaylin left the kitchen to go take a shower and change. Shane stayed in the kitchen, so he and I could talk.

"I hope you're not upset with me, Nokea. I know Tiffanie is your friend, but I don't want to rush into anything with her right now. I hope you understand."

"I do. And you don't have to explain anything to me. I just want you to be happy, and I know what you've been through in the past. My only hope is that it doesn't stop you from recognizing a good woman when you have one."

"I'll do my best." He smiled and gave me a hug; then he thanked me for being concerned about him.

Shane went to the lower level, and as soon as the phone rang, I answered. It was Joy, implying that she tried to call Shane's cell phone, but he didn't answer.

"He's here, but let me go to the lower level to see if I can find him for you."

With the cordless phone in my hand, I headed to the lower level. Since Shane had the majority of the basement to himself, I rarely went down there. I wanted him to have as much privacy as ever, and when I opened the door to his bedroom, I understood why. I could see him in the glass shower, standing with his eyes closed, with water dripping down on his face and stallion-like caramel body. He, too, was a very sexy man, and this was the third time I'd walked in on him when he had no clothes on. I knew why Tiffanie couldn't let him go, and he was packaged up quite well. I closed the door, telling Joy that he was in the shower. She asked for our address and I gave her directions to our house, even though I didn't want to do that. After all, Tiffanie was my friend, but I also didn't want any of the others to be upset with me for interfering.

Afterward, I walked around downstairs, straightening the pillows on the pit couch, which sat in front of a wall-to-wall entertainment center. I went to the weight room and put the weights, which Jaylin, LJ and Shane had all over the place, back where they belonged. Next I went into the sauna and removed a few towels that needed to be washed, and then I searched in the wine cellar for a bottle of wine that Jaylin and I could drink tonight. I found the red wine that I wanted; then I went into the spacious theater room, which had six rows of comfortable black leather chairs. I checked the thermostat, making sure the room would be cozy.

The thermostat was set at seventy-two degrees, so I was cool with that. I left the theater room, and just as I was getting ready to go back upstairs, I heard Shane laughing. I moved closer to his bedroom door, eavesdropping on his conversation.

"I told you I got you," he said. "I enjoyed myself last night too, and you set it out there for a brotha. I look forward to seeing you tonight, and you can chill the night with me, if you want to."

I rolled my eyes, somewhat anxious to see what this chick named Joy looked like.

Later that night, Jaylin and I put the kids to bed, and after we had a few drinks, we all headed to the theater room to watch a movie. We'd all heard that *The Hangover* was pretty funny, and the moment it came on the screen, we were all cracking up. Shane and Joy sat cuddled up in one of the leather chairs, and Jaylin and I sat right behind them. The chairs were indeed big enough for two people, but for comfort, one person would do.

To me, Joy had nothing on Tiffanie. She seemed very materialistic and had a Gucci bag, purse, belt and shoes. A Gucci watch was on her wrist. The way her voice squeaked, it drove me crazy. She was slender and tall, like a runway model, and had no assets whatsoever. Backside had a small curve to it, and her breast size couldn't have been no bigger than a 32A or B. Shane was known for liking very plain women who resembled runway models. No wonder when Scorpio was dating Shane to make Jaylin jealous, she was capable of blowing Shane's mind.

"Hell nah," Jaylin said, slapping his leg and cracking up at the movie. "These muthafuckas are crazy."

"I could see us doing some shit like that," Shane suggested. I popped him on the back of his head and told him that wasn't possible.

As the movie went on, everyone was tuned in. We kept filling our glasses with wine, Rémy, and Patrón. I was getting pretty sick from eating so much buttered popcorn. I was so glad when the movie was over, and as soon as it was, Shane couldn't wait to get Joy into his bedroom. Jaylin and I headed to ours, and he fell across the California King bed, lying on his stomach. We hadn't made love since he'd returned from his trip, so I went into my closet to change. I put on a lime green stretch-lace nightie that hugged my curves and barely covered my meaty breasts. Since it was lace, he could see right through it. I was so sure he would love it. I sprayed a dash of perfume between my breasts and couldn't wait for Jaylin to make love to me.

When I left the closet, I sauntered his way. He sat up on his elbows, eyeing me as I lit some candles and turned off the lights to darken the room. I slithered my body on top of his, and as we kissed, his hands roamed my backside. He carefully rolled on top of me, placing passionate kisses on my neck and shoulders.

"Nokea," he whispered. "Baby, God as my witness, I love you more than anything and anyone in this world. You know that, don't you?"

"Yes," I whispered back. "I feel it every single day of my life, and you know how much I love you too."

Jaylin pulled the top part of my nightie aside, exposing one of my wobbly breasts. He began to pluck my nipple with his mouth; and with each pluck, my nipple stiffened even more. He massaged my other breast in circles, caressing it with his soft, strong hand. I was so into his performance, until he whispered something to me that stung.

"Why in the hell can we not make any more babies? I want some more babies, Nokea. Damn, I want another baby."

My entire body went limp. He knew darn well why we possibly couldn't have any more babies, and did I have to remind him that I'd fallen down the steps because of the tape I'd seen a few years into our marriage with Scorpio seducing him? I kept my cool, but his words hurt like hell. It was as if he was blaming me, and I wasn't feeling that at all.

"We just have to keep trying," I said. "That's all we can do. You don't mind if we have to keep trying, do you?"

He kept sucking my breasts, ignoring me. When I lifted his head to stop him, I saw something peculiar in his eyes, which meant trouble. The disturbing look shocked me, and I did not know my not getting pregnant was troubling Jaylin so much. Talk about a mood spoiler, this was it.

"Why didn't you say anything to me about how you were feeling?" I asked, letting out a deep sigh. "I thought you were okay and you know how difficult this—"

Jaylin reached over and held the sides of my face; he sucked my lips into his. "I know, baby, and I am so, so sorry for coming at you like that. Sometimes I get to thinking about another child, and we don't really know if or when it will happen. I'm hopeful, though, so no worries."

I rubbed my fingers through the curls in his hair. "I'm hopeful too. But please don't hide your feelings from me. You haven't said anything about a baby in a while, and that look in your eyes scares me."

"I'm okay. As long as I got you with me, I'm fine. You're my strength, Nokea, and I could never make it through life without you."

"Same here. I can promise you this. . . . You'll never be without me."

"You promise," he repeated.

"Never," I assured.

For whatever reason, that night, our lovemaking session felt different. I mean, Jaylin was always so into making love to me, but his strokes were not on point, like they had been. He stopped several times, just to talk to me.

"I love you, love you, love you," he said, tickling me to change the mood. "You know I've been the best husband I could possibly be, right? And I apologize for getting at you like that about a baby."

"Apology accepted, and I know you're the best, Jaylin," I said, feeling so unsure about where all of this was coming from, afraid to dig deeper.

"I hope so, because I would never let you go in a million years. We have the best connection ever, and you were definitely made for me."

He held me tightly in his arms, and after an odd situation, he made passionate love to me throughout the night. I was a bit unsure about the whole thing. Why was he saying all of those things to me, and did they, indeed, mean anything?

Like any wife who knew her husband well, and could feel it in her gut that something wasn't right, I started to pay more attention to Jaylin. He had been spending more time with Jaylene and LJ. Whenever he went to the office, he started taking LJ with him. He didn't seem to mind if Jaylene wanted to sleep with us at night. As a matter of fact, for the past two nights, he'd slept in her room with her. He had been taking more business calls than usual, and there were several times that he walked into another room to take a call. I saw him looking spacey a few times; sometimes when I called his name, it was as if he didn't even hear me. Then there were our intimate moments. Ever since the other night, Jaylin hadn't pursued sex with me again.

Now, only four days had passed by, but he always used to be saying something revolving around sex, every single day. He barely laid a kiss on me since that night, and if he did, I initiated it. Yesterday evening, I saw him outside on the hammock, staring off into the sky, looking as if something heavy was on his mind.

During dinner he was known for cracking jokes and keeping everyone at the table laughing. Lately he hadn't said much at all. Nanny B even asked what was wrong with him, and when Shane asked, Jaylin replied, "Nothing." He played it off. Afterward, he and

Shane went to the lower level to play basketball on the half-court. I wanted to cry myself to sleep that night, knowing that the man I loved so much was starting to change. Why? I couldn't put my finger on it just yet, but it wouldn't take me long to figure out what was going on.

SCORPIO

I said that I'd do anything for Jay Baby, and I meant every word I said. He was a serious businessman, and when it came to my move, he had every single *i* dotted and *t* crossed. According to the letter he'd sent me, he hired a round-the-clock nurse for Mackenzie and his son. He told me not to bring any furniture, as our new location would already be furnished. He hired a nanny to help me out, and said her name would be Loretta. He also gave me a new bank account number that was set up for the personal needs of the kids and me.

I took care of things on my end too. I turned over ownership of my hair and nail salon, Jay's, to one of my closest friends and stylists who worked there, Bernie. She was disappointed that we were leaving, but she definitely understood why I had to go. As for my sister, Leslie, I gave my house to her. Bruce's name wasn't even on the deeds, and I had purchased the house with my own money. Pertaining to him, I already had filed for a divorce, and I knew there was no way in hell he would contest it. Almost two weeks after Jaylin suggested the change, the kids were out of the hospital and I packed up our belongings. We were on our way to Miami Beach, Florida. The man whom Jaylin hired to help us, his name was Ebay. He was a tall, skinny African dude, with short beaded hair. He seemed to be about business too, and he made the transition go very smoothly. The kids, of course, had gotten very irritable in the car, but we made plenty of stops. For now, Mackenzie still had to be moved around in a wheelchair. According to Jaylin's letter, her therapy would start right away. My son was doing much better. He even recovered faster than Mackenzie had, and I was extremely happy about that. I had all of the necessary paperwork needed to change his name, and I decided to rename him Justin. Justin Rogers, but I wanted to run it by Jaylin before I proceeded to do anything.

As for me, I was ready for a new start, but I wasn't sure how this thing between Jaylin and me would pan out. I definitely wasn't up for a bunch of drama, and in an effort to avoid that, all I had to do was give him everything he wanted. To me, he was so deserving, and he had already done so much for me and my family. I knew much more was to come and I couldn't wait to see what living in a new city would offer.

The ride to Miami was long, but Ebay kept me busy with conversation. When he pulled in front of a tall white stone building with glass windows, I thought he was just making a stop. Jaylin said we'd be moving into a house, but Ebay said it was a seacoast penthouse. All of the buildings in the vicinity were beautiful, and I couldn't believe people could afford to live like this. Ebay helped me get Mackenzie situated in her wheelchair, and I carried Justin in my arms. The moving truck that had been following us drove around to the back, and Ebay directed the driver to park. The inside of the building was even more stunning than the outside. Shiny marble floors were everywhere. Glass mirrors and modern paintings covered the walls, and the elevators were polished with gold. I was in awe, and I saw Mackenzie's eyes getting bigger and bigger. Ebay inserted a card in the elevator to make it go up. The elevator read the card, and spoke to us. "To the twenty-first floor," it said. "Correct?"

"Yes," Ebay replied, and the elevator went up. It was surrounded by glass, so you could look down and see what was below. I was afraid of heights, but the scenery was hard to resist. Swimming pools and palm trees were everywhere. Restaurants were close by, and so were plenty of golf courses and ice-cream stands. When the elevator opened, Ebay rolled Mackenzie down the long hallway. I followed, with Justin still in my arms. Ebay stepped up to the dark cherry oak double doors. When he opened it, I was nearly in a state of complete shock. The open space was unbelievable. Had to be at least 5,000 or 6,000 square feet. The shine from the cream-colored marble floors lit up the place, but the glass windows that surrounded the spacious area were breathtaking. You could see the peaceful blue ocean, filled with exquisite yachts. As high up as we were, Miami could be seen from miles away.

An outside balcony stretched around the penthouse, and turquoise lounging chairs were placed out there too. Turquoise was one of my favorite colors, and obviously, Jaylin didn't forget. The paintings on the white walls had turquoise in them, and the modern kitchen, which sat in the middle of the floor, had both turquoise and white pendant lights hanging above the kitchen isle. In the living-room area sat a two-sided fireplace, which had plasma TVs on both sides. If you were in the kitchen, you could watch TV; and if you were in the living room, you could watch as well. A contemporary cream-colored leather sectional was in the living room, and a silver chrome table with glass sat in the middle. The décor was so perfect! When I looked at one of the pictures, I saw the name 4M2H Designs, based out of St. Louis, scripted on everything. Whoever those designers were, they had their shit together!

Ebay took us down the hall, showing us two of the modern bathrooms, which had sinks designed like blue ocean waves. The showers had buttons that slid the glass doors aside, and the numerous chrome faucets made sure every part of your body was clean. The children's rooms were too adorable. They were right next to each other, and Mackenzie's room was decorated in pink, green and white. Three fashion girls were painted on her walls: one black, one white and one Asian. *Diversity Girls* was scribbled above it, and again, the design was signed by 4M2H Designs. Justin's room was dark blue and brown. He had a modern bed with bookshelves and a computer desk inside. Comfortable beanbags were on the floor, and they sat right in front of a plasma TV mounted on the wall. In the corner of his room was a play area that had choo-choo trains, building blocks and race cars. The area was designed to build his motor skills and keep him busy. Needless to say, I loved it!

When it was time to go to my room, Ebay told me to take the spiral staircase to the upper level, directly above the kids' rooms. He, however, went to an elevator that went straight up and opened up to my room. The space was ridiculous, and right in the middle of the floor was a simple, neatly dressed king-sized bed that was raised off the floor. It had a white silk padded headboard, and tall crystal-like turquoise vases sat on each side of the bed. The bedding was white silk, and I simply couldn't stand to see any more. I sat on the bed, and put my hands over my face to hide my emotions. Jaylin had outdone himself, and it was ridiculous for anyone to live like this. A part of me was a little skeptical, only because I didn't know if I would become confined to this place, waiting for Jaylin to come by, only to take care of his needs. I didn't want to be classified as his sidekick. If it ever got to a point where I truly felt that way, I'd have to make some changes. For now, I was here and was eager to see how things were going to go.

Ebay held out his hand to me. "Oh, we're not finished yet. Come, come, you must see the outdoor view from your room."

I choked back my tears and followed Ebay over to the glass windows. The view from my room was even better. I am very afraid of heights, and when Ebay suggested that I go outside on my wavy-carved balcony, which had lounging chairs, a personal swimming pool and Jacuzzi, I declined. Definitely, being out there would take some time to get used to.

When all was said and done, I had a bathroom that was almost the size of my whole house back in St. Louis. My roomy closet had no clothes in it, but that wouldn't be for long. And like it or not, this was going to be the place that my family and I called home.

Ebay let the movers in to place our things where they belonged, but there really wasn't much to do. I think Mackenzie had more than anybody, and all I had was a bunch of clothes. The nurse, Beatrice, had already shown up, and so had my nanny, Loretta. She seemed really sweet, and I could tell I would enjoy having her around.

Once things got settled, it was way after eleven at night. The kids had been put to bed, the nurse had left, but Loretta had a maid's quarter, which was on the other side of the penthouse. Ebay was on his way out. He told me about the twenty-four-hour security on duty and gave me his number to call him, just in case I needed anything. For now, I really couldn't think of anything. I thanked Ebay for his help, and he said he'd see me soon.

Before going to bed, I checked on the kids and they were sound asleep. I hoped that they'd enjoy their new place as much as I anticipated we would. To be honest, deep down, I felt Jaylin would be every bit a good father to them. I knew that he would give fatherhood his all. That made me so happy inside. Thinking about him, I took the stairs to my room. I tiptoed on the shiny marble floors and lay across my bed. My eyes looked at the coffered ceiling and the recess lighting that made the room so cozy. I rubbed my hands on the soft silk comforter, wishing that Jaylin were lying right next to me. I didn't know when he'd show up, but I hoped it would be soon.

I wanted to get comfortable, so I went into my closet and found a button-down silk pink pajama top. My feet were cold, but since I couldn't find my house shoes, I threw on a pair of clean white socks. I flipped on the TV mounted above the fireplace, watching for only a few minutes. I was thirsty, so I went to the kitchen to get something to drink. The wide stainless-steel refrigerator was loaded with bottled water, fruit juice, V8 juice and food. Some of our favorites, I might add; yet again, Jaylin had outdone himself. I wanted so badly to call and thank him, but I remembered what he'd said about not reaching out to him. I couldn't wait to call Leslie either, just so I could tell her about the place I now called home. I knew she wouldn't believe me. Hopefully, she and her kids would be able to come here and see how spectacular Miami really was.

Still thinking about Leslie, I leaned against the kitchen counter with the bottled water in my hand. I took a few sips; then I wiggled my fingers through my long, wavy hair that was a mess. I yawned a few times, and then I tossed the empty bottle in the trash can in front of me. The bottle missed; and when it hit the floor, I heard an alarm go off. It quickly silenced. I turned my head, a bit frightened, and wondered what the noise really was. As I stood still by the counter, I could hear heavy footsteps on the floor. My heart raced. When I saw Jaylin swoop around the corner, I felt relieved. He was a sight for sore and tired eyes. He looked out-of-sight in a red Ralph Lauren T-shirt, which tightened on his muscles, and dark black baggy jeans. He said not one word to me, and all I saw was him removing the thick black Polo belt from the loops on his jeans. The belt hit the floor; he stood in front of me, undoing the top button on his jeans.

"Thank you," I said, searching into his eyes, which said he wanted me. "I love my new place."

Jaylin had a blank expression on his face and he did not respond. He ripped my shirt apart, causing each and every button to fly off and bounce on the floor. His arms went around my waist and he lifted my body to sit on the edge of the double sinks. His jeans dropped to his ankles, and he gripped the back of my neck, bringing my lips to his. We sucked in a heap of each other's saliva. As he began to finger fuck me, my entire body was on fire. My hips were moving to the motion of his fingers, and I was barely able to keep still on the counter. My breasts were poked out right in front of him, and it wasn't long before he started giving them some attention. I could feel the heat coming from the tips of my toes, to the top of my forehead, which had already started to sweat. To cool myself, I reached back for the faucet to turn on the icy cold water. As Jaylin sucked my breasts and jabbed his fingers into me, I splashed and rubbed water all over my body to cool it. He sucked my wet fingers, and it wasn't long before he started sucking something else. I jumped down from the counter, pulling my shirt away from my body and dropping it to the floor. While holding on to the counter, I bent over and Jaylin inserted himself from behind me. His dick filled my slippery suction hole to capacity, and he was slamming it into me good. My firm breasts were bouncing around, and he extended his hands to massage them. He started massaging my clitoris with the tips of his fingers, and that *always* did it for me. I curled my toes, trying to shake off the tingling feeling that was taking over my body.

"Fuck me good, baby," I shouted while licking my lips. "I love this big dick in me! I could live with it in me for the rest of my life! How about that? Would you like that, baby? I know you would."

Jaylin said nothing, but he didn't have to. His grunts responded for him. As he picked up his pace, I exploded, covering his shaft like a heavily glazed doughnut.

"Gotdamn!" he shouted, then jerked backward. I felt his warm juices running down my legs and my pussy felt swollen from the beating it had just taken. We both remained in our positions, trying to regroup and taking deep, long breaths. Jaylin lightly smacked my ass and rubbed it. I stood up and turned around to face him.

"Why didn't you warn me that you were coming? Had I known, I would have been prepared."

He hungrily licked around his lips. "You're always prepared, Scorpio. And I thought you liked spontaneous sex?"

"Oh, I do, especially when it's with you."

Giving me a wink, he lifted his jeans, then zipped them. Afterward, he picked up his belt and tossed it over his shoulder. He walked toward the kids' rooms. Nearly ten minutes later, he came back out. Standing at a distance, he looked over at me still in the kitchen.

"I'll call you in a few days. I'm glad you like your place, and I hope the kids like it too."

"They do. Thanks again."

He nodded, and swaggered his way toward the door to exit. I stepped out of the kitchen and watched him.

"Also," he said, turning to me before he got to the door, "I want you to start taking birth control pills. I don't want any more babies. As you know, I already have enough. Okay?"

I slowly nodded.

"Don't be lying to me, Scorpio, I mean it. I don't want you playing games with me."

"I won't, as I do understand your concern. By the way, what about the name Justin Rogers? I already took care of that, so what do you think?"

He paused for a moment, then winked. "Good choice. Now, good night."

"I love you," I rushed to say before he walked out the door.

He turned those gorgeous gray eyes to me, leaving me in a trance. "I know. Me too."

The door closed and I hugged my waist, squeezing it tightly with my arms. This had to work out for my children and me. Seemed like Jaylin had saved the day, once again. With Bruce leaving me with all of the bills and responsibilities, he very well could have left me broke. No way in hell was I going back to stripping or taking my clothes off for money. It could easily have gotten to that point, and I'm so glad it didn't. I dropped to my knees, thanking God for my many blessings, especially for Jaylin.

JAYLIN

Fuck all of the naysayers and outsiders. This was my life. For now, this was how I chose to live it. There was no other way for me to have contact with my kids on a daily basis. I had to make sure that I kept Scorpio satisfied. Even though I could feel some changes about to happen with me and Nokea, she couldn't deny that since we'd been married, our lives had been drama free. A big challenge was now facing us, and I was hopeful that we would pull through, as we had done so many times in the past.

For the last couple of weeks, I kind of noticed some things about Nokea. She had been very observant and seemed to question some of my moves. My routine had changed up a bit, so I intended to be careful. I wasn't trying to be slick. After all, I had planned to tell Nokea *some* of what had been going on.

The timing, however, just wasn't right. Scorpio and the kids came in last night, and I wanted to see them. I had thoughts about fucking Scorpio again, and, like always, slamming myself into her backside just always did something to me. I got home about one twenty-five in the morning, and I was lucky Shane hadn't made it home either. I called his cell phone, and he was just leaving Joy's house. We met up, and walked into the house together. Nokea didn't suspect a thing. I told her we'd been out for drinks, and she seemed cool with it.

My lies, however, were getting very much out of control. I felt bad about the shit. This was so unlike me, but there was a time and a place to spill the truth. I'd always done my best to be honest with Nokea, but this situation required some lies to be told. By all means, and there was still no doubt whatsoever in my mind . . . I loved the hell out of my wife. Yes, through some people's eyes, I had made some bad choices, but nobody had to deal with my choices but me. It was hard for me to explain the deep need I had for my children, and that also applied to the love I had for their mothers. One love, of course, was stronger than the other. But the truth of the matter was, I cared deeply for them both. How I would ever get Nokea to understand what I was feeling, I wasn't sure. Some way, or somehow, I had to do it, and do it soon.

Shane had been questioning me about where I was last night, as well as my new attitude. He also knew my routine had changed, so I decided to come clean to him about all that was going on. As my true best friend and dedicated business partner, I needed his advice. Of course, I didn't expect for him to embrace what I had done. After all, he had been in love with Scorpio too.

After our morning workout in the weight room, we sat in the sauna with our shorts on and towels draped over our heads. The room was filled with hot steam, and sweat rolled from our bodies. I wiped my wet face with a soft towel, then placed it back over my hanging head. My hands were clenched together in front of me and I looked down at the floor.

"I need your advice about something," I said to Shane. "But you've got to keep an open mind about it."

He removed the towel from his head, placing the towel on his shoulders. "I'm always open-minded, especially when it comes to business."

"This ain't about business. It's more personal."

"Shoot," Shane said. "I'm good with that too."

I finally looked up and cocked my tense neck from side to side. "I've been seeing another woman behind Nokea's back."

Shane's eyes shot open and he looked at me as if he'd seen a ghost. "You what?" he immediately shouted. "Nah, Jay, quit playing. Don't be fucking with me like that."

My blank expression implied that I wasn't playing. "At times, I wish I were playing, but this shit is real. Real as it can get."

Shane shook his head in disbelief. "I—I can't even comment. If I do, I will offend you. Man, you know better! Nokea . . . some muthafucking men would lay their lives on the line for a woman like her. She has made you so damn complete, and I know you ain't that gotdamn selfish where you just gotta have yourself another piece of pussy. You risking all that you have over some pussy! There has to be something more."

"I already feel like shit, okay? But this ain't really about that. It's about my child . . . my children. I have another son, and I just found out about him."

Shane's mouth dropped open. "Please spare me," he spat. "You mean to tell me, Jay, that you've had a child on Nokea's watch? Is that what you're saying? You had a child during the course of your marriage?"

"To put it simple, yes. I fucked up, and my chickens have come home to roost. I don't even know how to tell her, man. What in the hell am I going to do if she leaves me?"

Shane just kept shaking his head. "Man, you had my ass fooled! I was bragging about you and shit. Negro, I was looking up to yo ass . . . wanting to find somebody who could make me feel the way I *thought* Nokea made you feel. You still empty as a carton of milk. I cannot believe that you haven't been satisfied with the life the

Man Upstairs has blessed you with. What about LJ and Jaylene, Jay? Did you think about them?"

Shane's words were harsh, but I can't say that I hadn't expected them. "Of course, I've thought about them, and they have always been my number one priority. Nokea has been too, and you can't even sit there and say that I am the man who I used to be. We're talking about one woman, not ten or twelve. I fight off women's advances every single day of my life, so give a brotha a little credit. This particular woman is somewhat difficult for me to shake."

"Well, I can't wait to meet her. She must be a badass woman with money, a great personality, strong goals in life . . . and values—obviously, she doesn't have them if she knows you're married. You did tell her you were married, didn't you?"

"She knows. She knows all about me, and loves me, just as much as Nokea does."

"I doubt that shit. And there ain't no way I'm gon' let you sit there and even compare the love Nokea has for you versus the love another woman may claim to have. I thought you had more sense than that, Jay. You may need to see a psychiatrist for a psychiatric evaluation."

Now Shane was starting to piss me off. His comments were going a bit too far. "Look," I snapped. "I am human and I make mistakes. . . ."

"That's a cop-out, and you know it. Human beings have brains, which they're supposed to use too. I don't even know why you're telling me this shit. If you think I got your back on this—honestly, I don't. You're going to tear your family apart, and Nokea, LJ and Jaylene do not deserve this."

Yeah, the shit he said hurt. Just the thought of my family being torn apart disturbed me, but I had hopes that Nokea would see things differently.

"Calm your ass down. I'm not asking you to have my back. All I ask is that you listen. I have to tell Nokea about my son, and it is killing me because I need to get this shit off my chest. I don't know what her reaction is going to be, but just pray for me, all right? Can you at least do that for me?"

I hadn't seen Shane look this disgusted in a long time. He didn't even know yet that the woman in question was Scorpio. I was skeptical about telling him, but I wanted to get it out in the open.

"I'm always gon' pray for you, my brotha. In the meantime, you got some soul-searching to do. I can only hope that this woman ain't trying to get you for your dollars. Are you one hundred percent sure the child is yours?"

"A hundred and twenty percent sure. He looks just like me, even more than LJ. LJ is a shade darker than me, but he's almost identical."

"What's his name?"

"Justin. Justin Rogers."

"What about his mother? How did you meet her?"

"I've known her for a long time."

"How long?"

"Years."

"So you've been fucking around with her since you've been here?"

"Before that."

Shane's face scrunched up and his head cocked back. "Felicia?" he asked.

"No," I paused. "Scorpio."

Shane shot up from his seat like a rocket. "Scorpio?" he shouted, then placed his hands behind his head. "How? When—"

"That night I left your house and talked to you about moving to Florida, I dropped by her house. We had sex, and several weeks ago, I found out she had my baby."

Shane stood still, staring at me without a blink.

"I know this shit gonna take some time to settle," I said. "But at the end of the day, I have to do right by my son. You know me, Shane, and you know I'm not going to turn my back on him."

Shane finally blinked and rubbed down his face. "You weren't in St. Louis last night. Who were you with? Are you still fucking her, Jay?"

"I moved Scorpio, my son and Mackenzie here. They arrived yesterday, and yes, we have been intimate."

At that moment, Shane walked out. I heard his footsteps go upstairs, and it was pretty clear that he was upset. Shit, if that was his reaction, I could only imagine Nokea's.

NOKEA

Something was going on between Jaylin and Shane, but Jaylin told me it was nothing to worry about. They were barely speaking to each other around the house. Shane was usually gone, more than he was here. They hadn't even been going to the office together, and I eavesdropped on a conversation they were having in Shane's bedroom the other day. They were arguing.

"And I don't need you judging my ass either!" Jaylin yelled. "I'm not expecting you to take my side, but some of your words have been insulting. As a friend, you can get at me better than you have. That's all I'm saying."

"And all I'm saying is you are wrong! You hate for anybody to call you on your shit, but I have no problem doing it! I'm done trying to talk to you about what I think you should do, and the next time you find yourself in a jam like this, don't come to me with it! Especially, if you're not willing to listen."

"I'm always willing to listen, but advice that is followed by attacks and harsh words go in one ear and out the other. Come to me correct, brotha. And whether you agree with how I handle my business or not, that's the least you can do. It's a respect thing, no matter what."

Shane didn't respond to Jaylin. Before I got busted for listening in, I walked away from the door. I assumed their argument might have been about business. Just last night, I saw them standing by the outside Jacuzzi having a civil conversation. They both had drinks in their hands. When they slammed their hands together, I guessed they had reconciled whatever differences they'd had.

As for me, well, things weren't quite that simple. I backtracked Jaylin's steps from at least three and a half weeks ago, pretty surprised by what I found. First of all, whenever I stepped to Jaylin with my concerns, I always had to present him with the facts. He was the kind of man who would take the information I had and make it look like the opposite.

I wasn't sure how he could or would deny the reservation confirmation I'd found on his computer, clearly stating that he had taken a flight to St. Louis a few weeks back, not Chicago as he had told me. Then there was the receipt from the casino I'd found in his pocket. It was clearly from a casino in St. Louis as well, and so was the receipt I'd found for the hotel suite he'd paid almost $600 a night for. Lastly there was his Facebook page. He'd been discussing our business with a lot of women. They had plenty of questions about our relationship and about him. Some of the comments upset me, and Jaylin's arrogance had me shaking my head.

My main concern was about him admitting he'd spent some time with Scorpio. I couldn't read everything, because I heard him coming through the door. And when I tried to check his Facebook page later, his password had been changed. I had never been the kind of wife to search through his things; but surely if you seek, you will find. After finding all of that, I searched his cell phone records on the computer. Of course, I needed a password to log in to that too. After trying one password after the next, surprisingly, I was able to log in when I typed in *Mackenzie*. Not LJ, or Jaylene, or Nokea, or Nanny B, but . . . Mackenzie. I went through his phone records. During the time he was away, I noticed one number in particular. I called the number anonymously, and it was no surprise who answered. *Scorpio*. I hung up, and since then, I had said not one word to Jaylin.

He was already running around here being fake, but I knew his fakery wouldn't last for long. He'd tell me what was up. If he didn't come clean after the weekend was over, I would.

Our neighbors down the street were having another one of their dinner gatherings, which we always looked forward to attending. The reason was simply because Jaylin and Shane always made more business connections, and those connections turned into more money. I didn't mind going, as I had gotten pretty close with the other wives in the neighborhood. Sometimes we'd shop together, take the kids out together, go walk together, etc.

Tiffanie was going to be there too. For the night, Joy had been put on the back burner. According to Tiffanie, she was okay with Shane seeing other people, and she decided to back off. She said that she'd started seeing other people too. I was happy about her decision to do that. Besides, it seemed like I had bigger fish to fry, so Shane and Tiffanie's issues were no longer my concern.

I wanted to look my best tonight. I had gone to the hairdresser and had my hair hooked up right. My right side was cut low, but my left side was cut into a hanging bob that crossed over my forehead and almost covered my eye. The hairdresser called it "Rihanna style." My dress was a long-sleeved silk white minidress that had a plunging dip in the back. It clung to my curves all over and showed off my nicely toned caramel legs. The dress, itself, resembled the one Amber Rose wore at the music awards with Kanye West. Too sexy for my taste or not, when I saw it, I had to have it. I wore silver-strapped heels with rhinestones and had a purse that matched. My sweet perfume was working for me. When I looked in the mirror, I was delighted by what I saw. To heck with Jaylin, if he ever required much more than what I had to give.

I left the bathroom, only to find Jaylin and Shane sitting in the great room with their black suits on and white pressed shirts underneath. They had drinks in their hands, and I could tell they were waiting on me. Yes, they both looked gorgeous; and when I saw Jaylin glance at his watch, I stepped up my pace. I stood next to the tall, thick columns near the foyer, holding my tiny purse in my hand.

"Sorry it took me so long," I said, smiling at the awed looks on their faces. "I'm ready whenever you are."

Jaylin and Shane, too, continued to look at me as if I hadn't said a word. Shane slowly stood up, and Jaylin still hadn't moved.

"I—I'm going outside to get some fresh air," Shane said. He walked past me with approval, yet some lust in his eyes. "You look nice, Nokea. Real nice."

"Thank you," I said, blushing. "So do you."

Jaylin stood up and guzzled down his glass of Rémy. He kept his eyes on me, and then he placed the glass on the table.

"Do you . . . Are you wearing any panties?" he asked. "I can tell you don't have on a bra, and your nipple imprints are showing."

"Thanks for noticing my hair. I had it done today. My nails were done too, and my panties are, indeed, on."

Jaylin stepped up to me and took my hand. He placed it on his heart. "Can you feel that?" he asked.

"Yes. Now, why is your heart beating fast?"

"Because you are the sexiest, most beautiful, loving and dedicated woman I know. I don't know if I should send you back in our room to put on another dress, or be proud that I have you as my wife. You already know that if you keep that dress on, I'm gonna be all over you tonight. The men are not going to be able to contain themselves, and I already gotta go check that fool, Shane, for drooling at his mouth."

"Do what you gotta do," I said, turning around. "I'm not taking off this dress, and the only thing you can do is be proud to call me your wife."

I stepped away, and Jaylin couldn't resist pulling me back into his arms and kissing me. His hands swayed all over my backside, and he couldn't help but take a squeeze.

"I have got to be the luckiest man in the world. My dick already leaking, and we need to hurry back from this party—soon."

I took Jaylin's hand and we made our way to the car. We only had to drive about half a mile down the street. As soon as we parked, we could see how crowded the party was. Bentleys, Jags, Mercedes-Benzes—expensive cars were everywhere, and our neighbors definitely knew how to throw a party.

As soon as we got inside, everybody was being friendly. Along with Jaylin and me, and Shane and Tiffanie, there were only two other black couples there. We were very cool with them, so we stopped to talk to them first. Jaylin kept a tight grip on my hand, and that was a good thing. I didn't know if the dress was too much or not, but it was definitely bringing me attention, especially from the men. My neighbor's husband, Jerrod, who lived directly across from us, he was the first to pay his compliments. He looked me over; then he patted Jaylin on his back.

"You guys are so fucking awesome, man. Nokea looks magnificent."

He leaned over to kiss my cheek and I proudly turned it up to him. "Thanks, Jerrod," I said. "Your wife, Marsha, looks spectacular too."

"Oh, not like you do. You remind me of that, uh, Nia Long chick. She is hot!" He calmed himself and straightened his suit jacket. "Have an enjoyable evening and do not leave until you've tried some of the dip over there. Marsha made it and it is *the* best."

"I will," I said, releasing Jaylin's hand so I could walk over to the bar and try the dip. Surprisingly, he let my hand go. When I walked away, my sexy walk was on point. I purposely strutted my stuff. No sooner had I tasted the dip, another one of my neighbors came up to me. His name was Charles and he was known as the playboy of the neighborhood. George Clooney was written all over him; and for many women, he was hard to resist.

"Nokeaaa," he said, dragging out my name while holding out his arms for a hug. I hugged him and he slowly rubbed up and down on my back. "You look lovely," he said. "Where's Jaylin?"

I looked around Charles. As I had suspected, Jaylin's eyes were focused in our direction. Charles put his fist up at Jaylin, and all he did was nod. I was just about ready to walk away, but that's when I saw Tiffanie heading my way. She had arrived separately from us, planning to meet up with Shane at the party.

"Hey, you." She smiled, making her way through the crowd. "I love, love, love your dress. Where in God's earth did you get it from?"

"I'll tell you later," I said, looking her over. Tiffanie looked nice too. She had on a simple black strapless dress that gave her boobs an extra boost. "Did you see Shane?" I asked.

"I did, but he's talking to Mr. Milono right now. I know it's about business, so I stepped away to find you. Let's go get something to drink."

I looked back to see if I could see Jaylin, but he had walked away. Tiffanie, several other ladies and I were standing around talking about reality TV shows. We laughed at all that was going on with the shows that we loved to watch, and talked badly about the ones that we couldn't resist watching. As one of the ladies was giving her input, I looked behind her and saw Shane standing alone on the balcony, looking at the amazing scenery down below. His suit jacket was pulled back and his hands were in his pockets. "Sexy" was the only word that described him. I excused myself from the ladies and walked up closer to him.

"Are you having a good time?" I asked.

Before he said a word, his eyes searched me up and down. "Yes, Nokea, I'm having a great time. I was looking around for Jaylin, but I didn't see him."

"I saw him inside talking to Mr. Milono and some of his buddies. They sure do like you and Jaylin a lot."

Shane laughed. "As long as you got the money to fit in their circle, everything is fine. You should know that by now."

"I'm starting to get the picture," I said, chuckling. "But, uh, I've been meaning to ask you, is everything okay with you and Jaylin? I've noticed some changes with the two of you, and I hope you're still excited about being here with us."

"I'm good. Real good. Jaylin has been more than a friend to me, almost like a brother. We have our differences sometimes, but there ain't nothing we won't be able to work through."

"That's good to know. I know how much he cares for you, and he's been so happy since you've been here with us."

"I know how much he cares and loves you too, Nokea. I hope you know that he will do anything in the world for you and the kids."

"Of course. Why wouldn't he?"

I could tell Shane knew what was going on behind closed doors. For him to say what he'd said, that was just another clue. Everything was starting to add up, and I couldn't wait to present Jaylin with the facts, along with what I had suspected.

Everyone talked and danced the night away. Jaylin and I had a wonderful time fast and slow dancing on the concrete patio full of intoxicated people. Jaylin and Shane kept switching partners; and whenever Shane would get too close to me, Jaylin would cut in. He was so protective of me. As numerous men asked to dance with me, he made it clear that wasn't going to happen. He kept complimenting me throughout the night, and many of our neighbors stressed what an attractive couple we made.

"Oh, I would pay millions to watch the two of you make love," my neighbor Nancy said. "Jaylin oozes sex appeal, and so do you. I bet sex with him is *sooo* great, isn't it?"

Tiffanie and I looked at each other and laughed. I knew Nancy had had too much to drink, but what an inappropriate thing to say. When I didn't answer, she made a comment to Tiffanie.

"Stop laughing, you lucky bitch. Shane is just as gorgeous, and I hate you for nabbing that great piece of ass. Those two make me want to go black and never go back. My husband is such a lazy bum in bed. Boy, does that man need help in the bedroom!"

Nancy's husband walked up, stumbling right in front of us. He was drunk, like always, and his glasses were tilted on his face. As drunk as Nancy was, she had the nerve to cut her eyes at him. "Come on, cupcake," he said, "let's dance."

She smiled and snapped her fingers as she danced away. They were such an interesting couple to me, and were always blunt. Knowing how much money her husband had, I was sure she would make that horrible sex she mentioned work out.

The dinner party wrapped up about two o'clock in the morning. Shane drove to Tiffanie's house with her, and Jaylin and I went home together. He was borderline tipsy. As I stood on the balcony, outside our bedroom, Jaylin snuck up from behind me. He wrapped his arms around my waist. Like always, he placed passionate kisses on my neck.

"Why you out here?" he slurred. "Why don't you come inside so I can show you what I'm workin' wit."

I continued to gaze out at the ocean. "I already know what you're working with, and a sista getting a little bit bored with the same ole, same ole," I joked, but kept it real.

Jaylin halted the pecks on my neck. "Say it ain't so, Mrs. Rogers. Did you just try to say being with me was boring?"

I shrugged. "If that's how you want to put it, then yes, maybe so."

Jaylin stepped a few inches back; then he peeled the top part of my dress away from my shoulders. He rolled it down past my breasts and tightened his arms around my waist. His lips touched my earlobe.

"Let's go inside and make love *all* night long. I can almost promise you a baby tonight, and you know what? As anxious as I am to dip into that pussy, you don't even have to do any work. As soon as I pop my dick inside you, bam! We gon' make our baby."

"Hmm." I smiled. "Are you sure about that? I get to have *another* one of your babies, huh?"

"Yep. And being the loving and beautiful mother figure that you are, how can I go wrong?"

"You can't," I replied. "There's not a chance in hell."

Jaylin lowered the rest of my dress and I stepped
out of it. He lifted me and carried me to our bed. Carefully laying me on it, he looked down at me. I couldn't
believe when I saw that strange look in his eyes again. I
held his handsome face with my hands.

"Please tell me what's wrong," I begged. "I can tell
that something is troubling you, and I need to know
what it is."

"I just have a lot on my mind. There's nothing for you
to worry about, okay?"

"Are you sure? Your problems are always mine too."

"Positive" was all he said.

He knelt to the floor, taking off my shoes and tossing them aside. After he removed his clothes, he eased
on top of me and made love to me in slow motion.
Our bodies rocked in rhythm together. I gave him my
juices, while sucking in a heap of his. There were plenty
of juices to exchange, and one load after another swam
into me. Just like the last time, Jaylin had exhausted
himself with telling me how much I meant to him.
Whether I was willing to admit it or not, he meant a lot
to me too.

JAYLIN

Making love to Nokea was truly the best. She knew how to make me feel as if I had not a worry in the world. She provided me with the love and care I so desperately needed. She made me feel whole and feel as if I could conquer the entire world. Her touch was like a security blanket, telling me that I could hold on to it forever and never let it go. After the lengthy lovemaking session last night, I realized one simple thing about myself. I was one selfish motherfucker, and why did life always have to revolve around my needs? It was so hard for me to consider other people's feelings. After marrying Nokea, I thought I'd gotten beyond that shit. Obviously, I hadn't. I had to work hard on my selfishness, or if not, I knew I would lose everything.

The dinner party last night was an eye-opener too. I couldn't keep my eyes off Nokea, and there were many times that she didn't even notice me looking at her. She was so beautiful, sexy and classy at the same time. I loved the fact that she felt so confident in herself that she could dress as she did. The men couldn't keep their eyes off her, and her aura was lighting up the room. That's the kind of woman I loved to call my wife. After all of the dust settled, I intended for her status to stay that way.

On another note, Shane and I had settled our differences. He was a little uptight about Scorpio, and I truly understood how he felt. The only thing he asked of me was that I not use him as an alibi to see Scorpio. I promised him that I wouldn't. His other advice was for me not to tell Nokea. He felt as if it would devastate her, and he didn't want to see me lose out. I thought about that too, but I also knew how much Nokea loved me. Yes, she would be highly . . . severely upset, but walk away for good? I wasn't sure about that. We had a lot to lose if she did, and a part of me didn't think she'd be willing to lose so much.

For the first time, I got to sit down, relax and play with my son. Mackenzie was in physical therapy, and I had spent at least an hour with her earlier. Justin was a happy child, and I couldn't believe how much he looked like me. I couldn't wait for LJ and Jaylene to meet him. Once I broke a few things down to Nanny B, things would eventually come together.

Justin and I sat on the floor, stacking some of his plastic Lego blocks as high as they would go. I let him kick them. When they came crashing down, he laughed. I pulled him in my arms, kissing his soft cheeks.

"You think that's funny?" I said, tickling him. He cracked up and fell back on the floor while kicking his feet on me so I would stop.

"Okay," I said. "Let's put this train set together so you can see this bad boy do its thing. Will you help me?"

"Yes," he said, sitting down next to me.

After a while, all Justin did was watch me put the train set together. We were both excited, watching the trains roll quickly around the tracks.

"I told you, you would like that. Now, what else would you like to do?"

Justin stuck his finger in his mouth and looked around his room. He then pointed to his bookshelf.

"You want me to read a book?" I asked.

He nodded. I removed his finger from his mouth. "Don't nod, say yes. 'Yes, I want you to read a book.' Always be clear about what you want."

"Yes. Read!" Justin shouted.

I laughed, knowing that he liked to read because of Mackenzie. As much as I used to read to her, she now loved to read books. She told me she read to Justin every single day. As he sat on my lap while I read to him, he seemed tuned in. It impressed me how much Mackenzie looked after him, just as LJ looked out for Jaylene. I was so lucky to have all of them in my life. Even though I felt bad about what I'd done, this was one of the things I hadn't yet regretted.

It was getting close to dinnertime, and Loretta had the whole penthouse infused with the smell of Italian food. The four-layered cheesy lasagna almost smelled as good as Nanny B's, but not quite. I carried Justin out of the room, flying him like an airplane, causing him to laugh his butt off.

"Jaylin, please be careful with him," Scorpio said, standing in the kitchen with Loretta. "He's not one hundred percent yet, okay?"

I put Justin on the floor and he ran up to Scorpio. She picked him up and he squeezed his arms around her neck.

"Hi, baby," she said, kissing all over his cheeks. "Did you have fun?"

He nodded and Loretta gave him a Blow Pop he was reaching for. Scorpio unraveled it, and Justin put the sucker in his mouth.

"Are you staying for dinner?" Scorpio asked me.

"Nah, I'm getting ready to go. I'll stay for dinner some time next week."

Scorpio walked me to the door with Justin on her hip. I leaned in to kiss both of them.

"Be good," I said. "I'll be back sometime tomorrow."

Scorpio waved good-bye and so did Justin. Spending time with him truly made my day. I headed for home, seriously on cloud nine. I was anxious to spend time with my other two children. When I got home, no one was there. That kind of surprised me, because it was rare that we had a peaceful home. No one had left me a note, text or anything. I called Nokea's cell phone, she said that she was en route home. She said the kids were with Nanny B at the mall and they were going to a 3-D kiddie movie afterward. When I hung up with her, I called Shane. He was in a meeting with a potential client, who wanted to purchase one of our properties. I told him to hit me back later, to let me know how the meeting went.

Wasting time until Nokea got home, I changed clothes and headed to the lower level to shoot some hoops on my half-court. I kept thinking about playing ball with my sons, imagining them as they got older. When I started to sweat, I took off my wife-beater and played in my hanging basketball shorts. Time was flying by. I heard Nokea call my name on the intercom, I rushed over to it, pushing the button.

"Yeah, baby," I said breathing heavily.

"Where are you?"

"I'm on the court. I'll be upstairs in a few minutes."

"Hurry," she said.

I took two more shots, missed one and made the other. When I got upstairs, I stopped by the fridge to get a bottled water. I drank it halfway down, then poured the rest over my sweaty face. I caught the dripping water with a towel, then rubbed it on my chest. I saw Nokea leaning against the arched kitchen's doorway with her arms folded, I walked up to kiss her cheek.

"What's up?" I said. "I can't believe we're all alone. If you want, we can definitely take advantage of the time."

Nokea smiled, but she took my hand and led me into the great room. I didn't want to sit on the leather couches with my sweaty body, but she asked me to have a seat. She sat across from me, crossing her legs.

"First, let me say that we're alone on purpose. I asked Nanny B to take the kids out for the day, and Shane already told me that he had an appointment. I—I've known you since I was six. I think after thirty plus years, I have gotten to know you pretty well, Jaylin. Even when you were a little boy, I knew when you were troubled, and I did everything in my power to help ease your pain. As we grew up together, that never, ever changed. When we became a couple, I knew the kind of man you'd grown into, and I accepted that because of your past. In time, I figured all wounds would heal, and eventually they did. With that, I am requesting that you tell me what is going on with you, right here and right now. I will not accept you telling me 'nothing,' as I know that is not the truth."

I hesitated, but I spoke up. "Like I said, I just have a lot going on. I'm trying to close some of these deals I've been investing in. Even though I didn't want to go back to work to this extent, I'm finding myself getting more involved. My time away from you and my kids is starting to bother me. Yes, the fact that we haven't had another child is disappointing. I'm doing my best not to let all of this get to me. In due time, everything will be okay."

Nokea stared at me and then cleared her throat. "Were you ever able to close the deal in Chicago? I know you've been working hard on that one in particular. I hope you didn't lose any money on that deal."

"I'm still working on it. The properties were pretty decent, and Shane and I may shoot down there in a couple of weeks to see what's up."

Nokea reached over to the table beside her and picked up several papers. She flipped through them; then she reached out to give one of the papers to me.

"Can you explain that to me? I printed it from your in-box, and there must be some kind of mistake."

I looked at the paper, and it was the reservation confirmation for my trip to St. Louis, not Chicago. I couldn't even think fast enough. When I had no reply, Nokea got up and stood in front of me. She let me see the other papers, two of which were my cell phone records and some Internet confessions on Facebook. She pointed to a number on my cell phone bill.

"While you're thinking about your response, tell me who that phone number belongs to. Tell me why this paper shows you were at the Four Seasons Hotel the days you told me you were in Chicago. And just to be clear," she said, giving me a money ticket from the casino, "how did you get this in your possession, when, according to you, you were in Chicago?"

She went back over to the chair, crossing her legs as she sat. "Think fast, as I have more questions for you, when you get finished answering those."

I sat back on the couch, unprepared to lay all of my bullshit on the line. Yeah, it was now or never, and I really didn't have a choice, other than to come clean. My stomach was already turning in knots, and the deep breaths I'd been taking weren't really helping. I placed my hands behind my head, ready to tell the love of my life *some* of the truth.

"Several weeks ago, do you remember when a phone call came in the middle of the night?" I asked, but Nokea made not one gesture. "Well, the call was from Scorpio. She told me that Mackenzie had been in a terrible car accident and asked if I would come to St. Louis to see her. I did, and when I got there, Mackenzie was pretty messed up. I . . . There was no way that I could leave her. She was happy to see me, Nokea, and I just couldn't turn my back on her again. I wanted to tell you, but I know how you feel about Scorpio and Mackenzie. There was no way you would understand what I was feeling, so I lied. I felt as if I didn't have a choice, and please forgive me for not being completely honest with you about this."

"What would make you think I would be against you going to St. Louis to see about Mackenzie? Don't you know me at all? Am I really such a cruel and vengeful person that you think I would want you to say, 'To hell with Mackenzie'? You have only assumed that I have something against her, and I never have. What I am concerned about, however, is your ongoing connection with Scorpio. Did you spend any time alone with her, while you were in St. Louis?"

I rubbed my goatee and my eyelids lowered. My whole body was tense and I held my breath before blurting out, "No, I didn't."

Nokea uncrossed her legs and sighed. "Have you forgotten that I can tell when you're lying? Yes, you did spend time alone with her. Do I need to share with you how I know what happened between the two of you?"

I wasn't sure if Nokea knew the truth or not, but since she was pulling out all of these papers and shit, I wasn't taking any chances on her pulling out photos, confirming the truth. I closed my burning eyes, rubbing them with the tips of my fingers. "She—she stayed one night with me," I admitted.

"Did you have sex with her?"

I couldn't even open my eyes to see Nokea's reaction. I waited before answering; then I came out with it. "Unfortunately, yes. Yes, I did, but it . . ." I paused, not being able to find the right words to say.

Nothing but silence fell over our great room, and the only thing you could hear was a mouselike squeak that was coming from a hanging ceiling fan. When I opened my eyes, I saw a tear roll down Nokea's face. Her lips quivered as she spoke. "Was that the only time you had sex with her since we've been married? Be honest, Jaylin, and do not lie to me anymore."

I nibbled on my bottom lip, trying to decide if I had the guts to go through with this conversation. When I noticed her eyes continuously fill with water, a tingling feeling rushed through my body. I regretted that I had to sit there and watch her next reaction.

"I—I had sex with her when we went to St. Louis for Pat's baby shower. She, uh, Scorpio"—I cleared the thick mucus from my throat—"got pregnant that time, and I . . . I just found out the baby was mine. He almost died in the car accident too, and, uh . . ." I paused, squeezing my eyes and rubbing them again.

"What!" Nokea shouted loudly, causing my ears to ring. Her voice was tearful and shaky. "Did . . . are you telling me she has your baby?"

I had no words right now as I watched tears drip from her chin.

"*Why*, Jaylin? How could you ever do something like this to me? What did I ever do to you, for you to continuously inflict pain on me?"

I wiped my hands down my face. "Baby, I swear to God that other than those few times with Scorpio, I have never been with anyone else. I didn't know she was pregnant, and it surprised the fuck out of me. I made a huge and costly mistake, and my intentions have never been to hurt you."

Nokea's cries started to become rapid. By the way her body was trembling, she looked to be on the verge of a nervous breakdown. I tightened my fist, pounding it on the couch and trying to get her to understand that I did this with no intent to hurt her.

"I love you, baby, and you have got to hold on to that right now. Please forgive me for fucking up. I can't take back what's happened, and I . . . I just got to deal with it. Damn!"

She moved her hands away from her face, allowing me to see the damage I'd caused. Her tears were falling like a constant rain, and the look in her eyes was turning ice-cold. I could have killed myself right now, watching her begin to fall apart. She gripped her stomach and spoke with a shaky voice while rocking back and forth. "How are you dealing with it? I'm almost afraid to ask, but I already have an idea, since your daily routine has changed. She's here, isn't she? That—that bitch and your babies are here, aren't they?"

I couldn't even respond. I leaned forward, placing my elbows on my knees and massaging my forehead with my hands.

"Oh, my God!" Nokea screamed. "You made arrangements for her to live here! In Miami! Did you really? You are still fucking her, aren't you?"

I was speechless. At this point, the baseball-sized lump in my throat was so huge that I couldn't even respond.

Nokea rushed up to me and snatched my hands away from my forehead. She smacked the shit out of me, causing both sides of my face to burn. One smack on the left cheek, then on the right. My head snapped to the side both times, and that's when she punched me between my eyes and nose. The blow caused my eyes to water from the sting, and my nose felt as though it was bleeding. I couldn't even defend myself, or my actions. She pulled my hair back so tight, forcing me to lie back on the couch, as she lay over me. I squeezed my eyes together, trying to fight back my anger and the pain I'd felt from her aggressiveness. She demanded more answers.

"Why, Jaylin?" she yelled through gritted teeth, yanking at my hair. *"Whyyy?* I—I swear to God, I hate you! I hate your fucking guts, you bastard!"

This time, she kneed me in the groin. When I grabbed my dick, she released her grip on my hair. She slapped me again, and started pounding my back and kicking me wherever she could. She was all over me, and I had to take that shit like a man who had, no doubt, wronged his wife. I grabbed her waist to calm her, but she dug her nails into my skin, piercing it. I snatched my arms away, and that's when she kneed me in the groin again. This time, that shit hurt really, really bad. I grabbed myself and dropped to my knees.

"Fuck," I shouted. "Stop it, Nokea, before I hurt you!"

She halted her punches. "You horny muthafucka! You've already hurt me! You could never hurt me more!"

Her kick went into my side and she pushed my head to the side as hard as she could. I lost my balance, trying to soothe my nuts with my hand. Nokea turned around, picked up the crystal vase on the table, slamming it into the glass. Shards of the glass shattered everywhere, including all over me. As she rushed over to the expensive painting on our wall, I got up and grabbed her from behind.

"Baby, stop. Please stop!" I yelled, trying to calm her with an embrace. "I'm so sorry, and I promise I'll make this up to you!"

She turned, shoving me backward. I had never seen Nokea react like this. Where in the hell was my wife? She picked up a mirror-framed picture of our family, throwing it into the glass wall unit, which stretched from one wall to the next. More glass shattered, and so did the tall floor vases as she sent them crashing to the floor. Allowing her to let out her frustrations, I fell back on the couch, covering my teary eyes with my hand. All

I heard was more glass breaking, and I wasn't sure if she had broken any of the glass windows that viewed the ocean from the back of our house. Each crash, though, made me feel as if an electrical shock was rushing through my body. She stormed through the entire first level, tearing up shit and breaking everything in her sight. Words of hate for me were being spewed my way, and her harsh words hurt like hell. It especially pained when she stressed how much she wished I were dead and she hated me. I don't care how bad it had ever gotten between us in the past; I couldn't remember a time when she had said that to me.

I listened to her going all over our house, basically destroying it. After she went into the kitchen, she came back into the great room, with a butcher knife in her hand. I watched as she slashed one of the couches and then stood in front of me with the knife in her trembling hand. Mascara was smudged underneath her eyes, and they were red as fire.

"Now you go ahead and move your bitch up in here with you. I've made room for her, and I'll be out of your way soon. I can't believe you've done this to us, and I hate your fucking guts for taking me down this road again!"

I looked up at her, feeling so horrible for what I had done to her . . . to us. "I don't need her here with me. I need you," I said calmly. I looked at the shaking knife in her hand. "If you're going to leave me, then go ahead and use that knife. Put me out of my fucking misery. I don't deserve you, baby. I never have."

Just then, the front door opened and Shane rushed in. He saw the knife in Nokea's hand and ran up to her. From behind, he grabbed her waist and she dropped the knife from her hand. Her body was shaking from her crying so hard. Shane cradled her body from behind as she slowly eased to the floor. He kept a tight embrace around her, asking her to calm down.

"I hate him, Shane!" she yelled, while rocking back and forth on her knees. "How could he do this to *me?*"

Shane looked up at me. Seeing the look on his face, all I could do was shamefully drop my head again.

"He made a mistake," Shane said, defending me. "One that I know, for a fact, he regrets."

Nokea held on tight to him, and the continuous echoes from her cries and her desperate asking of "How could he do this to *me?*" would stay with me forever.

NOKEA

This had to be the fastest I had ever moved from one place to another. There was no way possible for me to live in our home with Jaylin, so I packed my bags and left that night. My bank account was sitting pretty, so I wasn't too much worried about finding another place to call home.

Still, I was so unstable, and I hadn't seen my kids for at least a week. They were still with Jaylin. I had been in touch with no one and I lay alone, soaking in my tears, in my new partially furnished condo. The condo set Jaylin back a lot, but I could only imagine the place he had for Scorpio and her kids. I couldn't believe he had taken us down this road, and did he really think that I would go along with the plan? Maybe I could have somehow managed to handle all of this if the other woman wasn't Scorpio. Then I doubted that—because Scorpio or not, Jaylin had not taken his vows seriously. Then, to suggest that he'd only been with Scorpio a few times, and other than that, he had been faithful to me. Was I supposed to clap my hands and thank him? This situation was so messed up and I, more than anyone, wanted to wake up from this horribly bad dream.

Thing is, there was no waking up because this was as real as it could get. Jaylin had not only been unfaithful, but he also conceived a child during the course of our marriage.

How could I possibly deal with something like that? How do women with unfaithful husbands overcome? I couldn't even stand the sight of Jaylin right now, and how in the hell would we ever be able to piece our lives back together? I had to give credit to those women who could forgive, but God would have to forgive me for not being able to put this behind me. There was no way for me to do it, and the thought of what our future now looked like devastated me. I couldn't stop crying for nothing, and this was the worst feeling ever. Was this some kind of payback for what I had done to my ex-husband Collins? Yes, I abruptly ended our marriage to be with Jaylin and left Collins hanging, as well as devastated. I believed in Karma, but in no way did I deserve this. To think that Jaylin was capable of betraying me like this, I just couldn't understand. Was I wrong for believing that he loved me? Did he really love Scorpio that much and couldn't let her go? He had to. There was no way he would risk losing so much if he didn't care about her. I hated her, and I hated him. I had to turn him loose, just so he could be with the woman he obviously had desired to be with instead of me.

My thoughts left me curled up on the bed, hugging the plush body pillow with it tucked between my legs. I was miserable, but I had to get through this. I prayed day in and day out for my sanity. My children missed me, but I didn't feel stable enough to have them around. I knew they were wondering where I had gone. For now, though, I needed time to figure out how I was going to make it without Jaylin. Our life together was over. The bond that I felt we had, well, I wasn't feeling it anymore. Never in my wildest dreams did I think I could have so much hatred for him, and I truly did.

The following week, I couldn't go another day without seeing my kids, so I called Shane's cell phone to see if he would answer. He did, and I asked if he would bring the kids to my condo. I wanted to spend some time with them; it had been two weeks. I told Shane that I didn't want him to be caught in the middle, but there was no way I could turn to Nanny B. She always had Jaylin's back, and I didn't want to hear one of her lectures where she always wound up defending him. Shane told me he'd call me back, but Jaylin did, instead. I didn't even answer my phone; an hour later, Shane called back. He said that he'd bring the kids to see me, and I made him promise not to tell Jaylin the address where I had moved. At first he was hesitant, but then he told me that he wouldn't say anything.

About two hours after that, he showed up at my condo with the kids. My hair was slicked down to my head; I wore cotton pajama pants and a T-shirt. My face was without a drop of makeup, and my eyes remained swollen. The kids ran up to me excitedly; LJ grabbed my neck as I bent down to kiss him, and Jaylene was trying to get picked up. I smiled with happiness glowing on my face.

Shane stood in the doorway. "What time do you want me to pick them up?" he asked.

"Come back tomorrow, okay? They're going to stay the night with me. I'm not sure how we're going to work all of this out, but I know they don't want to be away from Jaylin or Nanny B for long."

LJ and Jaylene ran off, looking at the condo that I now called home.

Shane stepped inside and closed the door. "If you have a minute, can I please sit down and talk to you? I know you ain't trying to hear or discuss a lot of things, but I have to get some things off my chest."

We stepped away from the door and into the living room with asymmetrical ceilings. My condo could in no way compare to our house, and the whole place was kind of simple. It had three bedrooms, an updated kitchen, a dining room and two bathrooms. It was also near the ocean, and was at least four miles from home. For now, it gave me peace and allowed me time to think about what I intended to do.

Shane and I sat next to each other, and he covered my hand with his. "Listen, I just wanted to remind you that Jaylin really loves you, and he knows he has some major damage to repair. I hate to see the both of you like this, and we really, really miss you back at the house. I know you need time to sort through things, but don't give up on your family. No marriage is perfect, Nokea, and there are always challenges that every couple faces. Before you make any decisions, think hard about all that you and Jaylin have. Is it worth it to give up on it now? I don't know, but that's something you'll have to decide."

"Thank you for being the true friend that you are, Shane. But Jaylin and I are over. After all that he's done in the past, there was no room in this marriage for error. All I want to do is figure out what needs to be done with our children. I'm not staying with him because of them. The way I feel about him, I would make their lives miserable. Bottom line, I've been through too much and I am not going to stand by him again."

Shane looked disappointed in my response. I don't know why he expected me to say something different, and I knew what I had said would get back to Jaylin. I hoped so.

Jaylene and LJ came running into the living room, jumping all over me.

"Guess what we're going to do," I said. They looked anxious to hear what. "We're going to make some big ole chocolate chip cookies and put piles and piles of vanilla ice cream between them. Are you ready to help me?"

They nodded and LJ wanted to know exactly how big the cookies were going to be. He held out his arms wide. "This big, Mommie?"

Jaylene held out her arms, but they were in no way bigger than LJ's. "No, this big!" she shouted.

"Well, not that big, but definitely big enough for us to eat."

They jumped off my lap and ran into the kitchen. I walked Shane to the door, and he halted his steps before closing it.

"You're a beautiful person, Nokea. Don't allow bitterness to destroy you. After all that's happened, you've inspired me to get my act together. I was doing some things because I was hurt too, but those things weren't doing nothing but holding me back. Not anymore."

I leaned forward and kissed Shane's cheek. "You know I wish you all the best. I'll see you tomorrow."

Shane left and I hurried to the kitchen to make cookies with my kids.

Later that day, we were lying on the floor and putting together a huge puzzle, which I had bought. The kids kept questioning me about where I'd been. Even though they really didn't understand why I had to live in another place, I told them that this would be my permanent home. I also told them that we'd be spending as much time as we could together; unfortunately for me, they stressed how much they loved their home. LJ wanted me to come back, and come back now.

"Maybe in due time," I said. "But I'm okay being over here. I'm not that far and I can see you-all anytime I want."

LJ frowned; then he slapped the top of his forehead and stood up. He dug his hands into his blue jeans back pocket and handed me a crumpled picture.

"Look, Mommie," he said. "I forgot to show you this."

I reached for the picture. However, when I looked at it, my face fell flat.

Jaylene's arms were around my neck and she pointed to Mackenzie in the picture. "Those are our new friends, Mommie. She's *sooo* nice, but he's a crybaby," she pouted.

"Nuh-uh," LJ said, sitting on my lap. "Those aren't our friends. Daddy said they were our brother and sister."

"Nuh-uh," Jaylene shouted, "they're not!"

"Yes, they are," he fired back. "Aren't they, Mommie? Aren't they our brother and sister?"

Tears rushed to my eyes as I looked at the little boy whom Mackenzie was holding. He could have been Jaylin's twin. Even though I hated to break down in front of my kids, I couldn't help it. Even they started to cry, and this was not what I wanted to happen. I couldn't let them see me like this, and that's why I needed more time to get myself together.

JAYLIN

Nokea finally called for the kids. I couldn't believe she had been away from home for two weeks. She hadn't called and said nothing to me. At first, I didn't know if she was dead or alive. Each time I called her cell phone, it went straight to voice mail. Since we'd been married, she'd never been away from me this long. My mind kept wandering back to that day when all of this unfolded.

I did not know Nokea had that kind of rage inside her. It pained me that I had taken her to that level. When I had gotten up to see the damage she had done to our house, I couldn't believe my eyes. It was like a tornado had run through it. When all was said and done, thousands and thousands of dollars' worth of furniture had been destroyed. I had the place cleaned up, but I hadn't replaced anything yet. Didn't quite feel like rebuilding nothing, especially without my wife being around.

Truthfully, I wasn't doing so good. Sleeping alone was no fun at all, and I missed having her soft body next to mine. I lay in bed for hours, thinking about all that I'd done, asking myself if any of this was worth it. Having my kids together for the first time, yes; living in my home without Nokea, no.

I was determined to have it both ways. When she called Shane for the kids, I just knew she was ready to talk. To my surprise, she wasn't ready to talk to me. Shane told me what she'd said to him. When I asked him to give me her address, I couldn't believe he had the audacity to tell me no. I thought we were supposed to be boys, but he told me that he made a promise to Nokea that he intended to keep.

It was almost eleven at night, and LJ and Jaylene were still with Nokea. I took Mackenzie and Justin home, and Scorpio had asked me to stay the night. After the hurt I had caused Nokea, I couldn't. The guilt I felt inside . . . no way would I keep doing things that hurt her. I mean, I had some love for Scorpio, but not like I loved Nokea. Continuing to betray her didn't make sense to me, and running to Scorpio for comfort was something I didn't want to do. She could see the wounded look in my eyes, and I appreciated her being there for me again. Her comfort, however, wasn't what I needed right now.

I sat outside on the balcony at my house. I was lying on one of my lounging chairs. For the sixth or seventh time today, I used my cell phone to call Nokea. I hadn't left any messages, but decided to leave her one now.

"We gotta talk, baby. We are going to have to work through this. I know you're angry with me right now, but we can't go on like this. I need you here with me and the kids. Fuck, I need you! Period! Come home. Come talk to me, or answer this gotdamn phone. I'm begging you, before I go crazy in this muthafucking house!" I paused to calm myself. "All right. Good night, Nokea. I . . . I'm so sorry for hurting you. I won't do it again. You can bet your life on it. Call me, okay?"

Three days had gone by, no response. Shane had already come back with the kids, and all I could do for now was cling to the love I had for them. I couldn't even look Nanny B in the eyes, and she was at the point where she simply didn't want to hear it. When I told her what I'd done, she replied, "I saved your ass one time before, and I will not do it again!"

Since then, she hadn't said much to me at all; but when Mackenzie and Justin came over the other day, she seemed to be in a better mood. Nanny B loved all of my kids, and I knew she would embrace each of them with open arms.

It was Saturday, and Nanny B and I had taken the kids to a carnival. They had enormous fun and it was like a breath of fresh air seeing them all play together. Mackenzie and Jaylene were getting even closer, and so were LJ and Justin. Justin was even starting to cling more to me, and I was very happy about that.

After we left the carnival, Nanny B wanted to get a new pair of tennis shoes, so we stopped by the mall. That didn't go over so well, because my kids were straight-up misbehaving. Jaylene was falling all on the floor because I walked by the jelly beans she wanted; Mackenzie was picking up everything she could get her hands on; LJ kept running off, hiding behind shit; the only one who acted as if he had some sense was Justin. That was because Nanny B pushed him in a stroller and he was sound asleep. I was doing my best to get some order. When my voice got loud, Jaylene covered her ears and started to cry. I picked her up so she would be quiet. By far, she was definitely the most rotten of all.

"What is wrong with you, girl?"

She wiped her tears, then pointed her finger toward the jelly beans.

"Would you go get that child some jelly beans so these folks can stop looking at us like we're crazy," Nanny B said, irritated. "All of this foolishness doesn't make any sense, and it's embarrassing."

Just then, two women walked by, waving at me. I gave them a quick wink. One of them stepped up to me, and Nanny B quickly spoke up. "Don't you see all these bad kids this man has? And he has a ring on his finger. What is it that you could possibly want with him?"

"His phone number," the woman bluntly responded, then looked at me.

I spoke up. "Trust me, you don't—"

"LJ, get back here!" Nanny B shouted as he ran off.

I told the woman I was happily married. She slowly walked away, and Nanny B rolled her eyes.

LJ came running back toward us, skidding into me like I was home plate. "Yes," he yelled, tightening his fist as if he'd made a home run.

I'd had enough and my frown displayed it. "Get off this floor and cut that shi . . . mess out. You should know better."

LJ jumped up, swiping any dirt from his jeans. Mackenzie suggested that they go look at some books in the bookstore, but I halted their steps.

"Listen," I said to them. "We gon' get these jelly beans, get two books, and then we're out of here. If anybody else starts acting up, there will be repercussions."

"What's a 'repercussion,' Daddy? What does that mean?" LJ asked.

"Keep on acting up and you'll see what it means."

After Jaylene got her jelly beans, Mackenzie talked me into buying all kinds of outfits for her. LJ got two new pairs of tennis shoes and four new video games. I, at least, got more books than anticipated. When we got back to the house, it was rather late. We all changed into our pj's, and they were anxious for me to read some of the books. I pretended I was sleeping and playfully snored while in my bed, which was roomy enough for all of us. Jaylene pinched my nose real hard.

"Wake up," she shouted in my ear. She was a true badass, and I definitely had my hands full with her. I raised my voice, telling her to sit down. I could see that her feelings were hurt. As I lay sideways on the bed, she placed her head as close as she could to my chest. I kissed her forehead, apologizing for raising my voice.

"Okay, now y'all be quiet and listen as I read," I said.

I lay on my back, holding the book up in my hands. Mackenzie rested her head on one shoulder, and Jaylene laid hers on the other. LJ was sitting next to me, and Justin was bouncing up and down on the bed. He didn't seem to be interested in the story, but LJ kept his eyes on Justin so he wouldn't fall. I got through the story, with very little ruckus. That was because Jaylene had fallen asleep, and so had Mackenzie. Justin was sitting between LJ's legs. Once I eased myself away from the girls, I picked up Justin.

I carried Justin into LJ's room, and he followed closely behind us.

After tucking both of them in bed, I gave LJ a high five. "I appreciate you watching out for your little brother. I love you very much, and there ain't nothing in this world that I wouldn't do for you. You know that, don't you?"

LJ nodded, telling me that he loved me too. As I headed for the door, he called out to me.

"Psst, Daddy," he said. "I got something in this world that I want you to do. Can you do it?"

"Anything."

He placed his hands on the sides of his face and sighed. "Make Mommie come back home, man. It's getting a little boring around here without her."

I couldn't help but chuckle, not wanting to display the sadness I felt inside. "I'm working on it. I'm doing my best."

He pulled the covers over his head and I left his room. I was on my way downstairs to the lower level, but I sat on the steps and pulled my cell phone from my pocket.

"Day sixteen and you still haven't called me. I've been calling you every single day, and I don't understand why you at least will not talk to me. I need to hear your voice say something to me. Even if you want to tell me how much you hate me, I'll listen. Can I just see you, please? I just want to see you—that's all. Talk to you, hold you, make love to you . . . something. Anything. Just call me. I love you. . . . Really, I do."

I closed my phone shut, then dialed out again. Scorpio answered the phone this time.

"I'll bring the kids home tomorrow. We had a long day, and they're all resting peacefully."

I knew she could hear the sadness in my voice, and she'd seen it for the past couple of weeks. "What about you?" she said. "Are you getting any rest?"

"A little."

"Can I say something to you, without you getting defensive?"

"What is it?"

"Maybe this wasn't such a good idea. I never wanted for you to be so down like this, and all I wanted was for Mackenzie and Justin to bring happiness to your life. As much as I love you, this is not about us. I'm okay with the way things are, but I want you to be okay with it too. Deep down, I don't think you are."

"I am ecstatic about my children being here. This is something that I always wanted, and Justin is bringing my life to a full circle. My kids aren't going anywhere, Scorpio, so I hope you are okay with the arrangements. My marriage is a totally separate issue. Just so you can't say that I didn't tell you, I intend for Nokea and me to reconcile. Soon."

There was a pause; then she spoke. "I'm doing my best not to interfere. I struggle with not being able to make love to you when I want to, but we all have some issues that we have to deal with. For now, you're in the

driver's seat. It's going to be up to you to put what is going on between us in park. I can't see myself ever doing
it, and I will ride this out until you put the brakes on.
I hope you know exactly what I mean. Good night. I'll
see you tomorrow."

She hung up and I closed my phone shut. I headed
downstairs and saw Shane chilling back on the pit
couch, with the TV almost blasting. He was on the
phone too, so I wasn't sure how he could even hear. I
used the remote to turn down the TV; then I sat on the
couch, lifting my feet on the ottoman. Shane quickly
ended his call.

"When y'all get back?" he asked.

"We've been back for a while. I'm surprised you
didn't hear us with all of that noise upstairs."

Shane stretched his arms on top of the couch. "I don't
hear a thing down here. It's like I'm far away, living in
another house. That's why I can't let this shit go. I got
my own bed and bathroom, entertainment area, theater
room, b-ball court, sauna, game and weight room, patio
with Jacuzzi, indoor pool, bar with drinks. . . . Man, I got
it made. And . . . when you look out at the ocean from
those glass windows over there, the scenery is awesome.
You should check it out some time. Plus I don't have to
pay no rent. Now, who can beat that shit?"

"I feel you." I smiled. "You damn sure got it made,
in my house. That rent, though, it's being taken out of
those fat checks we've been getting. I'm surprised you
haven't noticed, but I guess it should be my bad for not
telling you why *your* checks are always coming up a tad
bit short."

Shane laughed and massaged the side of his face
with his hand. "So what up?" he asked. "I know you
came down here to holla at me about something."

"I did. First of all, I want you to tell me where Nokea
lives."

"As much as I would love to, I can't. I promised her that I wouldn't tell you, and the last thing she needs is to feel betrayed by me. That would really mess up everything, and any chance that you have of finding out what she's been up to would be cut off. You'd really be fucked then."

"Have you talked to her?"

"Yep."

"When? Negro, why you ain't say nothing?"

"Because you and the kids had been gone all day. I intended to tell you what she said."

I was anxious, but Shane was fucking with me. "And? What did she say?"

"She said that she got your messages. When she's ready, you'll hear from her."

I rubbed my chin. "Okay, that's cool. I can roll with that. Did she say 'soon,' and is that all she said?"

"She didn't say 'soon,' only implied when she was ready. She also said that you needed to see a psychiatrist. Now, I'd made that recommendation before, but you shot me down."

"Muthafucka, are you crazy! You got me all fucked up and I'm not gon' sit in nobody's damn office telling them shit about me or my past. That's why I call yo ass my *best* friend. You're supposed to listen to my bullshit and give me some advice about what to do."

"I do give you advice, but you don't listen. You got this controlling thing about you, Jay, and I can't believe how selfish you are about some things."

I pretended to be in denial, because I recognized I had some issues with being selfish and controlling. "I am the most giving man you and I both know. I pay my taxes on time. I give to those in need. I make donations to charities. I buy my kids anything they want. Look at all I've done for you. How can you sit there and call me 'selfish'?"

"I said 'selfish about some things,' particularly when it comes to women. It's like you're only willing to give so much, and what they think or want don't matter. It's your way, or no way. You expect for them to accept whatever you dish out. After a while, Jay, that shit gets old."

I placed my hand on my chest. "Shane, you've insulted me. If I could get up from here right now and take you to Scorpio's penthouse, you would take back everything you said. Look at how Nokea lived. She didn't want for nothing, and how is it that I've been so selfish to her?"

He shrugged and smirked. "You should see that condo Nokea is living in, as that may set you back too. Pertaining to you, though, you don't get it. It's useless talking to you. You're referring to the material shit. I won't add my two cents about Scorpio, but Nokea don't give a damn about this house. That's why she tore this mutha up like she did, and kicked your ass in the process," he said, laughing.

She did kick my ass, but I didn't quite find it as humorous as Shane did. Either way, he continued talking. "You're selfish because you don't consider her feelings. And if you do, you always . . . always put your needs before hers. In a marriage, you can't do that." Shane pointed to his chest. "A single man like me can get away with it, but you can't. You have got to think about your wife's needs and feelings too. That's all I'm saying, bro, and you need to correct yourself on that shit."

I kept quiet for a minute, thinking. "I feel you. I definitely feel what you're saying, but it may be too late for me. I got myself all fucked up in love with two women. One, of course, way mo love than the other."

Shane cocked his head back, then stood up. He stood over me and leaned down close. "No, no," he said. "You

love only one woman and her name is Nokea. Let me
kind of straighten some shit out for you. Since I'm your
psychiatrist and all, I want you to do something for
me."

I inched over a little on the couch, 'cause Shane was
breathing down my neck. "Hold up. Why you all close
like that and shit? Nigga, back up."

He stood up and folded his arms. "Shut up and close
your eyes."

"For what?"

"Just do it, so your ass can learn something about
love. I want you to think about some things."

I sighed and closed my eyes.

"Okay, go back to the last three times you were intimate with Scorpio," he said. "Are you there?"

"Yes," I said, quickly thinking about our sex session
in her kitchen the day she moved to Miami.

"You can see it and feel it, can't you? She throwing that pussy at you, and your shit about to explode,
right?"

I nodded and smiled. "*Yes*. Definitely yes."

"Them pretty-ass titties rolling around, and that
pussy so wet you can't hardly stand to be in it."

"Dripping wet, and my dick glazed like a Krispy
Kreme doughnut. I'm getting hard right now just from
thinking about it."

"I'll bet," Shane said, patting my back. " Been there,
done that, but go to the moment when y'all just about
to see fireworks. The pace increasing and she screaming how much she loves you. You may or may not be
saying shit, right? Other than moaning, of course."

"Oh, by now, I'm saying a lot. I may have tossed the
'love' word around, but I'm not too silent either."

"Fine. But here it comes," Shane said, getting closer
to me. "Pay attention, all right?"

I nodded.

"You come and all of your juices are rushing into her. When it's all over, you take a second or two to regroup. Then . . . what do you do? Think hard, Jay. This is crucial."

In my head, I played out the last three times Scorpio and I had had sex. Two out of the three times, after I got my nut, I left.

"I left and went home. The other time I was at a hotel, but I left the hotel early."

"And?" Shane said.

I opened my eyes. "And what? So what, fool, I left."

Shane smiled, but I was still confused. All this thinking bullshit made me hard as ever. Honestly, I was anxious to go get a late-night snack.

Shane sighed, telling me to close my eyes again. Just for the hell of it, I did.

"Now switch your thoughts to Nokea. Think about the last three times you had sex with her."

I smiled, thinking about that dress she wore at the party and the lovemaking we did that night.

"Are you there yet?" he asked.

"Yeah, I'm in there. I'm deep, deeply in there."

"Go deeper. Suck them titties, lick that pussy and think about how you felt when that ass was bent over and you could view your insertions from behind. You were crazed, weren't you?"

"*Yes,*" I admitted. "Damn near losing my *miiind.*" I thought about Nokea's perfect arch in her back, which always raised her titties so I could suck them. Her slit, which I loved to watch myself go into. And the way I sucked her clit, which I referred to as her "sweet raisin in the sun."

"It's good to you. Ain't it, dog?"

"Spectacular."

"Okay, now take yourself to those final moments. Y'all about to wrap it up. Think about what's happening."

"The last few times, we were kissing each other, barely able to catch our breaths. Words of love were being exchanged, and tears were definitely in our eyes. My sperm shot out like water from a fire hydrant. . . ."

"Bam!" Shane said. "Your juices were swimming, and after they found home, what did you do? Think hard."

"We . . . We went at it again, and again. . . ."

"After the 'again, and again' was over, what did you do?"

"I cuddled my wife in my arms. I constantly kissed her throughout the night and I dreaded leaving her side in the morning."

Shane smacked me hard on my back. "Nigga, that's love!" he shouted. "You don't walk out on love, once you get what you want! You stay there with it. If you go back to the many, many encounters you and Scorpio had, most of the time, you got up out of that bed and walked! Even while she was living with you. She was there for convenience, and there were times that you couldn't even stand to be in the same bed with her. In this house with Nokea, how many times have you found yourself breaking off to another room to sleep? Are you in a rush to depart from her? Hell nah! And one more thing," Shane said, poking my shoulder, "go back to your first thoughts of both of them. I bet you one thousand dollars, you said, in your head, that you had sex with Scorpio and made love to Nokea. Tell me it ain't so."

I went back to my thoughts, and Shane was correct. I thought about Scorpio's and my *sex session* in the kitchen, and thought about the last time Nokea and I *made love.*

I smiled, for this fool had seriously messed with my mind. He leaned his head over my shoulder and asked, "Who you love, Jay? What's her name again?"

"Nokea," I answered, chuckling.

He put his hand behind his ear. "Say it again. I can't hear you."

"Nokea, nigga. Nokea muthafucking Rogers."

Shane patted his hand on my chest—hard. "That's what I'm talking about, partna. Now stop talking crazy and go fix that shit. I'll give you her address tomorrow, but for now, I'm going to bed. You done wore my ass out, and since you've been sitting around all choked up about your wife, I gotta go take care of some business tomorrow so we can make some money. Good night, and I'll send you an invoice in the mail for my services."

Shane went to his bedroom and closed the door. I was still confused as ever. Lust or love, I had been feeling something deep for Scorpio. There was no way I would have allowed any woman to come in and cause the damage she'd done *if I didn't love her,* would I? Maybe I was in denial and couldn't acknowledge my feelings because I didn't want to. I had to fess up. Whether Shane believed me or not, I definitely had love for two women. No one could convince me otherwise. Besides that, I, Jaylin Jerome Rogers, knew what was deeply in my heart, so case closed.

SCORPIO

My nanny, Loretta, was a Mexican diva, and even though she was in her fifties, she and I had become good friends. I didn't know where Jaylin had found her, but she was a true joy to be around. Whenever the kids were with Jaylin—lately that had been quite often—Loretta and I would go places to hang out. She took me to a lot of the exquisite shops in Miami, and we enjoyed relaxing on the beach. I'd been trying so many different foods that it was starting to make me gain weight. The food was delicious, and those few pounds that I had lost came back on easily.

Things with Jaylin and me were going as expected. He really was all about his kids, and we hadn't spent much time together at all. I had started taking birth control pills, but it really didn't seem necessary. After that first day I'd moved here, he hadn't even approached me about sex again. I knew he was going through some things with Nokea, and I wondered how she was handling all of this. Mackenzie told me that they'd been spending most of their time at Jaylin's house. She even told me Shane was there. I had not known he had moved to Miami too. Mackenzie mentioned how excited she was to see Nanny B. As far as Nokea, though, she was not there. With that information, I knew all of this was hard on Nokea.

It was hard on all of us. To be honest, Jaylin never should have proposed to either one of us. He was a man who liked to do whatever he wanted to do, and it was just a matter of time that their marriage would get to this point. Pertaining to me, even if Jaylin tried to put a ring on it, as much as I loved him, I wouldn't accept it. Being married to him didn't make sense, and we all knew that it was a big risk living in his world. As long as he continued to be there for me in the way that he was, I wasn't being stupid. Just the opposite—I was doing what worked best for my children and me.

The other day, Justin had finally turned two. I had to hurry up and celebrate my day with him, because Jaylin was here before noon to pick up the kids. He didn't return with them until almost midnight that day, and they were all so excited about the party Justin had at Jaylin's house. According to Mackenzie, Shane and his girlfriend Tiffanie, and some of the neighbor's kids, were there. They went swimming in the outdoor pool that had slides; then they played games, took a ride on Jaylin's yacht, and ate lots of cake and ice cream. Mackenzie said they even rode on Jet Skis, and she talked about how well LJ could already ride one. She said that she wanted to learn, and Jaylin had shown her how. It sounded pretty dangerous to me, but I was glad that they all had fun. Afterward, Jaylin had brought me a piece of cake, and it was so moist and delicious. He said Nanny B had made it, and it was good to know that she had accepted my children. I wasn't sure how she felt about the whole thing, but I knew she would have Jaylin's back, no matter what.

That same night, Jaylin seemed so happy, especially because Justin was calling him "Daddy" now. Justin actually got a little antsy when he knew Jaylin was leaving; and as always, Mackenzie had an attitude too. That's just the kind of connection he had developed with his kids. Even though he was going through his issues with his marriage, I knew his kids were preventing him from going insane. As much as I tried, I didn't have what it took to keep him happy. And to be honest, I didn't think Nokea did either. It was his children, and maybe Jaylin would start to figure that out.

As giddy as he seemed that day, I thought he'd stay the night with me. He said he'd catch up with me next week, and I wasn't sure if that was to celebrate my birthday or not. Mine was a week later than Justin's and I couldn't believe I was turning thirty-four years old. Time had definitely gotten away from me. I had known Jaylin now for six years. To me, it seemed like a lifetime.

The day of my birthday, Jaylin called and said he was on his way to get the kids. I waited for him to wish me a happy birthday; but before I knew it, he hung up. When he got here, he seemed to be in a rush. He was doing something with his BlackBerry, and barely even said hello. I knew he'd forgotten about my birthday, but I made it clear to Mackenzie that she was not to say one word to him about it. She promised me that she wouldn't, and she gave me a beautiful card that she'd made herself. I kissed the card and placed it on the refrigerator with a magnet.

Around noon, Loretta took me to lunch. She invited two of her friends to come along. We sat outside the restaurant, under a huge umbrella, having a blast. We talked about our lives, politics, reality-TV shows and men. I couldn't remember the last time I'd had so much fun. When the waiters came outside to sing "Happy Birthday" to me, I was too excited. We all tore into the three-tier double-chocolate cake they gave me and clinked our wine glasses together.

As the day went on, I went shopping with the ladies, and then we had dinner together. By eight o'clock that night, we decided to go out dancing. I stood in my closet, picking through one after-five dress to another. I reached for my turquoise silk minidress that was sleeveless and had a diagonal cut across my chest. It wrapped around my curves and fit my waistline perfectly. My backside looked especially good in it. If the dress had been cut any higher, I would definitely be in trouble. I brushed my hair over to one side, leaving a flow of fluffy curls to rest on one shoulder. "Too sexy" was displayed on my forehead, and I couldn't wait to have even more fun than I already had earlier.

The nightclub that Loretta took me to was more like a bar-and-grill joint that had a dance floor and loud music. More Mexicans were in the place than anyone, but the club also had its share of Blacks and Whites as well. Nearly everyone had on sombreros, and a man sitting on the stage with one on his head was working the heck out of a Mexican maraca and drums. Everybody was clapping along with the music, and he had the place rocking. We sat at a table that had an array of martinis, tequilas, beer, and wine covering it. I drank so much. Before I knew it, I was up on the floor with everyone else, shaking my rump, clapping my hands and swinging my hair from side to side. The men were all over me, and Loretta kept encouraging me to go dance. After a while, sweat was dripping from my body. I had to sit down to take a break.

"This is fun, isn't it?" Loretta asked, sampling the tortilla chips on the table.

"Too much fun," I said, wiping my upper chest and forehead with a napkin. "Thank you so much for bringing me here. Do you come here often?"

"I've been coming here for years. It's relaxing, you know." She snapped her fingers and wiggled her shoulders. "You can come here to get loose, have fun and let your hair down."

I took a sip from my glass of tequila and cleared my throat to help the burning. "Hey, Loretta," I asked. "How did you get to know Jaylin? You're such a wonderful person, and I often wondered how he managed to find a nanny of your caliber."

She spoke loudly over the music. "I cleaned house for his neighbors. He and I would always speak, and he approached me about working for him. The people I worked for gave me good references and"—Loretta rubbed her fingers together—"the money he offered to pay a little woman like me, I could not deny."

"Well, I'm glad he found you." I reached out to give Loretta a hug.

"Me too," she said, patting my back. "Me too."

A few minutes later, my cell phone rang and I pulled it from my purse. Straightening my hair, I pulled it back over to one shoulder and answered the phone.

"Hello," I said, knowing it was Jaylin.

"Hey. Just wanted to let you know that the kids are staying the night with me. I'll bring them home in the morning."

"Okay. Did you-all have a good day today?"

"Don't we always?"

"Yes. But I was just making sure, that's all."

"We good. All good. Sleep tight, and I'll see you tomorrow."

"Sure. Kiss my babies for me, and I'll see you soon."

Jaylin hung up, and I was somewhat disappointed that he'd forgotten about my birthday. I knew he had a lot on his mind, so I didn't take it personal. Instead, I continued my conversation with Loretta. A couple of hours later, we decided to shut it down and go. Loretta had gotten a little tipsy too. For such a short woman, she could hold her liquor better than me. She threw her sheer shawl over her shoulder and laughed because we had to take a taxi back home.

When we entered my penthouse, we couldn't stop laughing our butts off. Nothing was really funny, other than the security guard who had the biggest nose we'd ever seen. With the alcohol in our system, his nose looked even bigger. I could barely catch my breath. When Loretta got to her room, she fell back on the bed, gripping her stomach.

"Whew," she said, throwing her hand back. "He really needs to get some plastic surgery. That nose was out to here, like Pinocchio." She gave an example of how long it was and kept laughing.

"Thank you again," I said, trying to contain my laughter. "I had a good time and I'm taking my butt to bed."

"Me too."

I stepped away from the door and could still hear Loretta laughing. It took me a minute to get from her room to the kitchen. I opened the fridge to get me a bottled water, but I noticed there weren't any cold. I closed the fridge and stumbled my way to the elevator. Normally, I would have taken the spiral staircase to my bedroom. The way my sore feet were feeling, though, I didn't think I'd make it. I took off my shoes, holding them in my hands. I then pushed the button for the elevator to open. When it did, my tired eyes were focused on the shiny floor. I slowly lifted my head; and when I looked up, Jaylin stood on the elevator, leaning against the back wall. His arms were folded, and he was naked. Every muscle in his body was on display. My eyes scanned down his tanned body, observing his cut abs and smooth shaven hair above his dick, which had a neat red ribbon tied on it. A tiny round birthday cake was balanced in his hand, and one candle was on top.

"Happy birthday," he said. "I thought you'd never get here."

I stepped onto the elevator, dropping my shoes to the floor and taking the cake from his hand. Unfortunately, that hit the floor too, as I obviously was in no mood for cake. I squatted, carefully opening my present by removing the ribbon tied to his dick with my mouth. As soon as I sucked in a taste of the best gift I'd ever had, Jaylin backed away from me. He picked me up, and my legs wrapped around his waist. He raised the hem of my dress. Since I didn't have on any panties, the access was easy. While plunging into me, he sucked down my salty neck and massaged my breasts. I wanted more, so I hit the up button on the elevator. It went up to my room, and we inched our way off the elevator and fell back on the bed. I didn't have to tell him how great the sex was. Jaylin made sure I had a memorable birthday that I would never forget.

The alcohol from the previous night had me dead as a doornail. When I woke up, Jaylin was gone. A pretty pink rose and card sat beside me. I couldn't wait to open the card, but first I placed my hand between my legs to touch my tender coochie. Jaylin certainly tore it up. As I thought about last night, I realized he just couldn't get enough. He had never sucked me for so long, and all I could remember was the multiple orgasms I'd let loose. I smiled from the thought; then I opened the card. It read: *I know you thought I'd forgotten about you, but there isn't a chance in hell that I would ever forget about a woman who has given me so much. You are the bomb! Happy Birthday, Scorpio. I hope your drunk ass enjoyed your night. By the way that pussy talked to me, I can tell you did. See you soon. Love, Jay Baby.*

Like I had said, I couldn't remember the last time I'd been this happy. I was starting to get the picture about what our relationship meant. I rescued him in his time of need, and he rescued me. It seemed as if he would be there for me, always, and I would always be there for him. I knew Jaylin's love for me had limitations . . . so what? I was satisfied with it and with his support and relationship with our children. What woman could ask for more? I couldn't. And with all of the cheating, lazy and good-for-nothing men out there, I doubted that I would find a man of Jaylin's stature anywhere else.

NOKEA

I had just gotten out of bed and pulled back the tall linen curtains to let in the bright morning sun. I reached for my cell phone on the nightstand and listened to Jaylin's daily message. "Day thirty-eight. This is getting ridiculous. I came by to see you, and you wouldn't even open the door. You won't leave your condo. As soon as you come out, I am going to be waiting. The kids have been asking about you, and how could you do us like this? What kind of person are you, Nokea? Our issues will never be resolved if you keep hiding behind closed doors. Call me, please. Please call me. FYI, I love you and always will."

I closed the phone and laid it back on the dresser. He had no clue how much I had been missing my family, and the thought of not seeing them made me sick as ever. I fought hard, every single day, not to go back home and tell Jaylin I'd forgiven him. Thing is, this time, I just couldn't do it. I had reached my limit, and that made me sad. Sad because even though I knew how much Jaylin loved me, I finally realized that he would never be the kind of husband I needed him to be. Years down the road, we'd be faced with the same thing, over and over again. I, in no way, considered him a dog or anything like that; and by all means, he'd made some major changes. But his changes weren't good enough for me. Maybe they were good enough for him, and good enough for Scorpio. At this point, they weren't good enough for me. It's as if he wanted me to share him. Now, what kind of mess was that? He hadn't taken our vows as seriously as I had. With that, I contacted an attorney the other day and filed for a divorce.

Just sitting and listening to the attorney talk to me about my options made me even more miserable. And no matter how hard I tried to calm the emotional roller coaster I'd been on, I couldn't. There was so much that I didn't understand: why, how and where did we go so wrong kept popping in my head. I even put the blame on myself, thinking what if I could or should have done this or that a little differently. I quickly tossed that thought aside. Everyone who had known me knew I had given my marriage my all.

When I left the lawyer's office that day, I stopped at the mall to fill out some applications for employment. I had to start making a living for myself. As long as Jaylin's money took care of me, he would feel as if he owned me. I wanted my independence back, and the only way I could get it was by starting over. I always loved makeup, perfumes, and fashion. When I stopped at one of the perfume counters in a major department store, I asked the lady behind the counter if they were hiring. She just happened to be the manager, and she admired how beautifully my makeup was done, as well as my attire. She told me to go online and complete an application. When I got home that day, I did. She called me the following day, and I was due to start my new job next Wednesday.

I knew that working would keep my mind off what was going on, and it would allow me to get out of this cramped condo, which was really making me crazy. That's why I didn't want the kids here with me. Knowing that my sadness was affecting them, I just couldn't stand to have them around. In addition to that, I now had myself an even bigger fish to fry.

Recently Jaylin had made me a promise, and that was one promise he'd kept. The last time we had made love, he promised me that I'd get pregnant. Lo and behold, I missed my period. I made a doctor's appointment right away. When my doctor came back into the room, I could tell by the look on his face that I was with child. "It's almost a miracle," he had confirmed. "And I'm so glad that you and Jaylin did not give up!"

At any other time, I would have jumped for joy. And I later found out that it wasn't the last time we'd had sex that I'd gotten pregnant, it was the time before that. I struggled with calling Jaylin to tell him about the baby, and debated if I should consider an abortion. I knew how difficult it was for me to get pregnant, and this could have been my last opportunity to have a child. The timing was so bad for me. If I called Jaylin, he would see this as a sign that we needed to stay together. Unfortunately, that's not how I saw it. I didn't want to use this baby as an excuse for us to get back together. Not this time—it wasn't going to happen.

With that said, I . . . I terminated the pregnancy. It was one of the worst experiences of my life. I kept having flashbacks of it in my head: from the white gown that I wore, to the sound of that suction noise that happened when the doctor was between my legs, all of it made me sick to my stomach. When it was over, I rushed to the bathroom to throw up. I could barely catch my breath and immediately regretted my decision.

Since then, I had been walking around my condo like a zombie. When Jaylin came by the other day, I could in no way face him. I hadn't left my condo since. When I listened to his message this morning, obviously, he was waiting for me to leave.

***

After taking a long shower, I got myself ready to start my first day at work. I had a degree in marketing, so I intended to start looking around for a job that paid more. But for now, this position was allowing me to be a part of something I always wanted to do.

As soon as I got to work, I was asked to complete several forms and was given a tour of the department store.

"Just in case the customers ask where the other departments are, we want to make sure our employees have some type of idea," said the manager.

"That's fine," I said, using my perfectly manicured nail to move my hanging bangs away from my forehead. I was cleanly dressed in a white pantsuit and three-inch black heels. My perfume infused the place, and my manager couldn't wait to put me in front of the store so I could connect with the customers.

"You are so perfect," she said, handing me a decorated basket full of sweet-smelling perfumes. I asked every customer who came in if they wanted a sample, and most did. Many of them went to the counter to purchase the perfume I was wearing. Talking to them about perfumes and fashion helped put my mind at ease. My manager gave me a thumbs-up. I smiled and continued to do my job. A few minutes later, I stepped backward and bumped into someone. When I turned to excuse myself, Jaylin stood close behind me. He was casually dressed in a black-and-gray-and-white Rebel for Life T-shirt from the Sean John collection of Diddy's favorites. His jeans were black and faded in the front, and white leather tennis shoes covered his feet.

"What in the hell are you doing?" he snapped, removing the dark shades from his eyes.

"Working," I said, turning to a customer who made an entrance. "Would you like a sample of perfume?"

The lady took the sample, and Jaylin tried to snatch the basket from me. "I can't believe you!" he shouted. "Why you out here doing this stupid shit?"

"Look," I said, turning to him. "I'm at work right now, and we'll talk about this later. Can you please just leave me alone? Please?"

With his hands in his pockets, and his sunglasses resting on his head, he gazed at me. As I moved, he moved. "You gon' talk to me right now, Nokea. Now, this shit has been going on for too damn long."

"Can't you see I'm busy? Quite frankly, there isn't much else that needs to be said. Did you get your papers yet?"

He snatched my arm. "What fucking papers? I ain't got no damn papers, and you'd better not be talking about what I think you're talking about."

His demanding tone had upset me. I turned to him with true anger in my eyes and pointed my finger in his face. "If you haven't gotten them yet, you'll be getting them soon. This is over, Jaylin. It is *so* over! Go marry that bitch who you can't stop sticking your dick into. Let her have more of your babies, and give her your last name, because I don't want it. Maybe it means something to her, and I truly hope the two of you live happily ever after."

Jaylin snatched the basket from my hand and tossed it like a flying saucer. My manager had been eyeballing us. When she came from behind the counter, she asked if I needed her to call security.

Jaylin stroked his goatee—hard. "Do you mind staying the fuck out of my business? I'm speaking to my wife, if you don't mind."

My manager looked at me and I told her security was not necessary. She watched as Jaylin grabbed my arm again, tugging me in the direction that he wanted me to go. I was skidding through the mall in my heels, trying to pull away from him. We seriously looked like Ike and Tina Turner, when she was trying to get away from him. People were looking, and the whole scene was quite embarrassing. Jaylin's grip on my arm was so strong, and he didn't let it go until we reached his truck, where he shoved me inside. He got in, locking the doors.

"Now that I have your attention," he said, looking over at me, "what's going on with you, Nokea? Why are you playing this game and won't even talk to me? What kind of shit is that? As a married couple, we're supposed to talk about shit and work through our troubles. I can't believe you've just given up on us like this."

I sat, looking straight ahead, with my hand resting on the side of my face. I'd already said what I had to say, and the divorce papers said the rest.

"Do you hear me talking to you?" he yelled. "Say something! Are you really going to divorce me? Is that what you really and truly want?"

Still ignoring him, I closed my eyes and wiggled my fingers on the side of my face, humming to myself inside. I wanted to tune him out. As loud as he was, I couldn't.

He hit the dash with his hand. "Woman, would you stop ignoring me like that! Let's talk this shit out. Now." His voice calmed and I opened my eyes. "I can't say I'm sorry enough," he said. "I'm sorry, and I will never put you through this again. I—I feel so alone and I can't even sleep at night anymore. You're on my mind, day in and day out, baby, and I don't want to proceed in life without you. You are my everything, Nokea, and this is just the one and only mistake I'll ever make in our marriage. Give me a chance to make it up to you. I will spend the rest of my life doing it, and I don't want to be alone anymore. Not anymore," he said, pausing to swallow. "Just come home."

Seeing Jaylin so upset always made my heart go out to him. He rarely showed his emotions by crying. Instead, he showed what he was feeling inside by his anger and by throwing tantrums. His tantrum had ceased, but his words were not enough to make me change my mind about divorcing him. I touched the unlock button on the door. "I'm sorry too, Jaylin. I'm so sorry it has to be this way. You've made your bed, and now you must lay in it."

Jaylin reached for my arm and dropped his head on the steering wheel. He used his arm to shield the pain in his eyes.

"I can't live without you, and I won't live without you. All I want to do is sleep, and I can't sleep, can't eat, can't think—nothing."

"Surely, you can fuck, though, can't you? I'd bet any amount of money in the world that through all of this you've made time for fucking your whore. That there is Jaylin's style, baby. No matter how much it hurts me, that is definitely how you do it. And you will continue on doing it."

He didn't respond. I knew what that meant, and I was glad that our conversation was over. Jaylin remained in the car with his head on the steering wheel; I went back inside to see if I still had a job. Unfortunately for me, I didn't.

JAYLIN

I had been in denial and finally realized . . . this was some serious shit! What in the hell was wrong with me for not even thinking that something like this could happen? My life as I had known it was destroyed! I had my money, my kids, my nanny, but in no way did I have possession of the woman I loved. She was done. No matter how hard I tried, Nokea was not changing her mind about divorcing me. I had underestimated her, and shame on me for taking her for granted. I didn't realize just how much damage I'd done, until I actually sat on the edge of my bed with the divorce papers in my hand. I didn't intend on signing nothing, and I would drag this on for as long as I could. Maybe she'd have a change of heart and realize that we were destined to be together. She had to, and she had to do it real soon.

Why? Because I was seeming a bit unstable. I hadn't done any work with Shane; I kept forgetting to do shit because my mind was so preoccupied with the thoughts of Nokea; I was feeling depressed. I got tired of putting on my game face for the kids, but they were counting on me. The constant questions they were asking were driving me insane. Whoever said that during times like this, the kids are the ones most affected—well, they didn't lie. I had not been going to get Mackenzie and Justin every day, like I'd done in the past, and I had started to make it every other day. I was just getting tired, and the entire situation was draining.

Scorpio picked up the slack on her end, and Nanny B was doing her best, too, to make sure the kids were okay. Even at a time like this, I could always turn to Nanny B. Regarding her attitude toward me, she was still acting shitty about the whole thing. I was like . . . fuck it. If she didn't want to listen, oh well. The only person I wasn't catching any gripe from was Scorpio. She was nice and understanding. She wasn't pressuring me about any-thing, not even about having more sex with her. I knew she wanted more. Every time I went inside her, though, the guilt from what I was doing was eating me alive. I didn't like the way I felt afterward, but I had some major needs that had to be met. As a man, I couldn't deprive myself, and I didn't know if Nokea would ever come around. The divorce papers implied that she wasn't, and that was very bad news for me. I picked up the phone, dialing Nokea's number, expecting to get voice mail.

"Day fifty-seven. No, I am not giving you a divorce. It ain't happening, and that's all there is to it. I miss you very, very much. Call me." I hung up.

About an hour later, I got a phone call. It was not the one I had been waiting on, nor was it one that I had pre-pared myself for. It was Nokea's mother, calling from St. Louis. I heard her father in the background talking shit, and he definitely had every right to be upset.

"Jaylin, we trusted you," her mother said. Even though she wasn't in front of me, I visualized her dis-gusted face over the phone. "Lord knows that I've been praying for the two of you to work things out. Nokea knows how we feel about divorces, and God will not ac-cept any excuses for it. Talk to her, Jaylin. Get off your behind and do whatever to save your marriage! Do you hear me?"

"I've been trying, Mama. She won't even talk to me. I just got the divorce papers today." I rubbed my forehead as I looked up, staring at the sky-view ceiling in my bedroom. "I don't know what else to do. Talk to her again for me. Doesn't she know how you feel about divorces? I know she'll listen or talk to you."

"I have tried to reckon with her, and I hope that I've not been wasting my time. Have you repented to God and prayed for him to save your marriage?"

"Yes, I've done all of that. He ain't hearing me, though. She's getting further and further away from me. I feel it."

"Jaylin, I really hate it that you messed up. Why would you do something like this to my daughter? She gave her all to you, and I know darn well she did. Either way, God will forgive you. Let's just hope that Nokea can too. Kiss my grandbabies for me, and I want you to bring them here real soon. I hate that you-all are so far away, and Lord knows I want to be there for my child, who, I know, is going through something. My legs been bothering me real bad, and flying or driving right now would kill me. Y'all need to—"

"We'll work it out. I will fix this, Mama. Someway or somehow, I'm going to do it."

Her father took the phone, adding his two cents. "What kind of man are you?" he shouted. I knew where this conversation was going. Even though he had cheated on his wife before, I figured he would sit there and judge my situation. "My daughter deserves so much better than you, and I warned her that you'd hurt her again. I don't give a damn if she doesn't reconcile with you. How much do you expect her to put up with? I mean, this isn't your first time being unfaithful to her, is it? You've been cheating since the two of you have been married, and your shit has just now caught up with you. If she decides to divorce you, she and those kids are coming back home to me."

That fast, he pissed me the fuck off! "My family ain't going no damn where, Mr. Brooks. And how dare you sit there and talk that shit to me, when you've had your share of problems as well. I had been faithful to my wife, and you should know better than I do that sometimes shit happens. I don't mean no disrespect, but I'm not in the mood to listen to your false accusations about me. Get the facts, and then talk to me, man-to-man, like you got some sense. Until then, I have nothing else to say to you, or to anyone whom I classify as a hypocrite. Or for that matter, someone who sounds like a damn fool!"

He hung up, leaving me in a rage and trying to calm down. I hated people who always tried to point the finger at others. Their shit wasn't right, but they were always trying to tell you how to correct your life. Mr. Brooks had always been guilty of that, but Nokea's mother seemed very understanding. Her words did make me feel horrible, though. I wanted to prove to her parents that Nokea had made the right choice. I knew her father was wishing she'd stayed married to Collins. For now, her mother seemed to have my back, and that was very good news. I hoped she'd make some kind of progress with Nokea and do it soon.

Shane was doing his best to keep me afloat. He knew I had backed off the business end of things, but he was still going strong. The other day, he showed me a check for $750,000, which he was going to deposit into our business account. Now, that was one of the lesser checks that we'd gotten, but I felt good about Shane going ahead and handling things. He was proud too, and he and I, along with Tiffanie, went to celebrate that night. Shane had been spending much more time with her, and I guess he had learned from my mistakes.

When you had something good, do not let it get away from you. The two of them seemed to connect well. Being with them made me think of Nokea the entire night. Tiffanie and Shane both were hopeful that we would work things out.

The following day, I was in the kitchen with Nanny B and the kids. They all had on chef hats and aprons. They were supposed to be baking some sweet and sugary treats and candy, but the kitchen was a mess. Justin was sitting on Nanny B's lap, while the rest of them sat around the table talking loudly. Jaylene got mad because LJ took her red dots, and she didn't want the white ones to decorate her treats. Mackenzie reached over and gave Jaylene some of her red dots.

"Here, you can have some of mine. I'll go get some more from the pantry."

Of course, that wasn't enough for Jaylene, and she sat at the table, pouting. "Daddy, LJ took my dots. Will you make him give them back to me?"

I closed the fridge and set the V8 juice, which I planned on drinking, on the counter. "No, Jaylene. Mackenzie is in the pantry right now getting some more. All of you have to learn how to share, okay?"

Her cheeks blew up like a balloon. When she let go, she wailed out loudly. She cried ferociously. When I told her to get up from the table and go to her room, she cut up even more. LJ paid her no mind. As she continued to throw her fit, he reached over and took some more of her dots. Today I really wasn't in a good mood. I loved Jaylene to death, but she had been working me. I ordered LJ to put her dots back. Then I removed her from her seat, pointing to her room.

"Now, Jaylene!" I said. "Go now!"

My mind traveled back to those days with Mackenzie, when she used to get out of control. When I looked at her, all she did was smile. Jaylene sat in the middle of the floor with her arms folded, like she wasn't going anywhere. She wiped her tears and had a mean mug on her face.

"Ooh, look at her," Nanny B teased. "She vicious, ain't she?"

LJ and Mackenzie were cracking up. They should have known better than to pick on my baby. I swooped her up from the floor, placing her on my back. She was all smiles by then. After I removed the mail from the mail tray, I carried Jaylene to my room. I sat on the bed, and she stood up behind me. As I looked through the mail, she kept peeking her head over my shoulders. I turned my head from left to right, kissing her cheeks on every turn. She laughed and told me she loved me.

"I love you too, but you'd better stop all of that clowning with your brother, all right?"

She quickly nodded; then she jumped off the bed. She was on her way back into the kitchen, but I called her name. "I mean it, Jaylene. Don't make me have to come into the kitchen and get you. Be good. Be good for me, okay?"

"Yes," she said; then she sprinted off to the kitchen. She was such a good mixture of Nokea and me. There was no doubt that I had the most beautiful kids in the world.

I opened the mail, and nothing seemed to interest me. Not even my investment statements, which showed how much my stocks had increased for the month. That was, until I came across an explanation-of-benefits letter from our health insurance carrier. According to the invoice, Nokea had gone to her doctor, and the list of services given was a pregnancy test. I quickly reached for the phone to call her doctor's office. I knew they couldn't discuss anything with me, due to patient confidentiality. However, when her doctor got on the phone, the first thing he said to me was "Congratulations on your miracle baby!"

Lord knows, this was very good news to me, as the Man Upstairs had finally answered my prayers. "Thank you, Dr. Kline," I said, playing it off. "Nokea wasn't feeling good today, and I wondered if there was anything she could take."

"I'll be happy to prescribe her something for the nausea she's having, but for the most part, she may have to ride it out. She'll be fine, and I know the two of you are very excited about the news. I should be able to tell if it's a boy or girl soon. Which one are you hoping for?"

"At this point, Doc, it don't even matter. Thank you so much. And if you wouldn't mind sending that prescription to our pharmacy, I'll be sure to pick it up."

"You betcha."

I hung up and could have jumped for joy. I couldn't change clothes fast enough, and I was on my way to see Nokea. I stopped by the kitchen to check on the kids, promising LJ that Nokea would be home sooner than expected.

When I got to Nokea's place, I anxiously knocked on the door. I figured she wouldn't answer, but I wasn't leaving until she did.

"I'm not leaving," I said through the door. "I know about the baby, Nokea, and you need to open up the door so we can talk."

Nothing came of my demands, and I couldn't hear anything inside her condo. "Baby, come on and open the door. We got ourselves a baby on the way, and I told you we could do it. This is a miracle that we should celebrate together."

Nokea would not budge. I stood with my back against the door, hitting it with my elbows. "I'm staying right here until you come out. If I have to stay here all night, I will."

Fifteen minutes had gone by, and she still hadn't come to the door. I put my hands in my pockets, letting out a deep sigh. As soon as I stepped away from the door, I saw her getting off the elevator with two plastic bags of groceries in her hand. I rushed up to her, taking the bags from her hand.

"Damn, where have you been? I've been out here for hours," I lied. "Banging on your door so we could talk."

Nokea said not one word. She put the key in the door; then she tossed her keys on a table when we got inside. I locked the door, and then I carried her groceries to the kitchen. I wanted to bring up the baby, but first I wanted to know if she would tell me. She wasn't yelling and screaming at me yet, so maybe that talk with her mother had done some good.

"Did you get a chance to talk to your mother?" I asked, taking a seat at the kitchen table.

She put a frozen steak in the refrigerator. "Yes."

"And?"

"And what, Jaylin?" She turned and folded her arms as she leaned against the counter. "What my mother wants doesn't matter. It's what I want."

"And what do you want?"

"You left a message telling me you got the papers. You know what I want."

I threw my hand back at her. "Baby, you don't want that. Stop all this madness and let's have some for-real talk. Besides, I tore up those damn papers. I'm not going to sign my name to no bullshit like that. What the fuck do I look like?"

Nokea left the kitchen for a few minutes; then she came back with papers in her hand. She laid them in front of me. "All I'm asking for is a dissolution of our marriage and joint custody of our kids. I don't want a dime of your money or spousal support. The quicker we get this over with, the faster we can move on with our lives. All you have to do is sign and be done with it. If you need to take a day or two to have Frick look it over, please let him do so. He will tell you that there is nothing tricky about what I am asking."

I wished Nokea would stop with the games. I knew what I'd done was wrong, but damn! This was going too far. "What about the baby, Nokea? You mean to tell me you still want a divorce when you're going to have our baby? This is our miracle child, and that baby is in your stomach for a reason. I'm not giving up on us. If I loved another woman as much as you seem to think I do, then I would walk with no problem. It ain't like that, baby, and my love is with you."

She gazed at me, looking surprised that I'd known about the baby. "Sign them, Jaylin," she said in a soft tone. "Sign the papers and let's end this."

I inched the papers away from in front of me. "Not a chance in the devil's lonely hell. Never."

"Fine, then. If you're contesting it, then I will soon see you in court. We'll let a judge decide what to do. If you think any judge is going to side with you, Jaylin, you're crazy."

"I'm willing to take my chances. In the meantime, Mrs. Rogers, are you coming home to your children. Will you let me take care of you and my baby?"

Nokea had a cold, disturbing look in her eyes. "There is no baby."

I pulled the insurance invoice from my pocket, knowing that she would lie to me. "Let's see," I said, pointing to the paper. "You had a pregnancy test done on this day, and when I spoke to Dr. Kline today, he confirmed it. Are you calling Dr. Kline a liar?"

She sounded like a broken record when she snapped, "Sign the papers, Jaylin. I said, for the last time, there is no baby. Got it?"

Her voice sounded hard, and her neck twisted on the words "got it." At that point, I had gotten it, I thought. I looked into her eyes and saw nothing but deviousness. I finally had seen how much she hated me. I sat for a moment, thinking. Now, if there wasn't no baby, then what in the fuck happened to it? I politely asked Nokea just that, quietly waiting for her to answer.

She was blunt. "I terminated the—"

Before the words even left her mouth, I jumped up from my seat. I could have killed her, and as I gripped her throat, I wanted to do just that. Anger, hurt, pain—all of that, and then some, was running through me. My blood was boiling over and I could feel the tightness in my skin. As my head started to spin, that's when I heard Nokea gagging and I shoved her away. Her back slammed into the refrigerator and she tightly squeezed her stomach. Her chest was heaving in and out, and her cries were as loud as ever.

"I hate you!" she spat out. "To hell with having your gotdamn baby! I didn't want it!"

My fists tightened and I punched it into my chest. "I hate your ass too, Nokea. You went too fucking far! I swear to God, I could kill you right now! How . . . could . . . you?" I paused, turning around and squeezing my eyes together.

"Why did you make me hate you, when I loved you *so much!*" she shouted. I swiftly turned to look at her as she continued. "Didn't you want me to love you? Didn't you need for me to love you? After your mother died, nobody loved you, Jaylin, but me!" She punched her chest with her finger. "*I* loved you! Not your father, not your aunt, not her boyfriends, not Stephon, not your other cousins, and damn sure not that bitch, Scorpio! How could you do this crap to me!"

I swung my fists in the air, spit flying from my mouth. "Don't you think I know that shit! I'm well aware of how much you've been there for me, but don't you ever forget that I've been there for you too! I made one fucking mistake, Nokea! One! I am in no way perfect, and the last time I checked, neither are you! So what! We didn't have the perfect Cinderella life you always wanted, or the one your hypocritical-ass daddy told you you'd have! We have had a good—more than good—life together, and, unfortunately, sometimes shit happens, baby!" I held out my hands and moved closer to her.

My voice calmed . . . a little. "Aye, it's time to woman up and get over it. You had no muthafuckin' right to terminate your pregnancy without my consent. That baby was a blessing to us, and I don't care how upset you were with me. You should have consulted with me first. I will never, ever forgive you for this, and you knew how much joy that baby would have brought to us. So go ahead and hate me all you want. But at the end of the day, you're still not getting your fucking divorce."

She kept on spewing her harsh words at me, but I tore up the divorce papers, throwing that shit at her. The shreds of paper fell over her and onto the ground. I wanted so bad to punch something. Instead of hitting her, I picked up a chair. In a rage, I slammed it to the ground, breaking it. I could barely catch my breath as I angrily eyeballed Nokea. I had no sympathy for her. I left before I did something that I'd later regret.

I weaved in and out of traffic, barely able to see straight as I blinked away the tears forming in my eyes. I thought about what Nokea had done to my baby. How could she do something that was so damn damaging to me and to her? She had to know that something like that would send me over the edge. It did, and the rage inside me was taking over.

Minutes later, I walked through the door of Scorpio's penthouse. After taking swift steps, I saw her sitting on a bar stool, watching Loretta cook. Scorpio saw the disturbing look in my eyes, and she quickly stood up. My eyes turned to Loretta.

"Exit now!" I ordered. "Thank you."

She moved as quickly as she could, and I reached out for Scorpio's hand. I stepped toward the living room, but she squeezed my hand to halt my steps. I turned with no expression on my face, just blazing-red, fiery eyes.

"What's wrong?" she said, pulling me to her. She rubbed her hands through my hair. "Are you okay?"

I looked into her eyes, wanting to spill my guts. Instead, I pulled my shirt over my head and took her over to the couch. She lay back on it and I lay over her. I closed my eyes, pecking her soft lips with mine and letting my tongue turn circles in her mouth. My hands touched up and down her sweet-smelling body, and I broke open her shirt so I could see her nakedness. Scorpio continued to comb her fingers through my hair and wipe my sweat.

"Why are you doing this to yourself?" she softly asked. "Baby, you've got to stop this or you're going to make yourself crazy."

I kissed her again; then I pecked down her neck. "Stop . . . Stop taking your birth control pills. Don't take them anymore, all right?"

She lifted my head, causing my eyes to stare into hers. "No. No, we're not going to have any more kids. You can't keep doing this to me, Jaylin, and what in the hell is going on with you?"

My dick couldn't even get hard from the turmoil I'd just experienced. I dropped my head on Scorpio's chest, releasing my anger. "She killed my fucking baby. Why she do that shit to me, huh? I fucked up, but how could she do that to me? Damn!"

Scorpio lay still, slowly rubbing up and down my back. "You didn't fuck up. You may have made some questionable decisions, but one of those decisions turned into a son that will be with you forever. Stop referring to him as a 'mistake,' because he's not. How could you be disappointed about your son?"

"I'm not" was all I could say as I lay there being comforted by a woman who had given me her all.

SCORPIO

Needless to say, Jay Baby had been tripping. He was cursing people out and acting a fool again. I listened to him yell at somebody over the phone. When I asked who it was, he told me it was his lawyer, Mr. Frick. Jaylin told me that Nokea had filed for a divorce, and I really couldn't believe it. I do know, however, that he was simply not right. He had been late and slacking on picking up the kids. And for someone who was always prompt, I knew he was having a difficult time coping.

As far as his money was concerned, he told me he was sick of making money. Now, if there ever became a time that Jaylin was sick of making money, this was getting pretty serious. He briefly mentioned Shane doing a lot for the business, but Jaylin seemed as if he was done with work and wanted no part of the business he had basically turned over to Shane.

Earlier he'd picked up the kids, and was late as usual. Mackenzie told me that she had smelled alcohol on his breath. When he picked up the kids, I smelled it too. He assured me that he had taken only one drink; he promised me that he would take no more. But when I got a phone call later that night from a police officer at the police station, I almost lost it. The officer asked me to come get my children, because Jaylin had been arrested for a DUI. I drove Loretta's car, flying like a bat out of hell to get to the police station. They were nice enough to hand over my kids, but they said that Jaylin wouldn't be released until morning. The officer said that Jaylin needed time to sleep off the alcohol, and that's exactly what he was doing. I was mad as hell about his actions.

The next day, he showed up early in the afternoon. When I asked what had happened, he blew it off, acting like it was not a big deal.

"I can't believe you don't recognize how serious it is for you to ride around, drunk as hell, in the car with my children."

He placed his arm on the couch, gazing at me from across the room. "I wasn't drunk. I was tipsy. That officer was just fucking with me. When he gave me a Breathalyzer test, the shit was a tad bit too high. He wanted to arrest me because I was 'driving while black.' Frick gonna handle that shit for me, so I'm cool."

"No, you're not. You should really consider some type of counseling. I'm getting so worried about you. I don't want my kids ever to be put into a situation where they're faced with being in another car accident, like the last one. I'm not going back down that road again, and it was too devastating for my family."

"They're my kids too, and I wouldn't put them in no fucked-up situation like that. As for counseling, what's up with all you stupid-ass people talking that mess? Why don't you muthafuckas go to counseling? Silly-ass shit," he said, getting off the couch and calling for Mackenzie. She came into the living room. "Go and get your things. Let's go. Where's Justin?"

"He's coming. He's right behind me."

Justin came running into the room. Before Jaylin got to him, I did. I picked him up and put him on my hip.

"They're not leaving with you right now," I said. "Go home and chill for a moment. Think about what I've said to you. If you're becoming an alcoholic, you need to seek some help before it's too late. I would be a fool to let these kids go with you, especially when you're not even willing to admit that you were driving drunk last night. Maybe it's the first time that something like that has happened, but I can't take the risk."

Now, of course, Jaylin was going to challenge me. I didn't always listen to everything he suggested, and there were some things that I remained firm on. When it came to our children, that was one thing. We started arguing, and it was the first argument we'd had since I'd been here. He was yelling so loudly that Mackenzie and Justin started crying. I asked him to get out, but he threw that back in my face.

"What a joke!" he said. "How you gon' order me out of something I paid for? What kind of shit is that?"

"Look, don't be mad at me because you did all of this. I didn't ask you for one gotdamn thing, so don't going throwing that crap up in my face."

I sent Mackenzie to her room, and I made it clear to Jaylin, again, that she wasn't going anywhere. Boy, did he hate to be told no. When he left, he called me something underneath his breath. Since he didn't say it out loud, I didn't trip.

"Coward," I spat out, saying it right before the door slammed.

For the next few days, Jaylin hadn't called or shown up. Did he realize that he was hurting no one but himself? I guess he realized it eventually, because he called to talk and explain. I leaned over on the kitchen counter to listen to him.

"Look, you know I've been dealing with some stuff, and you were right about me drinking and driving. I assure you, though, that it was a onetime incident. I love my kids too much, and I would never harm them in any way."

"Accidents happen, Jaylin. Before my accident, I said the same thing too. I could have lost Justin and

Mackenzie in an instant. I'm glad you understand what I was saying, and please don't ever do that again."

"I won't. Where my babies at?"

"They're sleeping. We drove to Loretta's cousin's house today and she barbecued. We hung out with them for a while and pretty much enjoyed ourselves."

"That's good. Glad y'all had fun. Are you in the mood for some more fun?"

"You mean to tell me you actually asked me this time. Normally, you come busting through here, dropping your clothes at the door. You don't even give me time to prepare myself, and one day you're going to mess around and dip yourself into something that ain't right."

"You always right, baby. I like that sweet tang on your pussy, and that spontaneous shit turns me on."

"Sweet tang? Is that really what you want to call it?"

"I call it as I see fit."

Jaylin hung up. When I turned my head to the right, he was standing in my view.

"I'm warning you," I said, laughing. "You'd better stop this. I haven't even had my shower today."

He nudged his head to the right. "Then let's go shower together. How about that? And this time, I'm asking."

Since Jaylin had been so stingy with the goods, I was always gaming. He chased me upstairs to my shower, and the water had turned cold on us. Even so, I couldn't ignore that Jaylin had a hint of alcohol on his breath. This was definitely becoming a problem.

The next few days left me worried sick whenever Jaylin took the kids. He seemed fine, but I was skeptical about what was happening when he got home. I was so worried that I felt a desperate need to speak with Nokea. She had his children too, and I would truly regret if something happened to any of them. The other night, I had gotten Shane's phone number from Jaylin's phone. I called Shane and he answered, thank God. I expressed my concerns to him and told him about my desires to speak with Nokea. At first, he didn't want any part of what I wanted to do. I begged him, swearing that I in no way wanted to cause any trouble. This was all about doing the right thing. I felt relieved when he gave me Nokea's address so I could go talk to her.

The following day, I prepared myself to pay her a visit. I threw on an orange T-shirt, blue jeans and wore my hair in a ponytail. Surely, I could look much nicer, but this issue with Jaylin was so serious to me that I didn't want Nokea to feel intimidated in any way. It had been a long time since we'd last seen each other, and yes, there was still a lot of jealously and envy between us.

I went to the door, taking a deep breath before I knocked. I wasn't sure how she would react. At the end of the day, though, Nokea had always been a pretty sensible woman. With that, I lightly knocked on her door and waited for a few minutes. She didn't respond immediately. When I knocked again, I heard her softly ask who I was.

"It's Scorpio, Nokea. If you have a minute, I'd like to speak to you."

There was nothing said for a minute, maybe two. Then she opened the door. It was ten o'clock in the morning, and she was still in her cotton pajamas. Her hair looked freshly done, and she was still as pretty as I remembered her. I had never been jealous of another woman in my life, but I was of her. She widened the door, looking me over.

"Scorpio, what is this about? Jaylin and I aren't together anymore and—"

"I just need to talk to you. I'm deeply concerned about some things, and you know I wouldn't be here if this wasn't important."

She sighed and let me inside. The condo she lived in was decorated with modern furniture, and I must admit, she had good taste. She invited me to take a seat on the microfiber cocoa brown sofa and I did. Nokea sat in the matching chair, tucking one of her legs underneath her. She placed her hand on her cheek, waiting on me to say what I came to say.

"It's been a long time, Nokea, and I regret that I have to come to you like this, considering the damage you think I may have caused."

She couldn't wait to chime in. "You have definitely caused a lot of damage, and I don't understand how any woman can continue to chase after another woman's husband for so many years. It's ridiculous! And if all you've come here to do is gloat about your trifling actions, you're wasting your time."

Yes, I was taken aback by her tone, even though it was what I expected. I kept my cool. "Your tone is fair, but I hope you don't forget about Jaylin's participation in this as well. I have not been chasing after him, and you are so wrong about us. I don't know if you've spoken to him lately or not, but he seems to be getting somewhat out of control. I know he's going through a lot because of the divorce or separation, but I'm here because of the kids. He's been drinking a lot. The other night, he was arrested for a DUI. My kids were in the car with him, but I figured yours were not. I don't know if he's driving around with LJ and Jaylene under those conditions or not, but I just wanted to warn you. He's not stable, and I sense something very tragic may happen."

"I know about some of the things that are going on. When the kids come here, they tell me. I wasn't aware that Jaylin had been doing any heavy drinking. I will definitely find out what is going on with him on that end. Thanks for the warning."

There was silence, and I could tell she was ready for me to go. But having so much more to say to her, I looked down at my nails and fumbled with them. "You know, I'm glad I've gotten this opportunity to speak to you, and I—I really want you to know a few things, Nokea." I looked up and could see the daggers being shot at me. She still remained calm as ever. "What happened between Jaylin and me several years ago was not supposed to happen. I was getting married soon, and when he came to my house that night, I had a difficult time letting him walk away. When I found out I was pregnant, I was so sure that the baby belonged to my husband. But then, when I had my son, I knew that not to be true. I never wanted to break up your marriage and—"

She cut me off again, and her lips were slightly pursed. "I find that hard to believe, Scorpio, and you are such a liar. You've always wanted to be married to Jaylin, and you have never respected his decision to marry me. He made his choice. Why in the heck couldn't you just live with it?"

I sighed, trying to cope with her attitude. "The marriage was difficult for me to accept, and with that, I couldn't respect it. I thought our last time together would be it, and no one would ever find out. I kept my son a secret. No matter what you think, I intended to do so forever. I wanted no one to know the truth but me, and that's when the car accident happened. I wanted Jaylin to be there for Mackenzie, because my husband, her own biological father, had abandoned her again." I took a deep breath, pausing to wipe a falling tear.

"He found out the baby wasn't his, and I still struggled with telling Jaylin the truth. I knew how much damage it would cause, Nokea, and I didn't want that. Jaylin, being Jaylin, found out Justin was his. I felt so bad for betraying him again. When he asked me to move here for the sake of being with his children, I couldn't say no to him, especially after all that he'd done for me."

Nokea snapped at me again. "Saying no seems so hard for you to do, doesn't it?"

"At times. But I'm not trying to go on the attack here. We both know how persuasive Jaylin can be, and living in his world definitely ain't easy."

Nokea folded her arms and cleared her throat. "You got that right. I guess I really want to know, how in the heck did you-all think this would some way or somehow work out? You may as well have moved into our house with us, just so Jaylin could have access to you and me both. We've all been in turmoil over this. Things are going to get worse, before they get better. If I would have allowed Jaylin to move you into that house with your children, he would have gladly accepted my offer. This mess has been going on for too long, Scorpio, and I am so done with it. Once our divorce is final, please marry him and do whatever. I don't care anymore. I'm sick of it. As far as I'm concerned, his world no longer exists." Her voice cracked, but Nokea was doing her best to hold back her tears.

"He never would have suggested or accepted anything like me moving into your house. Our relationship is not what you think it is. I know that the only reason Jaylin is around me is because of his children. He and I don't spend a lot of time—"

"Are the two of you still having sex?"

I was honest. "Barely. But I will sit here today and make you a promise. If you do not divorce him, and if you can get him back on the right track that he needs to be on, I will never, ever let him touch me again. That is a huge step for me, Nokea. Whether you believe it or not—and I'm sorry to say this to you—I love your husband with all of my heart. He means the world to my children and to me. I can't stand to see the pain he is in from losing you, though. Eventually he will destruct and all of this will come tumbling down. My children will suffer, and so will yours. He needs you, and all I am right now is good sex, which he only wants on his time. I'd rather see him happily married to you, having a wonderful relationship with all of his children, and building a future for them. Don't you want that too?"

"No," Nokea said, straightforward. She removed her leg from underneath her and sat up straight. "No, because no matter what, Scorpio, Jaylin will always find his way back to you. If there were no you, there would be someone else. Do you even know what kind of man he is? Well, I recently found out. After all of our years together, he continues to be full of surprises. He is not the kind of man I envision myself spending the rest of my life with. If you have to sit there and make me the kind of promise you just did, how can I roll with that? How can I be in a marriage, always afraid of that one unfortunate time when you and Jaylin slip again? I believe that you love him, and I know what you will do for him too. He will make you do what he wants you to do, and I don't think you always would be willing to tell him no."

"For the sake of our children, I will do it. You're making him out to be something that he's not. I know you're angry, but from what I know, Jaylin has been totally committed to you. This isn't about him just wanting to play the field. The problem is with me, and it can be corrected. Yes, it's hard to trust my words, but even you know how much Jaylin loves you. I am so envious of the way he feels for you, and I can't compete with what the two of you have. To be honest, I never could."

Nokea sat silently for a moment, thinking about what I'd implied. She even reached out to give me a tissue when she saw the tears in my eyes. She took a few deep breaths; then she lightly massaged her forehead with her hand. "Neither of you will ever understand how painful this has all been for me. I've lost myself in the mix, and now I have to start all over. The man to whom I gave every ounce of my love has destroyed me. He took everything out of me, and I don't even know if I love him anymore."

"Yes, you do," I said. "All wounds heal in time. I felt the same way when he had gone off and married you, and there were times that I wanted to end my life. I'm so sorry for hurting you, him and myself. I just loved him so much, Nokea, and it was hard for me to imagine my life without him."

I didn't like expressing myself like this in front of Nokea, but what I spoke was the truth. I could tell she was holding back her emotions as much as she could. Every once in a while, she'd dab her eyes with a tissue.

"Can I ask you one more thing?" Nokea said. I nodded. "If I divorce Jaylin, then what? Will you continue to have sex with him and have more children with him? Or do you intend to marry him?"

I didn't hesitate to respond. "He'll never marry me, and I know that for a fact. He doesn't love me enough, and there's only been one woman who was capable of taking him to that level. I think you know who she is. If you don't go back to him, I doubt that marriage will ever happen again for him. As for us being intimate, the only thing that will stop that from happening is if the two of you reconcile. If not, I will make myself available to him, whenever he needs me. If I have to do whatever it takes to pick up the pieces, I will. I'll do it out of love, not because I desire to have sex. As for another child, who knows what will happen?"

Nokea cut her eyes at me, looking away while in thought. "I just realized how being in your presence, Scorpio, makes my flesh crawl. I can't help the way I feel and I don't quite understand your motive. Whatever it is"—she turned her head to look at me—"you've won. Good luck to you and Jaylin, and I hope he is everything that you want him to be."

Nokea slowly stood up and made her way to the door. I followed behind her. We stopped at the threshold.

"I don't have a motive, and I meant every word that I said. Whatever you decide, I'll respect your decision."

"Yeah, right. Just like you respected my marriage, huh?"

She opened the door and we stared at one another for a couple of minutes without saying a word. I guess I didn't have anything else to say, so I broke our stare and walked out the door. She slammed it behind me so hard, nearly knocking it off the hinges.

NOKEA

Who said that two women in love with the same man couldn't sit down and have a civil discussion without calling each other names or pulling each other's hair out? If it could happen between Scorpio and me, it could happen between any women. I appreciated her stopping by to talk to me, but I still despised her for interfering in my marriage. She did her best to explain that she'd done it out of love for Jaylin, but I wasn't sure about that. Scorpio knew that if Jaylin went down, she was going down with him. Jaylin having less money and no stability meant she would as well. No, she couldn't let that happen; from the day Jaylin had met her, he had become her sole provider. One thing I could say about our conversation was that she really loved Jaylin more than I thought she did. He had caused her a lot of grief too, and decisions were made without anyone giving much thought.

I was guilty of this too, especially for terminating my pregnancy. I had always been against abortions. How in the world did I bring myself to do something so out of character for me? I did my best to justify my actions by saying that my anger toward Jaylin was a good enough reason. Realistically, it wasn't, and I should have known better. At this point, all I could do was push forward and try my best not to look back on some of the mistakes that I had made.

In the meantime, everybody and their mamas were trying to save my marriage. Mama was calling, begging me not to go through with it. Even my friend Pat was saying I needed to hang in there. *What in the hell would the average woman do?* I thought. *Would she really let go of Jaylin so easily?*

I had spoken to Shane often and he still was trying to encourage me to work things out. And it definitely surprised me that Scorpio had wanted the same thing too, but I sensed a bit of fakery with her. Then, of course, there was Jaylin. He'd been calling every day, leaving messages and trying to make me feel guilty about what I had done to *his* baby. He repeated that he'd never forgive me and asked how I could be so cruel. One message after another, he went on the attack. He called me a hypocrite, said I was overreacting and blamed me for his behavior. I deleted some of his messages, until I noticed they started to calm down. Then he was back to telling me he loved me. From the slurs in his voice, I could tell what he had been going through. We all were going through hell.

When a knock came at my door, I was surprised to see that it was Nanny B. Lord knows I was in no mood to talk to her! But after all she had done for us, I could in no way play her. I invited her inside and we sat at the dining-room table. She had brought me some handmade cards from the kids, and I sat in the chair, smiling as I read over them.

"The kids really miss you," she said. "And I do too. I guess I don't have to tell you how much Jaylin—"

I dropped the cards in my lap and sighed. "Please, Nanny B. I really don't want to hear about how much Jaylin misses me, and why do you always take up for him? It is so frustrating. As a woman, you should understand how I feel."

Nanny B reached out and touched my hand, which I had placed on the table. "I do know how you feel. I've been there too, Nokea, more than you know. I don't

always see eye to eye with Jaylin, but I do have a connection with him that you've been unaware of. Jaylin
has never told anyone our secret, and that's because I
asked him not to. I'm his stepgrandmother, Nokea, and
I raised his mother up from when she was a little girl."

I sat in shock as Nanny B told me about her tumultuous marriage to Jaylin's grandfather, about her
struggles with his biological grandmother. History had
definitely repeated itself. When she told me that she
was the one who had given Jaylin the money she'd gotten from his grandfather's estate, I couldn't believe it.
I was speechless and I couldn't believe Jaylin had kept
this a secret for so long, and according to Nanny B,
Scorpio didn't know the truth either.

"So you see, Nokea, this is why I feel so connected
to him, to his children and even to you. The two of you
have got to work this out and we've all come too far to
give up now. It pains me to watch Jaylin suffer at that
house without you. I can't stand to see him so torn, and
I know you're miserable over here too."

I sadly looked down. "I am, but I would be even more
miserable with him. I don't know how to get over this
bad feeling that I have inside. All I can think about is
somehow getting back at him. I want him to feel what
I'm feeling. I don't think he even knows what this pain
feels like, and a part of me just . . . I just wish something
bad would happen to him. I never thought I could feel
that way about him, ever."

"No, you don't wish him any harm," Nanny B said.
"That's just that ole devil trying to get at you when
you're weak. His motive is to kill, steal, and destroy.
Don't let him win. Figure out a way to get from underneath his grip. With me, I eventually forgave my
husband for all of his wrongdoings. But the most important thing, Nokea, is I found myself during some of
my most difficult and challenging times. Take this time

to find out who you are and what you really want. Celebrate your life, as you have so much to be thankful for. Even at a time like this, you need to celebrate the good things in your life. I don't need to tell you what they are, and all you need to do is look around you. I talked to Jaylin the other day about the same thing. Life is too short for a bunch of nonsense, and whatever happened to people exploring their dreams? Have you been so wrapped up with Jaylin that you've forgotten about yours? Maybe so. I hope and pray that the two of you work this out, but don't stay in your marriage based on what others want. Do what feels right for you, okay?"

I nodded in response. To put me at ease, Nanny B started talking about the kids and all that they'd been getting into since I'd been away. It sounded as if she and Jaylin had their hands full, and I told her just that as she was on her way to the door. Nanny B gave me a tight hug, squeezing me. She told me that she loved me and encouraged me to be good and to stay well.

Later that night, I lay in bed, thinking about my talk with Nanny B and about Jaylin as well. I was kicking up a sweat, having some serious Jaylin withdrawals. I couldn't stop thinking about how bad he was suffering, and I wondered what he was doing. The thoughts of him being with Scorpio angered me. What if he was at her place tonight? Being without him was so difficult. However, since our day in court was coming soon, I guessed I'd better get used to being alone.

For whatever reason, I needed him to forgive me for what I'd done to our child. It was hard for me to forgive myself. As I thought about his messages, I felt terrible. Tonight, I was in a mood to celebrate life, as Nanny B had suggested. I needed to see Jaylin, and I wanted to release all that was inside me. Since we'd been married, it was hard for me to go two or three days without making love to him. To go this long without him being inside me, it made me crazy. I got tired of touching myself and thinking about all that he was capable of doing to my body. I couldn't go another day without the man I desired to have.

I pulled the covers back and got out of bed. Dressed in my knee-length peach nightgown, I got in my car and left. I drove to our house, parking my car in the arched driveway. It was one forty-five in the morning, and the house was partially dark. There were several lights that always stayed on, but I could tell that everyone was asleep. I crept into the house, tiptoeing my way to the bedroom. When I cracked the door, the television was the only thing lighting up the room. I could barely hear the light jazz music that Jaylin sometimes played to fall asleep. Surprisingly, he was not in the bed. My stomach tightened as I had a feeling where he might be. Water rushed to my eyes and I looked around at our bedroom, which was rather messy. The bed hadn't been made; two pairs of his pants were on the floor, and so were some of his tennis shoes. A half-empty bottle of Grey Goose was on the nightstand, with an empty glass beside it. Next to that was a porn magazine. As I moved to the other side of the bed to see what Jaylin had been indulging himself with, I saw him sprawled out on the floor. He was passed out with no clothes on. My eyes scanned down his chiseled, muscular body, causing my insides to moisten. I removed my nightgown and laid it on the bed with my keys. I straddled my legs over Jaylin, looking down at how handsome he appeared while sleeping.

"Jaylin," I whispered. He was so out of it, and all I could see was his chest heaving up and down. The smell of the alcohol was pretty strong. There was no telling how long he'd been out like this. Hopefully, not for too long. I whispered his name again, but he didn't budge. I then squatted down, resting my goods directly

on top of his limp dick. I laced his shaft with my wetness, and the feel of it made me so hungry for him.
Slowly, but surely, his nine-plus started to rise. Jaylin's
eyelids fluttered. When he saw that I was on top of him,
he shockingly jumped from his sleep. He squeezed his
eyes; then he widened them to look at me.

"Nokea?" he said, slowly sitting up on his elbows.

I rubbed his chest, feeling his heartbeat accelerate.
"Yes, it's me. Now relax."

His dick quickly shot up, hard as a solid rock. He
reached out to touch my breasts, but I pinned his arms
to the floor with my hands. I positioned myself, then
jolted down hard on top of him, swallowing every inch
of his dick inside me. My force was powerful, and it
caused both of us to grunt loudly. My insides felt as
if they'd been ripped apart, and he tightened his eyes
from the pressure.

"Take—take it easy on me," he pleaded. "And please
let me taste your pussy."

I in no way took it easy on Jaylin. I released his
hands, and started to do major work on him. A deep
arch formed in my back, and I rode him tough, like a
jockey fighting hard to win a horse race. I spewed loud
grunts from the feel of him holding down my hips and
pumping his dick inside me. I wanted to come so badly,
so I increased my pace. My pace was at a rhythm that
Jaylin couldn't keep up with. He was sucking in his
bottom lip, and his eyes were locked in with mine.

"This is so perfect, Nokea. Work that pussy, baby.
I like . . . love how you're fucking me and riding this
dick."

His words caused me to work even harder. As hot
beads of sweat rolled down my body, his hands had a
solid grip on my ass. He squeezed it tightly, lifting my
cheeks to the tip of his thick head. He was groaning
each time I slammed myself back down. It wasn't long

before he stopped moving altogether and dropped his head back to the floor in defeat. "*Ahhh,* shit! Don't stop, baby. Keep on popping that pussy like this. I love it, Nokea. Baby, I love it!"

I was loving this too. As I dropped back on my hands, I gave him more pleasure. I gyrated my hips, stroking him from left, then to the right. With each thrust, Jaylin's body lifted from the floor.

"Gotdamn it," he yelled, with his fists tightened. "Come home to me, damn it! I need you . . . this. . . . I need this every day for the rest of my life!"

The sounds of him stirring my juices and our sweaty bodies slapping together filled the room. I slowed my pace, but Jaylin started to pick up his. He carefully watched his insertions as he licked the wetness from his lips.

"Do you want to come now?" he whispered. "I'm dying to bust this nut, but I want you to come with me."

I nodded, and Jaylin quickly flipped himself on top of me. He held my legs apart and inched his way into my perfectly fit tunnel. It was always difficult for me to fire back with my legs being held so tight, but I didn't mind watching him go to work. As soon as his fingers and thick head shoved against my swollen clit, it was all over with. I was on the verge of getting what I came here for. My breathing was sporadic, and my body was near a convulsion-like state. I reached up, pulling my hair on both sides.

"Do—do you forgive me?" I panted and cried out. "Please tell me that you forgive me for what I did to our child. I need to hear you say it. I'm so sorry for what I've done."

Jaylin dropped my legs and leaned atop me. I felt his warmness flowing inside me and down my crack. "I forgive you. Yes, baby, I do," he whispered in my ear.

"And I—I need for you to forgive me too. Please say that you forgive me and come back home."

The intense moment was over and we stared into each other's water-filled eyes. This was so hard on both of us, but I could in no way form the words to tell him that I forgave him. I touched his chest, slightly pushing it back so he could get off me. He sat up, resting his back against the side of the bed. With a frustrated look on his face, he closed his eyes, running his fingers through his wet curly hair.

"You're not going to forgive me, are you?" he asked.

At the moment, I couldn't say a word. I stood up and slid my nightgown over my head. My keys were on the bed. After I reached for those, I made my way to the door.

"Nokea!" Jaylin yelled. I turned, looking at him as he knelt beside the bed. Confusion was in his eyes, and he pleaded for my forgiveness. "I need for you to do that for us. It's the only way we can work through this. I know you want that, don't you?"

I stood for a moment; then I softly replied, "No. I don't want us to work it out. I cannot forgive you. I'm sorry it has to be this way."

I left, feeling numb, and knowing that great sex would never solve our problems. It was dynamite while it lasted. However, at the end of the day, our divorce was moving forward and the so-called celebration was over.

Two days later, I received a letter from Mr. Frick, advising me that Jaylin would be contesting the divorce. With that, our attorneys received letters from the courts, advising us of a scheduled court date when the judge would hear our arguments and possibly make a decision. My attorney said that this was a good

thing because there were so many marital assets involved: the children, the house, the many properties
Jaylin had, his money and his investments. . . . Going
to court was the best route to go. I listened to his recent
call on my voice mail and could barely make out what
he'd said because his voice was so low.

"Day eighty-eight. How in the hell can you come over
here and fuck me like that, then divorce me? That's
some cold shit, Nokea. As you know, we're expected in
court tomorrow. Time is not on our side and I hope you
will see things for the way they need to be. I thoroughly
enjoyed myself the other night, and my body craves
for more of you. Don't make me live without you. If it
helps, I love you. Always will, Nokea. See you soon."

I'd gotten to the point where I looked forward every
day to hearing Jaylin's messages—good or bad. As angry as I was, my heart still went out to him. No matter
what, though, I had to do this for me. I had put Jaylin
before myself too many times, and look where it got
me. After my talk with Nanny B, I realized she was
right. I didn't care what other people wanted me to do,
or how they wanted me to live my life. My life was my
own, and this decision in no way came easy for me.

I got up early, showered and put on my long-sleeved
burgundy stretch dress that hung slightly above my
knees. My hair was cut like always, and it had a Dark
and Lovely shine to it. I didn't wear too much makeup,
but my flawless skin made the little makeup that I had
on look airbrushed. Just as I was getting ready to go, I
checked my cell phone. I had a new message that had
come in while I was showering. I was afraid to look,
thinking it would be from Jaylin. I didn't know if I
could deal with any communication from him on *this*
morning. Instead, the call was from Nanny B, trying to
make her final plea to me.

"Good morning, Nokea. You're about to come to the conclusion of one of the biggest decisions of your life. My only hope is that you've thought this out carefully. Whatever you decide, we'll all just have to live with it. I love you, and my prayer is that your heart and soul will be filled someday with the happiness you deserve. Keep your head up and do what they always say . . . 'keep on trucking.'"

I had already been so emotional this morning and Nanny B's message didn't help. I missed my family so much and I couldn't wait for all of this to be done.

I arrived a tad bit late to court; traffic wasn't on my side. When I got to the courthouse, my attorney was waiting for me. Jaylin and Frick were there as well. As soon as I opened the door, Jaylin turned his head and looked at me with no expression. The saddened look in his eyes, which I hated to see, was there, but I looked at my attorney to avoid it. Jaylin sure looked good, though, and his cologne infused the entire courtroom. There was no denying that he could wear any black suit and turn it into something special. Sure he'd gone out of his way to look spectacular for me, and I had done the same. I walked down the aisle, moving my hair away from my face as part of it covered my eye. I kept my eyes on my attorney. When I reached her, she stood to give me a hug.

"Are you ready?" she asked. "The judge should be here in a minute. I don't know if we'll be able to wrap this up today; sometimes these things take a little longer."

I nodded and took my place next to her. Just to get a glance at Jaylin, I turned to my attorney to start a conversation. Jaylin was bent over with his elbows on his knees and hands shielding his face. From his lowered head, I could tell he was praying. Frick was talking to him, but was getting no response.

"Don't you worry," my attorney said. "You're going to be just fine. He really has no basis for contesting this divorce. Let's hope this goes quicker than expected."

When Judge Kay Catrel came in, my heart dropped to my stomach. I slowly stood up; Jaylin was even slower, being the last person to stand. After we took our oaths, we were ordered to take our seats. Good thing, as my legs immediately started to weaken.

"Let's see," the judge said, looking at the documents in front of her. "What do we have here today?" She peered over her glasses, looking at me and my attorney, then at Frick and Jaylin. She looked at the documents again; then she addressed Frick.

"Mr. Frick, I'm not quite clear about your client contesting the divorce. On what basis?"

Mr. Frick came from around the table, clearing his throat. Full of arrogance, he eased his hands in his pockets and spoke clearly. "On the basis that Mr. Rogers does not wish to divorce his wife. He's always been a family man and has provided well for his wife and children. In the documentation that we have presented to the court today, you will see just how well he has provided. He does not wish to separate his family, and doing so would be detrimental to his children. I'll make this very simple, if I can, Your Honor. Mrs. Rogers has no justifiable claims for divorce, other than to disrupt a family that she, herself, will admit to you today, she dearly loves. Indeed, her request for dissolution of the marriage should be denied."

Well, I'll be damned, I thought. *How was I the one willing to disrupt my family?* Frick was way out of line, but I knew my attorney would clear up that mess.

The judge looked at Jaylin. He was still sitting with his elbows on his knees, shielding his face with his hands, and looking down at the ground. "Mr. Rogers, I understand that this may be difficult for you, but please sit up straight. If you would like to address the court, now is your time to do it."

Jaylin sat up straight; then he stood to his feet. He looked at her with compassion and sorrow in his eyes. I wondered if his look pained her as much as it pained me. Already, this wasn't looking too good for me.

"I—I really don't have much to say, Your Honor. I made a mistake—one mistake—and my wife wishes to divorce me." He turned to look at me. "That's not what a marriage is about. We're supposed to face our challenges together, not give up when things happen. I don't want this divorce to be granted. Even though my reasoning may not be good enough to stop this, I am hoping the love you can see that I have for my wife may be enough. I'm counting on you to make the right decision." He paused for a second, eyes still connected with mine. "Damn, baby, you all I got. Please don't go through with this. I'm begging you, Nokea. From now on, I promise to be everything that you need me to be. One more chance, that's all I ask of you."

I swallowed the lump in my throat and turned my head to look away. I swear, nobody knew how painful this was. Seeing him like this just made me crazy.

The judge asked him to take a seat. When I turned my head, she looked like she wanted to say "poor baby" and go stroke his head. She blinked, then looked at my attorney. My lawyer, Anna Delaney, stood up.

"Your Honor, the mistake that Mr. Rogers is referring to has to do with infidelity issues—issues that led to his conceiving a child outside the marriage. My client's life has been turned upside down in finding out the truth behind her husband's adulterous affair, which has lingered on with the same woman for years and years. Throughout the years, Mrs. Rogers has remained faithful to her husband and wholeheartedly dedicated to their children. Her requests are simple and should be immediately granted by this court of honorable law."

Anna removed her glasses, wiping the smudges from them. She then put them back on, picked up a piece of paper and continued. "Mrs. Rogers would like for her divorce to be granted immediately. She accepts joint custody where the children are concerned, and is requesting twenty thousand dollars a month in spousal support. When you review the marital assets, you will clearly see that the amount she is requesting is minimal. Before entering into the marriage, Mr. Rogers's assets exceeded well over seventy million dollars. Throughout the marriage, those numbers have tremendously increased, and the reason why I bring this to your attention is simple. Mrs. Rogers's request for only twenty thousand dollars a month shows the desire she has to move forward with her life and leave the past behind her. Stripping her husband of his wealth is not her intention. The only thing that she seeks is a peace of mind. We know you can't legally grant her that, Your Honor, but today we hope that you will grant her a path to her freedom."

I kept my praying hands in front of me. When the judge asked if I wanted to address the court, I declined. My attorney had already said what I wanted her to say, and I didn't want to make this any more difficult than it already was.

"Mrs. Rogers," the judge said, watching me wipe my tears. "Have you at least considered a legal separation, instead? Obviously, this is painful for you too. Do you still love your husband?"

I was under oath, so I couldn't lie. "Yes, I do."

"I can't tell you how many couples come in here requesting a divorce and later regret it. You can petition your superior or family court for a legal separation and they will grant it. Many people do it because of their religious beliefs or due to the morals and values they hold against divorces. Legally, you will remain married to Mr. Rogers, but you will live separately from him. In the months to come, if you decide the legal separation does not work for you, then you may proceed with your divorce. Let me make myself clear. . . . I'm never delighted about being in a position where I have to grant any couple a divorce. I prefer to bring people together, rather than tear them apart. The decision, however, is yours. Is it possible for you to consider a legal separation right now rather than a divorce?"

I hesitated, only for a brief moment, thinking about our long life together, down to our "celebration" the other night. Jaylin had been so good to me, but I was sure he'd been that good to Scorpio too. My head slowly moved from side to side. "No. No, I'm not interested, Your Honor. I would like for you to grant me a divorce."

She sighed and sat back in her chair. She looked at Jaylin, who said nothing, but had gone back to the position that he had been in throughout the hearing. Frick had reached over to rub Jaylin's back again.

"Is there anything else?" she asked.

Frick abruptly stood to his feet. "Your Honor, before you make your decision, I ask that you take a few things into consideration. The first one being that my client, as you can see, simply does not want this. He truly loves his wife, and has always loved her. For years, these two have remained together through the good and, unfortunately, sometimes bad. They have always overcome. In time, this situation will heal itself. I ask the court to delay this process, allowing Mr. and Mrs. Rogers time to consult with each other about a future, possible reconciliation. Mrs. Rogers has in no way permitted that kind of conversation to take place, and her decision to dissolve the marriage is a bit rushed. For the sake of saving a marriage, I ask that you consider a dismissal."

My stomach tightened as I expected Frick to bring up my abortion and really make me look bad. Thank God that he didn't, but he really was trying to make the case for Jaylin.

For the next few minutes, the judge looked at the papers in front of her. At first, she suggested going back to her chambers, but she changed her mind. She had a picture of LJ and Jaylene, compliments of Frick. As she looked at the picture, she smiled.

"Are these the children?" she asked, looking in my direction. I nodded. "Gorgeous. So gorgeous," she said.

She put the picture down and cleared her throat. A deep breath came afterward and she addressed Jaylin. "Mr. Rogers, if I could save your marriage, I would. However, on the basis that you have presented to the court today, your request for a dismissal will be denied. I will grant Mrs. Rogers her divorce, joint custody of the kids where she will have them on weekends and every other holiday. As for spousal support, I'll order it in the amount of forty thousand dollars a month. Mrs. Rogers, you will thank me later for that decision, as Mr. Rogers was willing to give you more. Good luck, people, and God bless." The judge slammed down her gavel.

Tears poured down my face, but it was in no way from feeling happiness. Jaylin was still looking down at the floor, but his eyes were closed. Frick looked upset because this was one time he couldn't give Jaylin what he wanted. After I thanked Anna, I rushed to leave the courtroom, thinking that Jaylin would come after me. He didn't.

JAYLIN

The drive home felt as if I were riding on air. My blurred vision caused me barely to see the road. I'm not going to lie when I say I felt like driving my ass off a cliff. The thoughts of my children prevented me from doing the unthinkable, but I was not prepared to tell them that Nokea wasn't coming home at any time soon. I just couldn't believe this shit was happening. I wished like hell that I were dreaming. Why couldn't she have given me another chance? The end result of what happened today left me distraught.

I walked into the house, trying to keep my emotions in tact. I unknotted my tie away from my neck and pulled out my shirt, which was tucked into my pants. I could hear the kids laughing and playing in their playroom. When I went to the door, I stood in the doorway, watching their teacher and Nanny B helping them with their paintings. Justin and Jaylene were making one big mess with the watercolor paints; Mackenzie was painting flowers, and LJ was painting a picture of our family. No one saw me standing in the doorway, until Nanny B turned her head in my direction. She stared into my red and swollen eyes, which gave her a clue as to how my day in court had gone.

"Everyone, it's time to clean up," she said; then she turned to Mrs. Mahoney. "Would you help the kids clean up? I'm getting ready to start on dinner."

Mrs. Mahoney started helping the kids clean up, and Nanny B headed my way. Mackenzie saw me and rushed past Nanny B to show me her picture.

"Look, Daddy," Mackenzie said, tightening her arms around my waist. She had no idea what her hug was doing for me right now, and her proud smile about her painting made me crack a tiny smile. I held one side of the picture up, while she held the other.

"It's beautiful, baby," I softly said. "Tomorrow I'm going to buy a frame for it and hang it in my office."

The others rushed up to me, showing me their pictures and asking if I would hang theirs too. "Please, Daddy," Jaylene said, grabbing my leg and holding it. "Mine is pretty too."

I looked at her picture, mixed with many colors. Then at LJ's, which just tore at my soul. I swallowed the oversized lump in my throat, clearing the mucus. "All of them are very nice. I'm going to hang up all of them."

"Yay!" they shouted, including Justin, who had ripped his picture from waving it around too much. Mackenzie and Jaylene awaited their kisses, which I always gave them when I came into the house. When I lowered my head down to them, they both grabbed tightly around my neck. I closed my eyes, for I didn't want them to question me about why my eyes were so red. I felt their lips peck my cheeks. I slightly cracked my eyes so I could see their cheeks to kiss them back.

"*Muah,*" I said, then hurried to stand up. They ran away to help Mrs. Mahoney clean up, and Nanny B stood next to me. She was saying something, but I ignored her while looking at Jaylene. All I could think about was Nokea, because they looked so much alike. Nanny B touched my back.

"Go get out of your clothes and get ready for dinner. I'm making one of your favorite dishes tonight, and I . . ."

I sighed, and walked away from the doorway. I felt more anger inside. I wasn't sure if it was at Nokea, or at myself for fucking up so badly. I went into my bedroom, looking at the huge bed in which I would now have to lay alone. I slammed the door, and my breathing started to increase. My fist tightened. After I swung it in the air, I punched my chest hard.

"Gotdamn it!" I shouted. I took a deep breath, sucking in a long heap of air. Wanting to tear up something, I looked at the TV, the lamps and even the glass windows that surrounded my bedroom. I then looked at a picture on the nightstand of Nokea and me. I walked over to pick it up. I held the picture in my hand and my emotions ran over. I plopped down on the bed, dropping the picture next to me. Sitting up, I covered my face with my hands. I sobbed, like I had never done before. And all of this over a woman? I couldn't believe I was losing my swag. It had been years since I'd last felt like this. Realizing that I had made one of the biggest mistakes of my life was, nonetheless, crushing. This wasn't just any woman. . . . This was Nokea.

I heard my bedroom door open, but I didn't want to lift my head to see who it was.

"I'm so sorry," Nanny B said sympathetically, "but you'll get through this."

I lifted my head, clearing my wet face with my hand and shaking my head. Justin was on Nanny B's hip. The Lord knows that I didn't want Justin to see me so broken. "How? How can I live without her? I can't do it, Nanny B. There is no way for me to imagine my life without her. Ain't no way!"

Nanny B put Justin down and came up to me. Without saying a word, she opened her arms, inviting me into them. I stood, embracing her, and feeling the strength and support from a woman who was much smaller than me, but powerful in her own way. As I staggered, she held me tightly, assuring me that everything would be fine.

"We will get through this," she said tearfully. "I promise you that I will never, ever let you or your children down." She removed my slumped head from her shoulder and held the sides of my face as I looked into her eyes. "I love you like my child, Jaylin. When you hurt, I do too. From now on, I want you to live for these beautiful children. Nokea did what she felt she had to do, and I don't want you to be angry with her about her decision. Continue to love her as you do. When all is said and done, I assure you that we will all be one big, happy family again."

I felt some comfort in her words and stood to gather myself. Justin was trying to get up on my bed, so I picked him up and put him on top of it.

"Thank you," I said, turning to Nanny B. "I love you too, and I am so blessed to have you in my life."

Nanny B smiled. "Me too. Dinner should be ready in about an hour. Settle down for a while and you can come help me, if you want to."

"I just might do that, as soon as I shower and change. In the meantime, do me a favor."

"What is it?"

"Please don't tell anyone about what just happened. I know you be talking a lot to some of your friends in the neighborhood, but, uh, don't make me look bad, all right?"

She chuckled and placed her hand on her hip. "Do you really think I would tell my friends about you being emotional? That's none of their business, and shame on you for—"

"I know. I was just making sure. I don't want anyone to think I'm soft, weak or anything like that, but—"

"Chile, please. Even Jesus wept! If He cried, who do you think you are?"

I shrugged. "I'm Jaylin Jerome Rogers, that's who I am."

"And?"

"And I'm not supposed to go out like this."

"Says who?"

"Says me. I'm a little embarrassed, but I'm so down with your support. Now, let's be done with this because I'm starving. I'll be in there to help you cook in a few."

Nanny B shook her head and reached for Justin.

"He good," I said, placing him on my lap. "I'll bring him to you before I take my shower."

Nanny B nodded and left the room. I lay back on the bed, straddling Justin across my chest. I held his hands with mine as he bounced up and down on my chest, laughing. As I began to tickle him, he laughed harder. His laughs made me laugh, and I couldn't help but tighten my arms around my son and softly kiss his forehead.

"Oh, I love you so much, son. Way more than you can ever understand right now."

All Justin did was smile, but I knew that he felt what I was saying. I put him down and he followed me into my closet. While inside, I removed my shirt and tossed a T-shirt and a pair of shorts over my shoulder. Justin was on the tips of his toes, trying to reach for my Rolex watches that sat on top of the island. I reached for one Rolex, putting it on his wrist. I knelt down beside him.

"I see you're already trying to be like me, but if you wear one of those, make sure you got the right suit on. No cheap mess, okay? You gotta have swag, too, and I'll tell you about all of that once you get a li'l older. As for the ladies, when you find one that you love, man, hang on to her tight! Treat her well and do not make the mistakes that I have." Justin nodded, pretty much ignoring me and trying to remove the glistening diamonds from my watch. He took it off, giving it back to me. "Thank you," I said, gathering the rest of my things to take a shower and watching him tear through my closet, putting on my shirts and stepping into a pair of my black leather shiny shoes. I tossed one of my hats on his head and held out my hand for him to give me five.

"Aw, man, that's you right there?" I said, smiling at how much he looked like me. "You already got the game and gone with it."

Justin kept looking at himself in the mirror, taking the hat off and putting it back on. He laughed some more and fussed when it was time to leave the closet. I picked him up, carrying him out the door. "Nanny B got the house already smelling good. Don't you smell that?"

"Yes," Justin said.

"I do too," I said, putting him down. He rushed to the kitchen, where Nanny B was sitting at the table breaking open some lettuce with her hands. She wiped them on a rag next to her, then reached for Justin so he could sit on her lap.

"I'm going to take my shower," I said. "I'll be back to help in a bit."

"Hurry," she said, smiling, and looking at Justin, who had already stuck some lettuce in his mouth. "As you can see, he's not going to let me get much done."

"I will."

I returned to my bedroom with the thought of Nokea still heavy on my mind. My shower took longer than expected, for I couldn't stop thinking about if there would ever be another time that she would join me. I visualized her being in the shower with me, but the fear of moving forward alone was fresh in my head.

Later that night, I tossed and turned in bed. I couldn't sleep at all, and my eyes stayed glued to the dark sky that had lightning occasionally flashing through it. I rubbed my chest, feeling as if I hadn't done enough to try to save my marriage. Yeah, for some people, it may have been too late, but I in no way could accept what had gone down in court today. I looked at the clock, and it was only ten-twenty. I had to see Nokea, just to tell her what a big mistake she had made today, and to see if there was any way possible for us to get back on the right track. She had been calling too many shots lately, and I didn't like the path that she had chosen for us. I tossed the cover aside, and put on my light blue pajama shirt, which matched my pants. As thunder crackled, I slid into my house shoes and grabbed my keys from the dresser.

On my way to her condo, the rain was coming down hard. The wipers didn't seem to be moving fast enough, making it difficult for me to see. I started to pull over, but I was anxious to get to her place. Unfortunately for me, when I got there, her Range Rover was not in its designated place. I called her cell phone, but she didn't answer. I wondered where she could be at this time of the night. Maybe she had parked elsewhere. When I drove around the entire parking lot to see if I could find her truck, no luck. Just for the hell of it, I ran inside to see if she was there. I was drenched as hell, knocking on her door, but got no answer. The thought of her being with another man was starting to consume my mind, but who in the hell was he? There had to be someone else, and I was fooling myself if I thought there wasn't. The insecurities that I felt inside were unbelievable. I had never felt this way before, but no woman had ever had a hold on me like Nokea did.

I walked outside, with my head hanging low. The rain seemed to be coming down even harder; water was dripping from my chin, hair, nose and eyelashes. I combed back my dripping wet hair with my fingers. When I saw headlights in Nokea's parking spot, our eyes locked together. I walked up to her truck, and she lowered her window.

"What are you doing out here?" she asked. "You're soaking wet."

"So? I needed to see you. Where have you been?"

Nokea looked irritated, tapping her fingers on the steering wheel. "It's really none of your business, but I went to the movies. Wanted to clear my head. Staying cooped up inside my condo was driving me crazy."

"Did you go alone?"

Nokea opened the door, standing out in the rain with me. She squinted, blinking fast so she could see. "Does it really matter, Jaylin?"

"Hell yes, it does! We have some unfinished business to take care of. If you think what happened in court today is final, baby, you're sadly mistaken. No way, no how, am I giving up on us. You need to tell whoever he is that we—"

"There is no one else, Jaylin, so stop sounding so darn insecure. I never wanted anyone but you. Don't you know that?"

I stared at Nokea, watching the rain beat down on her beautiful face. Her hair had gotten flat and her clothes were now drenched as well. I reached out my hands, holding her face and softly rubbing her cheeks with my thumbs.

"What must I do, baby? Tell me what I can do to help us erase what happened today and move on with our lives together. I know I didn't fight hard enough for you. I took you for granted, and shame on me."

Nokea touched my hand and I watched as water rushed to the brim of her eyes before flowing over. "This—this hurts so bad," she said, trembling as she spoke.

I rushed to hold her in my arms, laying her head against my chest. I softly rubbed her head and kissed it.

"I know it does. And I was one stupid muthafucka for putting us through this."

Nokea's cries increased and I could feel her heartbeat accelerate. I wanted to calm her, so I moved her head away from my chest and looked into her eyes. "Don't you love me anymore? Don't you need me like I need you?"

She hesitated, but then she slowly nodded. I took her confirmation as a sign to go for a kiss, so I did. I held her face, hesitantly taking one peck, then two. She didn't reject me, so I sucked in her wet bottom lip. When I felt her hands ease around my waist, that's when I went for it all. Her lips were so juicy; I could barely contain myself. My dick was hurting; it was so hard. I pressed my hardness against her so she could feel it. We backed up to her truck, sucking in each other's lips and barely taking a second to pause. The rain was still pounding down hard, and both of our clothes were sticking to our bodies. I felt Nokea's hands touch my abs, and then slide down to my goods. My hands roamed too. I reached underneath her skirt, raising it a bit and circling her perfect ass, which was barely covered with hip-hugging lace panties. We felt each other's bodies for a while, massaging, squeezing and touching in all of the right places. Nokea unbuttoned my thin pajama shirt, trying to peel it away from my soaking wet chest.

"Make love to me," she whispered while sucking the water from my lips and squeezing my hair. "Please."

In no way did she have to say "please" to me. I helped her remove my shirt, dropping it to the pavement. Nokea touched my chest and massaged my biceps.

"Let's go inside," I suggested.

She moved her head from side to side. "No, right here. I want to do it right here."

I wasn't going to argue with her about where to make love. I was just overly thrilled that she wanted to do it, but also surprised. She backed into the backseat of her Range Rover, where she quickly came out of her blouse and hiked up her skirt. I looked inside, not knowing where to venture first. Her breasts were so damn succulent and pretty, but not as much as her pussy was. I wiped down my face, trying to clear the rain from it. I didn't care that we would have to leave the door open; and if anyone saw us, too damn bad. I made my way inside, thinking to hell with foreplay. We were both so aroused. I knew Nokea wanted to feel me as bad as I wanted to feel her. I lowered my pajama pants, allowing my dick to flop out, long and throbbing hard. It entered Nokea's tunnel within seconds, causing both of us to gasp. Slowly my hips went into action, and her wetness stirred up my rushing semen, which couldn't wait to coat her walls. I could still feel her body trembling underneath me, so I placed delicate kisses on her shoulders and on her chest, just to see if I could calm her. Her hands gripped my ass, and her nails were pushed into it. She squeezed her eyes, letting out a bunch of moans, and then a loud ear-ringing scream. The scream caused me to halt my actions.

"Damn, baby, am I hurting you?" I whispered, releasing one of her legs that I held high. It felt as if her pussy had dried up on me, and that had never happened before. "I'll take it easy, but just work with me, okay? Relax."

She swallowed while staring into my eyes. "I can't do this," she said. "All I can think about is our divorce. I didn't want to go through with it Jaylin, but you being inside her, and making her feel the way you do me is..."

"*No,*" I said, feeling her about to renege on me. "I—I don't care how she feels. You . . . we can do this. Let's work hard at putting our lives back together and to hell with that divorce."

Nokea wasn't with it. Tears rolled from the corner of her eyes and I kissed them. I tried to calm her, but to no avail. She pushed my chest back, telling me to get up.

"Baby, calm down. Let's go inside and—"

"No!" she shouted. "I want you to leave me the hell alone and accept that our divorce is final!"

Seeing her like this was a disappointment. I thought we were making progress. "I ca-can't accept our divorce. I can't lose you like this, Nokea. To hell with Scorpio, baby! What is it about that, that you don't understand?"

She sat silently for a moment, waiting until I got my act together. I didn't want to come over here acting no damn fool, but she was very unsympathetic to what I had said.

"I needed you too," she said. "But you failed me, time and time again. I had no choice, other than to go through with what I did today. I'm sticking to it. So please get up so I can go inside."

I let out a deep sigh before I eased out of her dry pussy and backed out of the truck. I raised my pants, watching Nokea hurry to put her blouse back on. She stepped out of the truck, pulling down her skirt, not saying a word. How we went from being so excited about each other to this? I don't know. Nokea started to walk away. I called her name and she turned. Holding out my hands, I pleaded with her.

"So this is how you're going to treat me, huh? Let me know now, so I can stop wasting my time with you."

"I'm letting you know now, you will be wasting your time."

I knew I was seconds away from losing it—again. And saying not another word, she went inside the building, leaving me in more pain than I was in before I came over.

"Fuck it," I said, making my way back to my car. "To hell with it."

JAYLIN

The divorce was hard to swallow, but I was doing my best. Shane had closed on another deal, and that did bring some joy to me. Losing Nokea, however, was the worst feeling ever, and I couldn't believe that I had been so clueless about what she would ultimately do in a situation like this one. Never did I think she would make such a move. She did, and I was still trying to figure out how I was going to live with her decision.

I mean, my behavior was so out of character. Having thoughts about following her to see what she'd been up to? Thinking about her being with another man? That in itself made me angry. I couldn't seem to overcome this insecure-ass feeling I had inside. No doubt, when a man loves a woman and he loses her, it just makes him crazy. I was definitely feeling that way, and it frustrated me that I was making no progress with her whatsoever.

Shane had been on me about getting my act together. He knew how difficult this situation had been. I was pleased to have a friend who wasn't trying to stab me in my back at a time like this, but who was trying to be helpful. After work one day, we went to a crowded bar, just to sit back and chill. I needed to relax, and having a few drinks every now and then seemed to help. I sat on a bar stool with my elbows resting on top of the bar. I had just taken a shot of Rémy, and was feeling the burning sensation down my throat. I cleared it and looked over at Shane, who was sitting next to me. We were both causally dressed in jeans and button-down shirts. Mine was tan and his was white. I had on my Calvin Klein loafers, but Shane wore his Nike tennis shoes. We rarely got dressed up to go to work; and as low-key as we were, the women's eyes were still shifting around the room toward us. I was flattered by the attention and so was Shane. He did notice how quiet I was, and he reached over to grip the back of my neck.

"In time, my brotha, you will feel so much better," he said.

"Yeah, but I'm living for today and not for tomorrow. Today I feel like shit. I would do anything in the world to remove that day in court from my life. I can't believe Nokea is no longer my wife."

"That's what the courts say, but you know, as well as I do, that Nokea will forever keep her status."

"I agree, but I'm surprised by how quickly the shit went down. She didn't even allow herself time to think about it. She brought her ass to the house and damn near raped my ass; then she basically told me, 'Fuck you.'"

Shane cocked his head back. "What? I didn't even know she'd come to the house!"

"She did. I was knocked out, and she came in and fucked the shit out of me. Had me going crazy, and made me tell her that I'd forgiven her about killing my baby. I'm still pissed about that, even though I told her I wasn't. That hurt me like hell, man. Nokea never should have done that to our child. Then she got me hyped again. We were making love in the rain, and all of a sudden, she made me pull out. Man, her pussy had dried up on me, and that ain't never happened. She said it was over and she was satisfied with her decision. She's been fucking with my emotions, and I got a problem with that."

"You'll be all right. It just takes time, that's all. It was wrong for her to have an abortion, but neither one of us knows or understands what she was going through at the time."

"I know it's been hard on her, but something like that was difficult to swallow. She's got this look about her that says she doesn't even love me anymore. And when I look into her eyes and see it, man, it's the worse feeling ever. You should have seen her that day in court. She wanted that shit over with, and after the divorce was granted, she broke out of there like she was pleased. Later that night, I saw something different. I'm confused."

"I've spoken to her since then, and 'pleased' is not the word you'd want to use. Maybe 'ready to move on,' but she is just as devastated by this situation as you are."

"Then why go through with it? It didn't make much sense to me, especially if she's so hurt behind this. One day she's going to regret her decision. I know that for a fact."

"I agree. But in the meantime, I need for you to chalk it up, stop spending so much time in Jaylin's World on Facebook and get back to business with me. Can you do that for me?"

"I will do my best, but the love that I get from my Angels on Facebook helps me cope with what I'm dealing with. You have no idea how those ladies make me feel, and it's not about hooking up with anyone in particular either."

Shane gave me a stern look. "Are you sure about that? You don't need to inject any more women into this mess that you already have. You seem to have your hands full, and I don't want you to lose focus."

"I assure you that I won't. And even though a few ladies—well, one, in particular, has really caught my attention—I know it may stem from the neglect I'm feeling from Nokea. She reminds me so much of Nokea,

and she fine as hell too. But it is what it is. I damn sure
know what my priorities are now. Business and my
damn kids!"

We both laughed.

Since our glasses were getting empty, Shane called
for the bartender to fill them. An older black man, Raymond, came over to fill our glasses.

"Don't y'all youngbloods overdo it, especially if the
two of you aren't the ones paying."

We weren't sure what Raymond meant by that, until
he pointed to two chicks at the other end of the bar
who had told Raymond our drinks were on them. Both
of the women looked decent, and being offered a drink
wasn't going to hurt anyone. Shane lifted his glass to
the ladies and they smiled, lifting their glasses as well.
A few minutes later, they came to our end of the bar to
sit. One of the women kind of reminded me of Taraji P.
Henson, and the other had addictive eyes, like Regina
King's. She sat to Shane's right, and the other woman
sat next to me. I guessed they had already planned this
out.

Shane glanced at me, and then he smiled at the ladies. "Thanks for the drinks, but you really didn't have
to."

The one with the pretty eyes spoke up. "It's okay. We
didn't mind at all." She held out her hand, extending it
to Shane. "I'm Velvet."

The other one spoke up too. "And my name is Faith."

Shane spoke for both of us. "I'm Shane and this is
Jay," he said, pointing to me. I nodded my head and
sipped from my glass again. It was so easy for me to
pick up women; Nokea didn't know all of the women
I'd turned away because of her. Even at a time like this,
I could easily walk away, but conversation never hurt
anyone.

Faith cleared her throat to get my attention. I turned to her, while Shane started conversing with Velvet.

"I guess I don't have to ask if you're married, only because I already see your ring," she said.

I looked at my ring, turning it in circles. "Yeah, I'm happily married," I said, leaving it there.

"I have to be honest and say that I was hoping otherwise. Your wife must be one lucky woman. I'm not going to pressure you or anything; but if I give you my phone number, is there any chance you'll use it?"

Sometimes in these situations, I didn't know how to say no. Depending on what kind of mood I was in, I didn't like to hurt anyone's feelings. In this case, the woman was beautiful, she came to me like she had some sense, and she was confident about what she wanted. That always impressed me. "Sure, you can give me your number. Maybe I'll use it, maybe I won't."

She smiled and wrote her number on a piece of paper. "I love a confident and cocky man. That you are." She gave me the piece of paper, and then she moved in closer. "If you're happily married, then why the long face? I've been watching you all evening, and I haven't seen you smile once."

"I'm tired from work, that's all."

"Then you should be glad to be off work. Would you like to dance? I love me some Maxwell, and the dance floor isn't that crowded."

I glanced at the small hardwood dance floor, where four other couples were dancing. A disco ball turned from up above, along with yellow and white spinning lights. Shane was still talking to Velvet, so I shrugged my shoulders.

"Sure. Why not?"

Faith and I went to the dance floor; as we danced to "Pretty Wings" by Maxwell, my mind was all over the place. I'd thought about taking her to her house and knocking her back out, but the desire wasn't there. Thoughts of Nokea were crippling me, and I wondered what she was doing. I finally forced out a smile, spinning Faith around.

"Okaaay," she said. "I *knew* I'd get a smile out of you tonight."

I was sure she wanted to get more than a smile out of me. We danced through another song. When the DJ kicked up KEM's "Why Would You Stay?" the words really caused me to lose my swag:

Girl, I know you deserve a better man./ I was a fool to ever let you down, so why would you stay?/ Woman, I beg your forgiveness and I'll do whatever it takes./Sugar, your heart has been broken, but I can still see true love shining in your eyes.

"Thanks for the dance," I said, backing away from her in the middle of the song. "I need to go handle some business right now."

She didn't ask what, and all she said was "Su-sure."

As she walked in front of me, my eyes dropped to look at her ass. I couldn't help but think about what could have transpired tonight. She made her way to the bar. Before taking a seat, she flagged the bartender again. She asked if I wanted anything else, but I declined. I turned my attention to Shane, interrupting his conversation.

"Say, man, I'm getting ready to jet. Are you staying?"

"Not for long," he said, eyeballing Faith. "Why are you leaving so soon?"

"I need to go take care of something real quick. Need to get home to check on my kids too."

Shane turned to Velvet. "I'll be right back. I'm going to walk my friend to his car."

She nodded.

Before I left, I reached out for Faith's hand.

"Enjoy your evening, baby, and stay sweet. Thanks for the drink and the dance."

"You're welcome. Sorry you're leaving so soon. I wish you'd stay for a while longer."

"Maybe next time."

"Maybe so."

I left and Shane followed behind me. When we got to my truck, he folded his arms. "I wish you'd hang around for a while. I'm not saying that you should hook up with Faith or anything like that, but just chilling and talking may help put you at ease."

"My mind ain't with it, but I'll see you when you get home. Or will I?"

"Hey, I'm good. I will definitely be there tonight, but I don't mind having good conversations with females."

"Are you sure that's all it is? Tiffanie shouldn't be worried, should she?"

"Not one bit. These ladies are real nice and down-to-earth. Tiffanie won't be home until eleven o'clock, so I'm just wasting some time."

I nodded. After Shane and I slapped our hands together, I left.

I drove down the highway in a real shitty mood. I knew Scorpio could temporarily change my mood, but I didn't feel like seeing her. I called home to check on the kids, and Nanny B said that everyone was fine. I talked to LJ for a few minutes, then to Mackenzie and Jaylene. When I asked for Justin, Nanny B said he was asleep. I told her I'd be home soon.

I figured it would be another restless night for me, and if the thoughts of Nokea were keeping me up, I wanted to keep her up. I didn't want to seem like no stalker, but I missed having my wife around. My hope was that she would have something intriguing to say to me, and that would change my mood around. That led me to her condo, and I lightly tapped on the door.

There was no answer. I knew she was there, only because her Range Rover was parked in the parking lot. I'd also heard soft music playing from inside her apartment. I heard the volume go down. I leaned in to speak loud enough so she could hear me. I didn't want to sound like I was yelling, however. I kept my voice friendly.

"I guess by now you've already looked through the peephole and you know it's me. Why don't you just open the door?"

There was no response. I sighed and waited for a moment. Still, silence. Minutes later, I continued. "Can I tell you that being without your love is driving me insane? If you were out to make a point, you damn sure made one. I don't know how long you're going to make us suffer like this. If you don't give a damn anymore, why don't you just say it?"

She didn't say one word. I wanted her to open the door, so I did not raise my voice. "I will only stay for five minutes, and all I want to do is see you. A hug would be nice too, Nokea. If you're listening to me, just say something. Give me a signal. . . . Knock on the door. Something."

I waited, but no signal came. I stood for a moment, and then I sat down in front of her door, bending my knees. I fumbled around with my fingers, thinking about how things had gone so very wrong. "Damn, I just wanted to tell you about my day, and I miss not being able to communicate with you. So here I am, and I hope you're listening. I got up early and took my morning jog, which you sometimes took with me. Then I showered and looked for you, but you weren't there. Afterward, I had breakfast with Nanny B and the kids; and to see your chair empty ain't a good thing, baby." I swallowed the lump in my throat, pausing for a moment before I continued on. "I then drove to the office

with Shane, expecting to get a phone call from you,
telling me that I'd forgotten something and needed
to come back to get it. Or a call just to say how much
you loved me, and encouraging me to have a good day.
What—what about those notes that you sometimes
write me, sharing your thoughts and letting me know
what's waiting for me when I come home." I smiled in
deep thought. "All I can say is, plenty of times, Nokea,
you had my ass so anxious to get home. I miss all of
that, don't you?"

I would bet my life on it that she was on the other side
of the door, but wouldn't say anything. I wished like
hell that she would open the door. Since she wouldn't,
I kept at it. "After work, Shane and I went to a bar." I
smiled. "Can you believe two women bought us some
drinks, and one of them asked me to dance? Yeah, I
danced with her, but then that song by KEM came on,
'Why Would You Stay?' You should have seen me. I
couldn't even dance right. You have got to listen to that
song, if you haven't already heard it. Just pay attention
to the words. I know why you didn't want to stay, but I
want you to change your mind. When I listened to that
song, my mind was consumed with thoughts of us. I—I
know you think I'm bullshitting, but it's the truth. I had
a vision of us dancing together at our neighbor's party
we went to. We had so much fun that night, and that
dress you wore. . . . You really outdid yourself. That was
the night we made our baby. Or was it before that?" I
paused, knowing that she probably wouldn't want me
to go there.

"Anyway, baby, I just wanted to tell you that this
is . . . Being without you is tough. Lying in our bed at
night, alone, is the worst feeling ever. I'm starting to
have those bad dreams again about my past, and do
you remember when I used to call you in the middle of
the night so you could come over and lay in bed with

me? I felt so loved and protected. You always made me feel loved, didn't you?" I chuckled, thinking about when I was thirteen years old and got beat up for defending Nokea. "You know who I was thinking about the other night? That punk, Blake Jackson. Remember he kept messing with you? When he made you cry that day, I was so upset. I got my ass kicked; and even though I was embarrassed as hell, I remember you helping me off the ground and wiping the dirt from my clothes. That was the first time I held your hand on the way to school, and I kept thinking, '*Daaamn,* this girl may someday be my wife.' You were so fine, but Stephon, that fool, kept telling me that you liked him. I knew better, though. When you kissed me in my aunt's basement that day, I was like . . . 'Yeah, she feeling me.' That kiss was—was dry as hell, and you wouldn't even give me no tongue. Remember? You wouldn't give me no pussy either. When you did finally up it, I'll be damned if we didn't make LJ. I don't care what you say, but this shit was meant to last a lifetime."

I laughed and sat in silence as I thought more about our long history together. I had known Nokea for thirty plus years and was thinking about how she had been there for me too. And, how I had disappointed her. I lowered my head. "I fucked this up, didn't I? I regret all that I've done to you. Saying I'm sorry will never be enough, but let me show you that I can be all that you need me to be. Can you do that for me?"

I paused, and a few seconds later, my cell phone rang. When I looked to see who it was, it was Scorpio calling me. I ignored the call; the timing was way off. I had the nerve to be annoyed by the call, but I had no one to blame for this situation but myself. I slowly stood up, turning to face the door with my hands pressed against it. "I'm getting ready to go. I just wanted to say hello,

and I may come back tomorrow to share my thoughts.
I hope you don't mind, but you're still my best friend.
Meanwhile, can I get a simple knock to let me know
you're okay? Maybe two knocks just to tell me you still
love me. It really would mean the world to me."

I waited again for her to respond, but I guess I was
asking for too much. I put my hands in my pockets and
turned. As I walked away from her door, I heard two
light knocks. For now, that had to be enough.

Feeling just okay, I walked to my truck. When I got
inside, I returned Scorpio's call.

"What's up?" I asked.

"Nothing much. I was just calling to check on you
and the kids. Are you bringing them home tonight or
tomorrow?"

"Probably tomorrow."

"Okay. Then I'm going to Loretta's aunt's house with
her. If you need me tonight, I can be reached by cell
phone."

"Have fun, and we'll see you tomorrow."

Scorpio paused for a second. "You don't sound too
good. Is there anything that I can do to perk you up? I
can always cancel my plans with Loretta, and you know
I'd rather be spending my time with you any day of the
week."

"The invite sounds enticing, but I'll pass tonight. I'm
a little tired. I will see you tomorrow, though, okay?"

"Okay, honey. You still my Jay Baby. Whenever
you're ready for me, I'm all yours."

"Tomorrow. I'll be there tomorrow."

Scorpio hung up, and so did I. I wasn't sure what
tomorrow was going to bring, but I did know that I
couldn't go on feeling just "okay" forever.

SCORPIO

I couldn't believe that Nokea had really done it! She gave Jaylin his walking papers, but you'd better believe that he didn't walk too far. He came to me a few days after his divorce was final, and I had never seen Jaylin so torn. All I could do was lend him my shoulder, and seeing him so out of character caused me to be really hard on myself. I felt as if I were the one to blame for the entire mess. I apologized profusely for my actions. He didn't put the blame on me; rather he turned it to himself. He took responsibility for everything he'd done and simply said that he'd have to live with it the best way he could.

The weeks following had gotten even tougher for me. Yeah, Jaylin was spending a lot of time with his kids, so we rarely saw each other. Some days, he sent Nanny B to get the children, and his phone calls were always here and there. When I called to speak to him, he always seemed to be in a rush. I asked Mackenzie how he seemed; to her, Daddy was doing fine. She talked about how excited he was to be with them, and told me about all of the adventurous things they'd done. I guess I finally realized that this was not about him and me. Or, for that matter, about Nokea and him. Jaylin wanted to be with his children, even though he had suffered a tremendous loss with losing Nokea.

Nearly a month later, things had started to settle down. I saw Jaylin coming back to life. We'd only had sex once, but the performance he delivered was always everlasting. He was smiling more; he spent more time at my place with the kids; he talked about making money again. He mentioned Shane getting married and bragged about how much money they were making. I was feeling happy for Jaylin, and I couldn't believe Shane was getting married. I hadn't forgotten about our past history together. Whoever it was who landed him, she was one lucky woman. In a sense, so was I. I didn't have the relationship I wanted with Jaylin, but because of the damage we'd all done to each other, we all had to accept some losses. Nobody got exactly what he or she wanted or expected; but as long as Jaylin was a part of my life, I was okay. For now, anyway.

I sat on my balcony with my feet relaxing in the Jacuzzi, wanting to express my thoughts of late. Jaylin was sitting in one of the lounge chairs with Justin on his lap. Mackenzie was inside taking her piano lessons. We could hear her playing.

"What do you think about all of this?" I asked while splashing my feet in the water.

"About what?" Jaylin asked. "I think her playing sounds good."

"No, I mean about all that we've been through. Was this really how things were supposed to be?"

Jaylin tickled Justin to make him laugh. "Other than my divorce, I guess so. I believe things happen for a reason, but some things I can't accept."

"Have you spoken to Nokea?"

"Not much. There's been a word or two said between us when she comes by to get the kids, but nothing to brag about. I can't believe how much she hates me. I thought by now we'd at least be on good terms."

"She doesn't hate you. Not at all. I didn't tell you this, but I went to see her right before you went to court. We talked, and I told her how sorry I was for all that had happened. I expressed my love for you and told her that I would stop being intimate with you, if the two of you stayed together."

Jaylin sat quietly; then he and Justin came over to the Jacuzzi with me. "What else did she say? Did she believe you?"

I shrugged. "I don't know. But for her, my saying that wasn't enough. So much had already been done. For the first time, I saw the hurt in her eyes and I could see how much she loved you. This shit was *so* serious, Jaylin, and we'd all been playing around with it as if nobody had a care in the world. Do you think the day will come when we're all content and we recover from this?"

Jaylin put Justin on his shoulders and came closer to me. "I hope so. But in the meantime, thanks for being there for me." He puckered and I kissed his sexy lips.

After Mackenzie's piano lessons were over, we all went inside to eat dinner. Loretta made tacos, and Jaylin told her they tasted better than Nanny B's.

"Say it ain't so," I said. "If Nanny B heard you say that, she would disown you."

"The truth is the truth," Jaylin said, chomping down. "These tacos are really good."

Loretta looked proud. She ate dinner with us too. When Justin got irritable, she got out of her seat to get him. Almost immediately Jaylin took Justin from her hand.

"What's up with you, man?" he asked, picking him up over his head. "You ain't supposed to be crying like no little girl."

"He cries all of the time," Mackenzie said, rolling her eyes to the back of her head. "LJ cried a lot too when he was a baby, and Jaylene . . . she is really out there." Mackenzie placed her hand on her hip and started her sassy yakking. "My own sister took my purse and wouldn't give it back to me. Daddy spanked her real good and she calmed herself down."

"I did not." Jaylin grinned while sitting back in his chair. "I didn't spank Jaylene; I tapped her."

Mackenzie twitched her finger from side to side. "Nuh-uh, Daddy. You spanked her hard, and she had tears and snot running all down her face." Of course, Mackenzie described it. "I hugged her and was like . . . 'Girl, you gonna be okay.' We played with our Barbies, and I told her, 'Girl, you'd better watch yourself, because Daddy don't play.' I told her about when he spanked me, and I've been on the right track ever since."

Jaylin's brows were up. He looked stunned. "Mackenzie, why you lying on me like that? I have never spanked you. I should have, but I didn't."

Mackenzie quickly nodded her head, standing by her comments. "Yes, you have spanked me, Daddy. You were like"—Mackenzie deepened her voice, trying to sound like Jaylin—"'Girl, you'd better get yourself together. I'm warning you, or there will be repercussions.'"

I covered my mouth, trying to hold back my laughter.

Mackenzie continued. "Then you ordered me to my room and pulled out a big ole gigantic black belt that had holes in it. I was scared like Jaylene was the other day, and you—you . . ."

Jaylin sat with his hand pressed against his face, smiling and listening. "Then I did what? Finish telling the story, to your recollection, of course."

Mackenzie let out a deep sigh. "Then you sat on the bed and . . . and I think you gave me a big ole kiss on my cheek and told me to be good."

"Yeah, that's what I thought." Jaylin laughed. "But you said I spanked you."

"You did," she insisted.

"When?" he shot back.

Mackenzie closed her eyes and tapped her temple with her finger. "I need to do some more thinking. I'm sure I'll come up with something."

"Make it good," he said. "And if you lie on me again, there will be repercussions."

Mackenzie's grin became wider, showing her pearly whites. We continued to eat dinner. Because Justin had stood on Jaylin's lap, Justin had made one big mess. He had taco toppings everywhere. Jaylin left to go give him a bath, and Mackenzie and I cleaned up the kitchen. Loretta already had told us that she had plans for the night. After she left, I put Mackenzie to bed.

Jaylin stayed with Justin for a while. When he shut it down for the night, Jaylin came into my bedroom. He sat on the edge of my bed. I was surprised to see him remove his shirt. I moved to the edge of the bed, wrapping my arms around his neck and rubbing his chest.

"Are you spending the night?" I asked.

"Maybe," he said, slightly tilting his head as I pecked down his neck. He rubbed my arms as I touched his chest. "I was meaning to ask you," he said. "Did you really mean what you told Nokea about cutting it off with me, if she and I got back together?"

I halted my pecks on his neck and held my hair aside so it wouldn't fall over him. "Yes, I really would have. I guess the question is, would you have even come back to me again or accepted when I told you no?"

Jaylin sucked in a deep breath; then he let it out. "I know it's hard for anyone to believe, but I never would have betrayed Nokea again. As for you telling me no, you wouldn't have had to."

I wasn't sure if I believed Jaylin, but I knew that I didn't want to spend our night discussing Nokea. His mood had been just fine, and I definitely didn't want it to change. Already naked, I hurried off the bed and opened one of my drawers. I pulled out a box of feminine wipes. When I knelt behind Jaylin again, I gave the box to him.

He laughed. "What in the hell is this?"

"Read it."

"'Always Feminine Wipes. Feel fresh and clean all day and every day. Perfect for freshening up during your period, before and after sexual intercourse with Jaylin, and they're flushable.'"

We laughed as Jaylin made up his own words on the label and tossed the box over his shoulder. He laid me back on the bed, easing in between my legs. I wrapped them around his waist. "I haven't been able to use those wipes on a regular basis," I said, pouting. "I miss your spontaneous visits to see me. By any chance, can we work on getting your visits to increase? Just a little."

"We may have to see about that," he said, smirking and playfully biting my neck. "My kids just keep me so, so busy and—"

"And your kids claim you've been spanking them. Shame on you. I wish you would use some of that energy you got spanking me, instead. You would get so much more in return, and you'd have a lot of fun doing it too."

Jaylin turned me over, not spanking my butt, but massaging it real good. He lowered his pants; but like the last time we were together, I noticed that his dick was in no way hard. That was a serious problem; so I got off the bed and turned on some soft music. As I stood in front of the bed, he sat up against the headboard. My long hair was covering my perky breasts, so I moved my hair aside so he could see my hard nipples. His eyes lowered to my near hairless slit and to the gap that he had created. I could tell he was hungry for me, but it was rare that his dick wouldn't cooperate.

I crawled onto the bed. After minutes of intense dick sucking, I was in business. Jaylin slid into my wetness with ease. He stroked me at a slow pace. When I ordered him to fuck me harder, he did. He released a load into me that night. If I had not been faithfully taking my birth control pills, he could have possibly made himself another baby.

By morning, Jaylin was gone. I was stretched out in bed by myself. I was getting so used to this, and it was all about me accepting the situation that I had helped to create.

As expected, for the next couple of weeks, Jaylin had not given any consideration to increasing his visits to me. Things were left as they were, and how I expected them to remain for quite a long time to come. Yes, this was definitely Jaylin's World. I was the one who dared to live in it!

NOKEA

My life was very slowly but surely falling back into place. Without Jaylin being a part of it, I would never be whole again. I couldn't deny that simple truth, but everything going forward was what I wanted. This was how it had to be. I accepted that, and started making preparations for my future, as well as for my kids.

I didn't want to sit around all day doing nothing, so I'd finally gotten a job as a marketing director for a worldwide company that sold computer games. I was only required to work four days a week, so that gave me Fridays, if Jaylin allowed it, and definitely Saturdays and Sundays to spend with my kids. The biggest adjustment for me was being without my children on a daily basis. I was always so happy to see them, and they sat around telling me some of the funniest stories ever. Some of the stories were crushing too, like when LJ told me Jaylin got emotional at the kitchen table one day. "Mama, his eyes were almost fire red, and when I asked why, he got up from the table and left."

I guessed we'd been going through the same thing, as I'd had my setback days as well. And paying close attention to the song that he'd asked me to by KEM . . . oh, my God, it broke me down even more. I could feel Jaylin saying those exact words to me. The nights he came to my condo unexpectedly, pouring his heart out to me from the other side of the door, it made things even more difficult. I always looked at him through the peephole, taking in every word that he'd said. Sometimes I would sit low on the ground, my back against the door, but my emotions running high. At other times, I just walked away and couldn't bear to listen. I always wanted to open the door and tell him how sorry I was for all of this. There were times that I wanted to go home and throw my arms around him. I wanted to tell him how much I still loved him and tell him that I had forgiven him. Something inside wouldn't let me do it, and I didn't even have the strength to speak to him or see him face-to-face. Some days I regretted my divorce, and then there were other days that I felt at peace. I wasn't thinking about what woman he was with or what he was doing. I was doing my best to focus on Nokea.

After work on Thursday, my boss, Ralph Hoffenberg, invited me to dinner. It was strictly pertaining to business, and I had come up with some new marketing ideas to help with sales. As we sat at the small wooden table for two, I flipped through my folders, explaining ideas to make more money. The restaurant was filled to capacity and many voices echoed in the room. Waiters and waitresses were swiftly moving around, making sure everyone in the packed restaurant got served. Mr. Hoffenberg rarely blinked an eye as I spoke and he seemed impressed with my ideas. A huge smile was planted on his face and he kept combing his salt-and-pepper hair back with his fingers, nodding his head. He reminded me of Frick, Jaylin's lawyer, but without the arrogance. Even so, my mind was on how I, too, could make more money.

"Nokea, you are awesome," he said, looking down at the plans in front of him. "Where have you been hiding? I am so lucky that I found you."

I smiled, sipping from my iced water with lemon. I felt good about the marketing plan I'd put together.

"I'm glad you're pleased. I hope we can start implementing some of these marketing tasks soon."

Mr. Hoffenberg assured me that we would; then he looked at his watch. We were almost two hours into dinner. "We'd better get going. I don't want to tie up your whole evening, Nokea. I'm sure you have other plans."

I smiled, putting the folders into my briefcase. "No, no plans, but *Pretty Woman* comes on tonight. Seen it at least a million times, but don't want to miss it again."

Mr. Hoffenberg laughed. "You sound like my wife. She loves that movie too." He paused; then he touched my hand. "I—I don't mean to pry, Nokea, but you mentioned your divorce. I know it was tough on you. Are you dating again? If so, I have a wonderful friend whom I'd like for you to meet. He's single, makes very good money and is genuinely a nice guy. He's a workaholic, but a woman like you would be a perfect fit for him. Do you mind if I invite him to the office to introduce the two of you?"

I had run to another man before during my troubled times, and I wasn't about to do it again. In no way was I healed yet, and dating this soon would be one big mistake. "Thank you, Mr. Hoffenberg, but I'm going to pass right now. Check back with me in a year or so, okay?"

We both laughed. After he paid the waiter, we walked out together.

"Come to my car with me," he said. "I want to show you something."

I followed beside Mr. Hoffenberg, and he opened the car door to his silver Mercedes so I could get in. He got in on the driver's side and gave me a business card.

"Here, take this. I know what you said, but you're too nice and beautiful to be alone. The friend I mentioned is my son and I can't think of a better woman I would want to see him with."

I took the card from Mr. Hoffenberg's hand. "Thank you so much for the compliment, but I'm just not ready to date right now. I'll keep his card, just in case I change my mind."

Mr. Hoffenberg nodded and I leaned over to give him a hug, just for being so thoughtful and caring. No sooner had I released my arms from around him, there was a hard tap on the window, which startled both of us. When I snapped my head to the side, I saw Jaylin standing there. I wasn't sure if he was going to embarrass me again or not, so I hurried to say good-bye to Mr. Hoffenberg.

"I'll see you on Monday, Mr. Hoffenberg. That's my ex-husband. I guess he wants to talk about something."

Mr. Hoffenberg had a concerned look on his face. When I opened the door to get out of his car, he advised me to be careful. Jaylin had stepped several feet away from Mr. Hoffenberg's car and my boss drove off.

Dressed in my fuchsia sleeveless stretch dress, which hugged my curves, I walked up to Jaylin to see what he wanted. He peeled his shades away from his eyes, standing with his arms folded in front of him. He was dressed in black cargo shorts and a white Nike shirt and cap. I assumed he had come from working out.

I stood in front of him, noticing the wrinkled lines on his forehead that showed concerns. "What's going on, Jaylin?"

He looked at his watch. "Nearly a two-hour dinner, huh? Who was that joker you were with? Please don't tell me you're already dating again, especially a white man with wrinkles on his face and the looks of alcohol seeping through his pores. I'm letting you know now that I'm not having it. You opening up your legs to another man will in no way work for me. If you want sex," he said, removing his cap and pulling his shirt over his head, "you get sex from me. We can do this shit right here, if you want. So bend the fuck over and let me get at it." He started to unzip his shorts, showing his maroon jockey briefs underneath. I wanted to see how far he would go with this. When he dropped his bottoms to his ankles, I stood in disbelief with my eyes widened. I couldn't even trip off of the people who were slowly driving by, covering their mouths, or the ones who took their time walking into the restaurant.

Jaylin held out his hands. "Come on, baby, don't stand there speechless. Are you anxious, hot and bothered . . . what? Pussy been getting an itch, or are you just in the mood to fuck anybody? I hope like hell your taste hasn't resorted to old-ass white men with money. If it has, what a muthafucking disappointment."

I shook my head, putting my briefcase in front of his dick to hide it. "Being with a man of Mr. Hoffenberg's stature would be quite a step-up from dealing with black men, like you, who don't know how to get their shit together. But I'm not going to stand here and argue with you about my preferences and dating. I have a life to go live, and I'm letting you know that your days of controlling what happens with us are over." I lowered the briefcase and looked down at what used to excite me. "In addition to that, I'm in no mood to bend over. And even if I was, you'd be disappointed, because the sight of you doesn't wet my insides like it used to. Sorry. Now, unless you have something else important to talk to me about, I'm going home."

Jaylin stood for a moment, staring at me with a slight smirk on his face. Damn those addictive eyes! They were eating away at my soul. I turned around, ready to walk away.

"Nokea," he said, halting my steps.

I turned to face him, with a little snap in my voice. "What?"

"I just wanted to say that I love you, and you're a damn liar. Enjoy your evening and stop being so bitter. It doesn't suit you, and I apologize if I made you this way."

So angry with him for bringing us to this point, I darted my finger at him. "If you love me, get your shit together. Don't do it for me, rather do it for yourself. Becoming a stalker doesn't suit you, and neither does becoming an alcoholic or a stripper. Get it together. After all, your life is what you still do control."

I walked away, heading to my car so I could go home to a chilled glass of wine and watch *Pretty Woman,* as planned.

The weeks were going by quickly. During my last weekend with him, LJ hit me with something I wasn't prepared for. He had been spending a lot of time with his brother and sister, and he wanted to know if they could come over with him and Jaylene. "Please, Mommie," he begged, showing off praying hands. "We're always over here on the weekend, and we don't get a chance to see them. Can they come over here too? Daddy told me to ask you if it would be okay. I told him I would."

His request hurt like hell inside, but I realized that I couldn't deny LJ and Jaylene an opportunity to grow up with their brother and sister. They did nothing to be put in a situation like this, so I had to suck it up and deal with it. For me, it was just the right thing to do, but I also understood that many women in this type of situation would have some concerns. For the weekend, I made plans for us to go to the beach and have dinner on Saturday at the kids' favorite restaurant. Then on Sunday, I was going to take them to Sunday School with me. I told LJ to make sure Mackenzie and Justin brought their swimsuits. Hopefully, they would.

While I was in my room putting on my bikini, I saw the light on my cell phone blinking. I had an idea who the message was from. To no surprise, it was Jaylin. "Day one ninety-four, and you're still giving me the silent treatment. I heard the kids are coming your way today, and I hope you-all have fun. Thank you for accepting my children, and I know this may not be easy for you to do. That's why I love . . . You know what I'm about to say. Thank you for just being you. Call me so we can talk, whenever you're ready. Oh, by the way . . . did I tell you I love you?"

I closed the phone, thinking about Jaylin's messages. He was never one to give up on what he wanted, so I expected those calls to continue. The ones he'd left right after our divorce were very difficult for me to listen to, and I'd gotten to the point where I had to delete them. Slowly but surely, his messages were more pleasurable to listen to. Still, I couldn't understand why, after all this time, I couldn't bring myself to sit down and have a civil conversation with him. Any encounter would result in us harping on the past, blaming each other or possibly arguing. Right now, I just couldn't bring myself to do it. No one knew how difficult this was for me. When you loved someone as much as I had loved Jaylin, it was even harder.

The doorbell rang, and I knew it was Nanny B. She agreed to bring the kids over, and had even offered to stay with us. I'd already told her we'd be fine. I opened the door with my bikini on and a flowered wrap around my waist. LJ and Jaylene were all over me; they looked so adorable in their swimming gear and glasses. Nanny B held Justin in her arms. He had on swimming trunks and a pair of glasses; a beach hat covered his head. Almost immediately Mackenzie wrapped her arms around me. She had gotten so tall, and she looked just like Scorpio.

"Hi, Nokea," she said. "Do you remember me?"

I hugged her back. "Of course, I remember you. You don't think I forgot about you, do you?"

She shook her head; then she took Jaylene's hand. They ran off into the bedroom, because Jaylene wanted to show Mackenzie her *other* bedroom. Nanny B continued to hold Justin, and LJ was tugging at his feet, asking Nanny B to put him down.

"I will," she said. "I need to talk to your mother for a minute. Go get Justin some Kleenex, his nose is running."

LJ ran off, and Nanny B asked if I was going to be okay.

"I'll be fine. These kids have nothing to do with it, and I intend for us to have fun. Tiffanie is supposed to meet us at the beach too. She's been driving me nuts with this wedding, and I'm sure we'll be spending a lot of time discussing that."

"I know you will. She is so excited! She asked if I would make the cake for them. I've been trying to decide what I can come up with. When you get a chance, I want you to look at some of the designs for me."

I told Nanny B that I would. She put Justin down when LJ came back into the room. He wiped Justin's nose with a tissue. Nanny B squeezed my hand and told me that either Shane or she would be back late Sunday night to get them.

As soon as I closed the door, I went into the living room with LJ and Justin. I told LJ to go throw away the tissue and he rushed out of the room. Justin wanted to follow him, but I reached for him and carefully picked him up. My heart was starting to beat faster, but I took a few deep breaths. I eased into the seat behind me and stood him up on my lap. He was so darn cute. I could see the beautiful curly hair on his head underneath his hat. I removed his head covering and took off his glasses. My breathing came to a halt and my heart dropped somewhere beyond my stomach. I didn't know if I was jealous, angry, envious or a combination of them all. No matter what I felt, Justin was Jaylin all over again. LJ looked a hell of a lot like Jaylin, but just from the skin color difference, Justin was right there. I saw Scorpio in him too, and a part of me was uneasy because she had gotten her wish. Justin pinched my cheeks and scooted back from me, like he wanted to get down. LJ came to get him and they rushed off into another room. I smiled at how well they all seemed to get along. I couldn't help it that a few tears had fallen, and I quickly wiped my tears from all that I was feeling inside. Shortly afterward, I heard something break.

"What was that?" I asked, getting up and going into the other room. They all stood and pointed at each other. No doubt, this was going to be a long, long weekend.

A long day it was. I had not raised my voice this much in quite some time. We had spent the day on the beach; then we went out for dinner. LJ and Jaylene had shown their butts. They were clowning, and the only one who didn't give me any hassles was Mackenzie. She was sweet as ever; and being the oldest, she helped me out as much as she could. Justin was okay too, but he was really a fussy and spoiled child. He wanted me to pick him up all of the time. Of course, when I did that, Jaylene's big ole self started throwing a fit. She had to have the most attention, and I reminded myself to thank Jaylin for spoiling them so much.

That night, we had a slumber party and laid sleeping bags on the floor. The kids watched movies, ate popcorn, jumped around and danced to Michael Jackson's *Bad* CD. They loved Michael Jackson's music. Even though the "King of Pop" was now resting in peace, there was a new generation ready to carry on his legacy.

The Princess and the Frog had something going on too, and LJ sat gazing at the pretty princess until his eyes got tired and he fell asleep. It wasn't long before Mackenzie and Jaylene had gone to bed, but Justin was fighting his sleep. So everyone would stay sleeping, I picked him up and carried him into my room with me. I sat on the bed; then I laid him on my chest. As I started to softly read a book to him, his eyes faded. Before I knew it, he had shut it down, releasing light snores. This was, no doubt, a healing moment for me. I liked how he felt against my chest, and I got choked up thinking of the child I'd aborted. I swallowed hard; then I laid Justin on the bed next to me. I looked at my cell phone on the dresser and picked it up. It was almost midnight, and I wondered if Jaylin was awake. The phone rang three times, and he answered, sounding wide-awake.

"Day one ninety-four," I said. "The kids and I had a wonderful time together. You're so blessed, Jaylin. I hope you recognize just how blessed you are. Don't ever take your blessings for granted again."

"I won't, especially pertaining to you. I'm glad you had a good time. I suspected that you would."

"It wasn't easy, but I managed. All I can say, Super Dad, is you have some work that you need to do with your children. What is wrong with Jaylene and LJ? I haven't seen them this wound up in a long time. They really showed out, especially at the beach. Jaylene kept knocking down everybody's sand castles and had the nerve to get mad when they knocked down hers. LJ didn't listen to a thing I said, and I had to keep repeating myself over and over again. Mackenzie, she was so sweet. I would take her anywhere with me; she knows how to behave herself."

"Welcome to Jaylin's World, and they are a big part of it. Mackenzie, however, is playing you like a fiddle. She got issues too, and wait until she gets used to being around you again. You'll see, trust me." Jaylin paused; I knew he couldn't wait to ask, "What about Justin? Was he okay?"

"He's been a little fussy, but that's how two-year-olds are. I can tell he's on the same path as LJ is, and in a minute! I don't know what you're going to do."

Jaylin laughed. "I'm going to love the hell out of my kids, take care of them and teach them how to be successful in life. You gonna help me do that, aren't you?"

"Of course. And just because we're not together, I will never give up on my kids."

"I know you won't. I—I know you don't want to hear this right now, but I can't stop thinking about our baby. Did you hate me that much where you felt the need to do what you did? I just can't get that out of my mind, and look at how long we waited for that baby to come. Do you even think about—"

"I think about it every single day of my life. It's one of those bad decisions that I have to live with, and I'm sure you know all about those. 'Sorry' doesn't seem like it will ever be enough. Pertaining to some things, I guess not. With that, I'm sorry, Jaylin. From the moment I did it, I regretted my decision."

There was silence; then he spoke up. "I told you that I've forgiven you, and I have. Do—do you regret our divorce? Or have you completely given up on us? I hope not."

I hated to go there, but I had to. "Our divorce has been finalized and I'm satisfied."

"Do you really think that a piece of paper that a judge stamped her name on has that much power to override the love we have for each other? Legally, it is what it is. Through my eyes, though, you will be my wife forever. My heart will never know anything different, and I'm giving you all of the time you need to see that. I won't even ask you to marry me again, because it's not necessary. I know, and you know, that this thing between us is much deeper than anyone could imagine. All I'm waiting on is for my wife to come back home. I don't need a court order that allows her to do that, and neither does she. *You* can, and someday *you will,* come home on your own free will."

I paused, thinking about what he'd said. I was in no way there yet, and couldn't even envision living in that house with him again. "Good night, Jaylin."

"Thanks for calling me back. You gave me hope, and here goes another sleepless night for me. I know you're having them too. I will be so glad when we can lay in bed together, resting peacefully in each other's arms."

I didn't wish to comment, so I closed my phone shut. I scooted down in the bed next to Justin, holding his little hands. As I had done before, I played back in my mind the day Jaylin and I went to St. Louis and Justin was conceived. Jaylin was so out of character that night, and I should have known something wasn't right. I lay in bed, reminiscing about what his eyes had revealed to me that day.

Jaylin hadn't been answering his cell phone. When I got to the hotel room, I noticed his cell phone had been broken. I could hear the water in the shower running, so I entered the bathroom. I called his name several times, but he didn't answer. I then slid over the shower curtain. Jaylin looked at me as if he'd seen a ghost. His eyes were without a blink and he rubbed his chest.

"What?" he hurried to say. "Is—is everything okay?"

"Everything is fine, Jaylin. I saw your broken phone and called your name several times. You didn't answer, so I thought something had happened."

He took a deep breath and turned off the water. "I got mad at the damn thing because I couldn't get a signal. I tried to call you, but it wouldn't dial out."

I reached for a towel and slowly wiped his body. When I got to his back, I stopped. "Where did this red mark—this long scratch on your back—come from?"

He turned his back toward the mirror to see what I was referring to. There was a long scratch on his back; he seemed to be at a loss for words. My immediate thought was a woman had dug into his back during sex, but he cleared it up. "Shit, I don't know, probably from Jaylene climbing on my back yesterday. Remember when I was on the floor and she . . ."

He was trying too hard to convince me, but I didn't push. "Yes, I remember." I smiled and yawned. "I'm so tired. Pat's baby shower is tomorrow, and can you believe I'm already missing home? I can't wait to get back to my babies."

"I can't wait to get home either. I wish we could leave now, but I know how important it is for you to be there for your friend."

"Very important," I said. "Pat would die if I left this soon."

As I got undressed, Jaylin hurried and got into the bed. He had a very disturbing look on his face, and it was so easy for me to tell that something was wrong. What was it? I kept thinking. My gut was telling me something wasn't right.

"Out with it, Jaylin Rogers. What's on your mind?" I teased while climbing underneath the sheets with him. We cuddled, and as he held me, I laid the back of my head against his chest.

"I just had a long day, that's all. I'm glad that Shane and I worked things out. I'm looking forward to him moving to Florida. My mind's been preoccupied with our new business venture."

"I knew it was something. I've been here for almost thirty minutes and you haven't even kissed me."

I looked up at him. Just by looking into his eyes, I was positive that something was wrong, but what was it? Maybe I was just tripping, but Jaylin had never hesitated before kissing me.

As we kissed, he hadn't put much into it. It was over before it got started, and he pecked my forehead, giving me a forced smile. He then laid his head back on the pillow, staring at the ceiling as if in deep thought. His arm was behind his head, and I could tell something heavy was on his mind. Maybe it was in reference to the dream he'd had, so I interrupted his thoughts.

"Hey, baby, can I ask you something personal?" I asked.

"Of course."

"You mentioned that in your dream, you had millions and millions of dollars. I don't keep up with your financial status, but isn't it fair to me that you be a bit more specific about those kinds of things?"

"Yes, and if you ever want to know, all you have to do is ask. Anything you want or need, you can have it. What's mine is yours. It's not that I've been keeping our finances a secret, it's just that you rarely ask about our financial status."

"I do look at our bank statements, but you have accounts that belong solely to you. For the sake of our children, I don't know if that's a good idea."

"I agree. It's not."

"All I want to know is, is there more than fifteen million in your combined accounts?"

"Yes."

"Twenty-five?"

"Yes."

"Thirty-five?"

"You're onto something."

"Fifty?" My eyes widened. I couldn't believe what he'd said.

"You're very close. I promise you that when we get home, I'll reveal everything to you."

I laid my head back on his chest and rubbed it.

"Can I ask why, all of a sudden, you're inquiring about our finances?" he asked.

"Because I've been thinking about the yacht you purchased. That thing cost some serious dollars. I felt so foolish for not knowing that we could afford something like that. I don't like being kept in the dark, and I do want to know about all of our assets. A husband and wife should know those kinds of things. It's only fair to me."

Jaylin seemed uneasy about my questions, but he put me at ease. "Like I said, baby, it's whatever you want. Next week, I will make arrangements for us to meet with my financial adviser and Frick."

"Thanks," I said as I lifted my head to give him a tiny peck on the lips.

I reached in my purse and pulled out a silver picture book. When I lay back on his chest, I opened the book and it displayed many digital pictures of us.

"This was your anniversary gift," I said. "I was too embarrassed to give it to you."

"Why?" he said, admiring the cute and memorable pictures of us. "Woman, this book is priceless. We make an adorable couple, don't we?"

"Yes, and look at this one," I said, pointing to the picture. "This was taken when you were nineteen and I was eighteen, remember? You were so handsome and bad to the bone."

He smiled at the picture and couldn't believe that I hadn't shown it to him sooner.

That night, he said the yacht didn't compare to our memories together, and that the picture book was "priceless."

I guess that entire night for him was priceless.

Little did he or I know, he'd just made a baby with Scorpio. The weeks following, Jaylin wasn't himself at all. He seemed spaced out, and was very apologetic to me about every little thing. Our lovemaking didn't even feel right, and it felt as if we'd lost our chemistry. But when Shane moved in with us, things got better. I felt relieved, and was glad that I hadn't accused Jaylin of what I was feeling inside.

My gut told me that Jaylin had cheated on me that night. And yes, Scorpio had come to mind. Too bad I didn't listen to my instincts, but I was glad the truth had come to light. Two failed marriages: one with Collins, whom I didn't love but married because I thought it would suppress my feelings for Jaylin; and the other with the man I had loved my entire life, but he could not get his mess together.

I was satisfied with my decision and could never see myself living in Jaylin's World again.

JAYLIN

I was on a serious high after Nokea's phone call. I couldn't get back to sleep, so I went for an early-morning jog to calm myself. Later that day, I met up with Shane at the office. We both had been real busy with trying to sell some of the property we'd purchased. Luckily for us, we were about to close on another deal. Shane sat in my office, listening in as I spoke with the man who wanted to purchase the property. He said he could meet us around two in the afternoon to possibly close on the deal. I hung up the phone and rubbed my hands together.

"If I had known I could have made this much money, I would have asked you to move to Miami sooner."

"You're the one who retired early," Shane said. "If it wasn't for your retirement, you could have way more money than you do now."

"I agree, but my babies got me back in action. I gotta make as much money as I can for them."

"I'm glad to hear that, Jay. You seem to be feeling much better, and I haven't seen you this energetic in quite some time. What's up with the new attitude?"

I smiled and leaned back in my chair. "Nokea called me last night. I had been up, watching TV. When the phone rang, I thought it was you. I peeped the number and saw that it was her. I couldn't wait to push the talk button. She called to tell me about them badass kids of mine. You know she had all of them this past weekend.

I never thought I'd see the day that Mackenzie and Nokea would be hanging out together again."

"Now, that's all right. Did she say anything about y'all getting back together?"

"Nah, she didn't go that far. But it was something in her voice that gave me hope."

"Well, keep hope alive. Tiffanie told me that they were together yesterday. She said that Nokea was real good with Justin. I think Nokea and Tiffanie are going to meet the wedding planner later today. That will be the fourth or fifth time. I'm supposed to meet up with them too. Tiffanie said Nokea seems a little uneasy at times. Do you think her helping Tiffanie with the wedding may be too much for her?"

I shrugged. "Not sure. And if she couldn't handle it, I know she'd back away from it. I've been meaning to ask you too, are you really ready to do this? I mean, you only shut it down with Joy since this mess happened with Nokea and me. I hope I don't have you rushing into something you're not ready for."

Shane crossed his leg on top of the other. "I'm more than ready. I love Tiffanie, man. The only reason I was tripping was because I'd been hurt before. I don't have to tell you by whom, but, uh, I like Tiffanie's style. I love how she's got my back. She's always concerned about my happiness, and she was patient with our relationship. She turned up the pressure a little bit, but after a while, that's what a woman is supposed to do. When I showed that I wasn't ready, she backed off. When that shit happened with you and Nokea, I realized then that I didn't want to lose a good woman like Tiffanie. She and Nokea got a lot in common, and I didn't want to move forward with my life having regrets."

"I feel you on that. I can't keep saying how much I messed up, but this was a true lesson for me. If I could get my wife back, I would never do what I did again."

Shane hesitated; then he spoke out. *"Never* say 'never,' Jay. You don't know what the future holds. If somebody would have asked you or Nokea if y'all ever thought you'd be here, y'all would have said 'never.' Life is full of unexpected twists, and we just don't know what it really has in store for us."

"I agree," I said, standing up from my chair and stretching. "But life is about learning lessons too. Once you burn yourself badly, you never want to burn yourself again. If my wife returned to me, I would never again do what I did to her. Before you dispute that, let's go discuss it over lunch. We also need to discuss your bachelor party. Are you going all out or what?"

Shane stood and laughed. He gripped my shoulder. "You know what I want to do. The day before I get married, I want to share a wonderful evening on your yacht with family, friends and Tiffanie. I want you to call my mother and invite her, and please do your best to talk her into moving here with me. That would truly mean the world to me. Since you're my best friend, I am counting on you. You think you can handle that for me?"

"Are you doubting me? Man, I could do all of that, and then some. But you'd better have a place for your mama to stay, because she ain't staying with me. She and Nanny B would drive me crazy. I hope like hell that you are packed up and gone, soon!"

"In a month and one week, I'm out. I'll be a married man, and you are going to miss me when I'm gone. Don't be begging me to come back. Even though I'll be right down the street, please call before you come. My wife and me gon' spend a lot of time making some of those babies like yours."

We started toward the elevators. "Nah, you don't want no babies like mine. They would drive you crazy."

Shane pointed his finger at me. "You got a point. I love the hell out of your kids, but, man, they fuck me up. LJ and Jaylene done stepped up their game since Mackenzie and Justin showed up. When I dropped off LJ at soccer practice last week for you, I took the others with me too. They were fussing at each other one minute, then laughing the next. And that Jay—"

"Jaylene," I said before Shane could even get her name out of his mouth. "I know, she's something else, ain't she?"

"Yes. She was telling LJ, 'I'm gon' tell my daddy if you don't give me a piece of bubble gum.' LJ brushed her off and threw his hand back at her. She tried to take his cell phone so she could call you about a piece of gum. I was like, 'Come on, Jaylene.' I wanted to stop and get that girl a piece of gum myself. LJ was glad to get out of the car and go to soccer practice. I couldn't blame him."

I was shaking my head. "That's my fault, man. I'm gon' get her straightened out, but you should have stopped to get my baby some gum. I'm going to holla at LJ about not sharing too. And yes, she did call me on his cell phone that day. I bought her a big bubble gum machine for her room. When you get a chance, go check it out. It's nice, and she got all of the gum she needs."

"Terrible," Shane said. "I never thought I'd say this, but you are a true sucker."

We both laughed. When the elevator started going down, I defended my actions. "I can't wait for you to have kids. You gon' be the same damn way, and there is something about Jaylene that just . . ." I paused and patted my chest. "It's just all in here, Shane. More so since Nokea ain't around. I get to see Nokea every day, just by looking at Jaylene."

The elevator opened and a very attractive black woman in spandex workout pants and a half top got on. She spoke to both of us. Shane and I both leaned back a bit, checking out her curves and very shapely plump ass. I observed her while rubbing my goatee and nudging Shane. All he was doing was grinning and keeping his arms folded. As the woman moved her tense neck from side to side, her ponytail swung from behind. She wiped a few beads of sweat from her forehead with her hand and sighed. Her breasts rose from the sigh, causing me to bite my bottom lip. Going down on the elevator was pretty quiet. When we all exited to the lobby, she told us to have a good day.

"You too," I said, but Shane didn't respond. As soon as we were about to spark up a conversation about her, she jogged up from behind us.

"Excuse me," she said, handing me a card and smiling. "I struggled just a tad bit with my decision, but you're more of my type than your friend is. Besides, I didn't want to let this opportunity pass. Call me."

She jogged off; Shane and I watched until she was out of sight. I looked at her card and she was a workout instructor, who worked in our building. Her name was Chase Jenkins and a picture of her was on the card.

"See," Shane said, patting my back. "What did I just say? You never know what your future holds."

I held the card out for Shane. "If not me, it would have been you. I'm not gonna use it. If you want it, it's yours."

"I'm good," Shane answered, laughing. "Thanks, but no thanks."

As we walked by a trash can, I tossed the card inside. "Like I said, never again. I know what my future holds. I'm sure you know her name by now."

We walked off and I let out the biggest sneeze ever.

"Damn, bro, what you got? Swine flu or something?"

I sneezed again. "Hell nah. It's just that cheap-ass cologne you got on that's irritating."

We laughed out loud. Shane and I then walked down the street, debating the kind of cologne he insisted he didn't have on versus the expensive cologne he wore. We always made any simple issue debatable.

The next day, my cold had gotten worse. I was sneezing all over the place, but I wasn't going to the doctor. My head was starting to hurt and my body seemed to be achy all over. When I got home, Nanny B said that she'd had the same thing, but it was winding itself down. LJ and Jaylene were with their homeschool teacher. When they got finished, Nanny B said, she'd start on dinner. She took my temperature, and it was 101. Always seeing about me, she gave me some Theraflu and told me she'd make me some chicken noodle soup as well. Rest is what I needed, she said, and she ordered me out of the kitchen and into my bedroom.

As soon as my body hit the bed, I felt relieved. My mattress was so comfortable that I quickly got down to my jockey shorts and pulled the comforter over my head. Seeing nothing but darkness, I was out like a light.

What had to be hours later, I felt someone shaking my shoulders. When I quickly jumped up from underneath the covers, my body was sweating all over. It was dark outside, and the lamp next to my bed was on, giving the room a sliver of light. LJ stood with a tray in his hand, and Jaylene had a tall glass of frozen orange juice in hers. A napkin, a spoon and a smoldering bowl of chicken noodle soup were on the tray. I quickly sat up, smiling from the nice gesture.

"Here, Daddy," LJ said. "Nanny B made this for you. We already had dinner. Sorry you couldn't join us, since you are sick."

Jaylene was showing her pearly whites too. After I took the glass of frozen orange juice from her, I set the tray on my lap.

"Thank you," I said, tapping my cheek so they could kiss it. They did; then they sat on the bed to watch me eat. I sat up, closing my eyes and turning my achy neck in circles. I picked up the spoon, putting some of the soup in my mouth. Almost immediately my mouth started to burn. The spices in the soup were so strong that I started to cough. LJ and Jaylene sat with their hands pressed against their cheeks, looking at me with bugged-out eyes.

"Wha—what?" I asked, gagging. "What in the hell is in this soup?"

"Spices and herbs," LJ said. "Don't you like it?"

"And hot sauce too. Nanna include hot sauce in all of her food," Jaylene added.

I could barely catch my breath. I hurried to set the tray on the nightstand, and rushed to drink some of the frozen orange juice. It was almost too thick to swallow, but the coldness of it cooled my mouth down.

"Nanny B didn't make that soup," I said, with watery eyes. My throat was burning now. "Who made it?"

"She made it. But we added a little something extra to it," LJ admitted.

I stared at them with a blank expression. "Where is Nanny B?"

"She's sleeping," Jaylene said. "We didn't want to wake her."

I threw the covers off me and slowly staggered toward the door. My legs felt as if they were about to buckle. Because of that spicy-ass soup, I was sweating even more. I hit the intercom button by the door, yelling for Nanny B.

"Please come here!" I said, woozy and about to lose my balance. "These kids are trying to kill me!"

Jaylene tapped my side. "You didn't like the soup, Daddy? We'll go make you some more."

LJ had sense enough to exit. He eased by me, covering his mouth and then taking off. Nanny B didn't answer me, so I slowly walked to the kitchen. It was not only a mess, but it was a doggone mess. Spices, empty bottles of hot sauce, the blender, ice cube trays, eggs—all of that was on the kitchen table and some on the counters. Orange juice and the big pot with chicken noodle soup in it were sitting in the middle of the floor. Nanny B came into the kitchen, tying her robe and scratching her head.

She squinted, calling for LJ and Jaylene. Of course, now they were nowhere in sight. "What is going on in here?" Nanny B asked. "I thought I put them rascals to sleep."

"Well, they had other plans."

Nanny B saw how achy I was and told me she and the kids would take care of the kitchen. "I'm going to go get them right now. I know they're hiding somewhere, but they are going to clean up every bit of this mess. Don't worry and go lie back down."

She reached for a broom in the closet and started calling their names out loudly.

"Don't hurt 'em," I said, laughing. I struggled to walk back to my room. I dropped back on the bed and reached for the phone to call Nokea. Like always, I got voice mail.

"Day one ninety-six. Please, please come get your kids. They are over here trying to kill me, and Nanny B is about to whip their asses." I hung up; then I called right back. "Oh, by the way . . . I love you."

I lay across the bed for a while, feeling as if I was unable to move. I wanted to help Nanny B with the kitchen, so I tried to gather myself to go do it. I also knew I'd better go to the doctor to see what was up, but I hated that shit. After lying in bed for a few more minutes, I got up to take a shower. I sat on the seat, allowing the soothing water to pour all over me. I hadn't even lathered myself yet, but that was fine by me. The water felt good enough. As I sat for at least thirty or forty minutes, I finally stood to wash myself. A few seconds later, I turned and saw Nokea standing in the doorway to the bathroom. I couldn't believe my eyes. I squeezed them together; then I wiped them with my fingertips.

"Just wanted you to know that your kids are in big trouble," she said. "I can't believe they did that."

I smiled, just from seeing her. "Be easy on them," I said.

"That's the problem." She glanced at me; then she walked away from the door.

I hurried to wrap up my shower. Once I was done, I put on my robe and went into the kitchen, where Nanny B and Nokea were. They were finishing up, and I could hear Jaylene sniffling loudly from her room.

"What happened?" I asked.

Nanny B didn't look too happy. "What happened was, I made them help me clean up. LJ was fine, but Jaylene didn't want to do nothing. She wanted to stand there and pout. She got a spanking, and that's all there is to it."

I opened the fridge, looking for something to drink so I could clear the bad taste in my mouth. "Y'all need to stop being mean to my baby, and you better not have hit her with that broom. She just wanted to do something special for her daddy, that's all."

"True to the fact or not," Nanny B said, looking at Nokea and me, "y'all need to start putting y'all's foot down with these kids, especially you, Jaylin. You're the man of the house, and you need to take action. If you don't, in a few years, you're going to regret it. They're going to be so out of control, and then what you gon' do? As for the broom, who needs a broom when these hands I got can do a much better job?"

Nokea spoke up. "Are you suggesting that we spank them? I'm not for spankings, Nanny B. Even though you had to do what you felt was necessary tonight, I don't know if that's a good idea."

"I don't care what the two of you decide to do, but it's a discussion that y'all need to have. Time-outs and punishments don't work. Every time y'all do that mess, nobody sticks to it. I'm not Super Nanny, but maybe she should come here and show y'all how to be better parents."

Nanny B left the kitchen, but not before advising us not to go to Jaylene's room to baby her. "Let the sniffles flow, and eventually she'll get tired."

I took my glass of V8 juice to the bedroom and Nokea followed. She sprayed the room with Lysol; then she sat far away from me on the bed.

"You look awful. Have you been to the doctor?"

"I'll go tomorrow. I didn't expect for you to come over here, and I was just teasing you when I called. I'm glad you came, though. While you here, why don't you spend the night?"

"I have to work in the morning. I'll come pick up the kids after work tomorrow, just to give you a break."

I rubbed my nose with a tissue. "Work? I don't understand why you're working. It doesn't make sense for you to be doing that."

"It makes sense to me. I want my own money. Besides, working keeps me busy. I enjoy it."

"That's ridiculous," I said. I was upset that she was working, but I didn't want to get into it with her over—what I considered—a dumb move.

"Sorry you see it that way." She stood to go. I was disappointed that she was leaving. "I'm going to go say good night to the kids and see if they'd like to come home with me so you can rest. I hope you feel better, and whatever you do, get some rest."

"Would you mind resting with me? I would sleep so much better and—"

Right then, vomit rushed to my mouth. I hurried out of bed and went into the bathroom. My lunch from earlier, the spicy spoonful of soup, as well as the juice, had all come up. Nokea came into the bathroom as I bent over the toilet.

"I'm taking you to the emergency room. Tonight."

I was feeling so terrible that I didn't hesitate.

The visit didn't take long, and when all was said and done, I had a severe case of the flu. The doctor prescribed some medicine, gave me a shot and said what had already been told to me: "Get some rest." It was after one in the morning when we got back home and I really put on my sickness mode for Nokea. Shit, I wanted her to stay with me, so I lay in bed, making myself look extremely needy so she would stay.

"What if I die or something tonight? You gon' miss me when I'm gone," I stated with a pout.

Nokea rested her finger on the side of her face. "I can only wonder where Jaylene gets her actions from. *Hmm,* I really wonder."

"Jaylene be playing. I'm really feeling awful. I'm already having a hard time sleeping. If you were next to me, I would feel so much better."

Nokea stood for a moment, in thought. "I'll stay for one night, Jaylin. Do not try anything with me, or else I'm getting out of bed to go home."

I smiled. "I won't. I promise."

She hadn't removed all of her belongings from her closet, and there were still a few things in there. Not much to brag about, but some things that she had asked Nanny B to get rid of. Of course, I wouldn't let her. She came out of the closet with a long white oversized T-shirt on that had a sports team logo on the front. Maybe it was just me, but, I swear, I had never seen her look so sexy.

"I'm going to go kiss the kids good night. Do you want anything?"

I stroked my goatee as a quick thought came to mind. "Well, since you asked, I'm always feeling up to some of that action you gave me the last time you came over here. This time, I got something real special for you, and it is going to blow you away."

Nokea had no response; she left the room. Ten minutes later, she came back and got into bed with me. There was a huge gap between us.

"I thought you were supposed to be cuddling with me so I could feel better," I said, moving over to her side of the bed. I laid my head on her chest, throwing my leg over hers.

"Your body is really warm," she said. "Did you take your medicine yet?"

I nodded, and Nokea touched the top of my head. "Yes," I answered. "It may take a minute to kick in, though. If I'm making you hot, sorry, I just hope it's in a good way."

Nokea got out of bed and opened the doors to the balcony so the cool breeze could come in. We could hear the ocean waves. When she got back in bed, I got comfortable next to her again.

"Now, this is what I'm talking about," I said, squeezing my arm around her waist and rubbing my head on her chest. Her breasts were right there; I would have given anything in the world to suck them. She held me, and as her hands rubbed up and down my back, my eyes were starting to fade. Seconds later, I was out. I was sure so was she.

By early morning, I heard Nokea call in to work. She got back underneath the covers and I cuddled behind her. With my eyes closed, I rubbed her thighs and scooted myself closer to her. She felt my hardness pressing into her backside and used her elbow to move me back.

"Don't do that," she whispered. "You're too close, and definitely too hard."

"I can't help it," I said, easing my arm around her waist. "Can I please make love to you? It's been so long, Nokea, and I want to get inside you so badly."

She turned on her back. "I'm not ready to go there again, and I honestly don't know if I'll ever be. Don't force me, okay?"

I knew how Nokea felt about us, so I honored her wishes. I did, however, go to the bathroom to take a cold-ass shower. My dick wouldn't go down for nothing. After I worked it down myself, I was temporarily satisfied.

Rest was on my agenda for all day. Nokea left the room to go take care of the kids and she ordered them to leave me at peace. I was supposed to go pick up Justin and Mackenzie, but I called Scorpio to tell her I couldn't make it.

"That's fine," she replied, sneezing. "All of us messed up over here too. I don't know what's going around, but it's definitely something."

"I went to the emergency room last night. They said it was the flu. You and the kids should go get some antibiotics or something, and I hope my babies ain't too sick."

"Mackenzie not so much, but Justin's sneezing more than me. He's irritable, but he'll be okay. If I notice any changes, you can be sure that I'll take them to the doctor."

"Okay, baby. Take care of yourself too, and I'll see y'all. Hopefully, it will be by the weekend."

"Aw," Scorpio said, "I was hoping it would be before then. You haven't been to see *me* in a while. I'm starting to think you've forgotten about me."

"Never. You stay on my mind a lot. Just trying to figure out what I need to do with your pretty-ass self, that's all."

"You know better than anybody what to do with me. Whenever you're ready to *do it,* I'm here."

"I appreciate it. Stay sweet and I'll holla back."

Scorpio hung up and I pulled the covers over my head to go back to sleep. The day had come and gone. By nighttime, Nokea still hadn't gone home. She stayed another day with the kids and me. When she came to bed that night, she let out a loud sneeze.

"Oh shit!" I said, moving over next to her. "Looks like I'm going to be taking care of you for the next few days. You know how good I am at it, and you can definitely count on me."

"I knew it!" she shouted, and plopped back on the pillow. "I knew this was going to happen." She sneezed again.

For the next couple of days, I took care of Nokea, as she had taken care of me. I left for another day the conversation about us moving back in together, and I allowed her nothing but peace. I wanted her to feel comfortable at home again, and even though she was sick, I could tell she was happy. I was as well. I had spoken to Mackenzie and Scorpio, but I hadn't gone to her penthouse to see them personally. So, while Nokea was resting that day, I left.

When I got to Scorpio's place, it was real quiet, but I could hear soft music playing on the intercom. I also heard the shower running in the bathroom, so I walked up to the door to push it open. Steam poured out from inside and Scorpio was in the shower, facing the wall. Behind the glass, her soapy backside was a beautiful sight. I stood for a moment and watched her. About two minutes later, she turned. Startled, she dropped her body wash on the floor. She looked shocked to see me. She kept blinking the water from her eyelids.

"How long have you been standing there?" she asked, wiping back her long, wet hair.

"Not long. How much longer are you going to be, and where my babies at?"

"Loretta took them to get ice cream and to the park. I'm almost finished with my shower. If you want to join me, Jay Baby, you can."

She moved the glass door aside, allowing me to scan her naked body again. What man wouldn't want to join her? Surprisingly, though, my dick wasn't even hard. Without saying a word, I walked away from the door. I went into the living room and stretched my arms on top of the sofa as I took a seat. Ten minutes later, Scorpio came into the living room with no clothes on. She laid a pillow on the floor in front of me, dropping to her knees. With a slight smile on her face, she reached for the zipper on my tan cargo shorts. I touched her hand.

"Not right now, baby. I'm not in the mood."

Her face fell flat and her brows rose. "And why aren't you in the mood?"

"Do I really need a reason? I'm just not."

Scorpio stared at me for a moment; then she stood up. Like always, my eyes dropped between her legs. I observed her recently shaved slit. Having my attention, she took my hand, placing it between her legs. "Get in the mood," she said. "I would really like to feel you right now. It's so unfair that we always do it on your time, not mine."

I pulled my hand away, again. This time, feeling frustrated. "If I wanted to touch that pussy, I would. And the way you sometimes seduce me, I wouldn't necessarily say we always do it on my time, not yours. That's a lie. Now back the hell up. You're in my space."

She stood silently for a moment; then she straddled my lap. Her arms rested on my shoulders. "Okay, so what's the *new* plan? You're not going to fuck me anymore. Is that what you're trying to say?"

I in no way liked her tone; and for me, a woman acting desperate was a turnoff. Not only that, I also hated to be tempted and manipulated. "Get off my gotdamn lap, or else you will be on the floor. I told you I wasn't in the mood, Scorpio, and where you land from here depends on you."

She could see in my eyes that I wasn't playing with her, so she backed up. "Let me take a guess," she said. "You and Nokea must be getting things back on track, right?"

I stood up, moving her out of my way. "I'm not going to say all of that, but I think we're making progress. But if all you want to do is talk about Nokea and me, I'm not in the mood for that either. I came to get my kids. I see they're not here."

I started toward the door. Scorpio reached for my arm, scratching it. I quickly turned. "I'm talking to you, Jaylin, so stop being so arrogant and full of yourself. Are we off again, or what? If so, please let me know so I can call up some of these men who've been chasing after me since I've been here in Miami."

I shrugged. "You go ahead and do whatever it is that you have to do. Meanwhile, I'm not going to stay here and argue with you about *my* muthafucking dick!"

Her face looked flushed and she was speechless. Hurting her again was something I in no way wanted to do, especially since she had had my back. I calmed myself, looking into her eyes. "Look, didn't I tell you that I planned to work this shit out with Nokea? Our divorce doesn't mean anything to me. My love for her has not wavered one bit."

"For the one thousandth time, it's good to know how much you love Nokea. Honestly, I get tired of hearing it. And since you're committing yourself, once again, all I want to know is if you are done using me for sex or not?"

I sighed. "I haven't been using you for sex, and you know it."

Scorpio cut her eyes and turned her head to the side. Simply put, based on all that had happened, there were some losses we all had to accept. I moved forward, turning her head and stroking back her wet hair. I placed a tender kiss on her forehead.

"Baby, please calm down. I do not like arguing with you, and this has been about so much more than just sex. As I stand here today, I am a lost and torn man. I—I do love you, but I love another woman so much more. I can't help the way I feel. All I can do is be honest with you about what it is that I'm feeling inside. Bottom line, this situation is what it is, and what it has always been for a very long time. I can assure you that my feelings for Nokea will never change. If she decides to come back to me, I can't . . . I just can't do this with you anymore."

Scorpio stepped away from me. She walked over to the huge picture window, gazing outside. "I'm not going to be upset with you for being honest, but I sometimes regret falling so deeply in love with you. Then there are times that I'm grateful for what we share, and I could see my life no other way. I'm prepared to approach this, one day at a time. If you need me, I'm here. But don't in no way flatter yourself, because Miami is a very big city. I intend to start dating again. If you come in here with a bunch of bullshit about who I can and cannot see, we are going to have some serious problems. You know me well, Jaylin, and I can in no way sit around for the rest of my life being your house mistress. That doesn't work for me. As much as I love you, I love me more."

I walked up to Scorpio, taking her hand to ease the situation. "I never asked you to be my house mistress, and you'd better love yourself more than you love me. I can't even respond about the dating thing right now, but I guess I have to let you do you."

"Yeah, right, I'd like to see that." She laughed out loud. "You want it all, Jaylin, but like you said yourself, we will all have to accept some losses."

"I know. And even so, you know I'm going to set some rules about your dates, my kids, and this penthouse. Some things you'll have to be willing to abide by."

She folded her arms and smirked. "Like what? Don't bring my dates here, and don't have the kids around my men, right?"

"Exactly. I in no way want to walk up in here and catch you with your ass up in the air. Those are simple rules to abide by, and we won't have any problems if you agree to those things."

"Oh, I doubt that, but this is Jaylin's World, and you're the one running this show."

I kissed the back of Scorpio's hand and she hugged my waist. We stood, looking out at the ocean, enjoying the scenery, as well as our embrace.

"The—the kids won't be back until later," she said. "Are you sure you're not up to popping a quick cherry before they get here?"

I laughed. "I see I'm gonna have to buy you a vibrator. Scrap the dating bullshit and use a vibrator. I'll get you one of the best ones on the market and you can go that route instead."

"Oh, you would like that, wouldn't you? But I don't want a vibrator. It can't perform like you. I don't want to date either, but you leave me no choice."

"I know, and don't be mad at me for saying this, but I've been miserable without Nokea. You know I have, and my dick been acting kind of funny, anyway. I don't want it to disappoint you."

Scorpio shrugged. "Disappoint me? Never. I know how to revive it, and—"

My phone vibrated, interrupting her. It was Shane. Instead of answering, I told Scorpio he was waiting for me and I had to go. I walked to the door with her, and we continued to hug each other.

"Tell my kids I'll be back tomorrow to get them. As for you, you'd better be good, and please, please don't cause me more heartache." I turned at the door, letting go of Scorpio.

She smiled. "I love you too much to do that. See you soon."

I kissed her cheek. "I love you too."

I started to walk away, but Scorpio grabbed my arm. She was still smiling. "Do you know how many years I have waited for you to say those words to me and know that you really mean them? Don't think I'm not grateful for all that you've done, because I am."

I nodded. "I know, and vice versa. I truly do mean those words from the bottom of my heart. You know that I wouldn't say it, unless I meant it."

She agreed, and we hugged again before I left to go back home.

NOKEA

I couldn't believe how sick I'd gotten that day. With Jaylin being underneath me, I expected it would happen. I took the entire week off from work, trying to get myself together. Jaylin had gotten rid of his flu and spent his time catering to me. Surprisingly, LJ and Jaylene hadn't gotten ill at all. And when my flu was over, I thanked Jaylin for being there for me. Then I went back home. I can't lie and say that I didn't enjoy myself being back at the house, because I did. The kids were happy to see me every single day, and Jaylin and I had talked more than we had talked in months. The conversation he wanted to have, I wasn't quite ready for it yet. I was still uneasy about so much. When Scorpio had called the house one day, I answered the phone. She paused, but politely asked if she could speak to Jaylin. She talked to him about something with the kids. I guess to make me feel comfortable, he had the conversation right in front of me. He even mentioned my name, telling her I'd been sick too. Told her we were about to eat dinner and said that he'd be over on Saturday afternoon to pick up the kids.

I wasn't sure what kind of relationship they had, and I kept telling myself that it was no longer my business. All I wanted was for Jaylin to take care of his kids; thus far, he had been doing a darn good job at that. I understood Nanny B's concern with him about disciplining the kids more. But coming from the abusive situation that Jaylin had come from, he would never go down

that route with his kids. I don't care if they burned that
house down, Jaylin would find an excuse as to why they
did it. In return, he'd build them one even bigger than
the one before. I don't know why Nanny B couldn't see
that, but that was one of the things I had known about
the man I still deeply loved.

"Day two hundred twelve," he said on voice mail.
"How can you come over here, give a brotha a little
hope, and then not call him? You cold, baby, and I
can't believe just how cold you've gotten. You know I'm
anxious to spend some time with you again. You got me
all excited, and you really need to admit that you had a
good time with us too. It was perfect, just like it used to
be. If we could bypass the last seven months, I'm ready
to hook back up whenever you are."

I deleted Jaylin's message and went into a confer-
ence meeting at work.

For the next few weeks, my routine had pretty much
remained the same. Work was keeping me busy and so
were the kids. Jaylin had taken all of them to Disney
World. When the kids mentioned that Scorpio had
gone with them, I was livid. I couldn't get over the fact
that Jaylin was still spending time with her. Despite
his being there for his kids, I was troubled just knowing that the two of them were seeing each other on a
regular basis. I didn't care to have a conversation with
Jaylin about where things stood between them, and my
speculations made me keep my distance. I guess I was
mad because he didn't ask me to go to Disney World
with the kids. I didn't even know that Scorpio had been
spending time with my children. When I asked LJ, he
said that was the first time he'd met her. I wasn't sure
what to think or how to feel. During lunch, though, I

talked to Tiffanie about my concerns. She tried to sim-
plify it the best way she knew how.

"From what Shane said, Jaylin used that as an opportunity for Jaylene and LJ to get to know Scorpio. He
felt as if being at Disney World would make them comfortable with her, and I even think it might have been
Shane's idea. The kids do spend a lot of time together,
Nokea, and I wouldn't take it personal if I were you."

"But what are the kids thinking? I mean, they see
her, and then they see me. They probably think their
father has two wives. That can't be a good thing. I know
they're confused."

Tiffanie placed her long hair behind her ears and
dipped into her cheesy nachos. She licked the cheese
from her finger and sipped from her glass of water.
"When you get finished talking, my stepmother is awesome. My brothers and I grew up with her as well, and
so many families are doing it like that. Now, I don't
know what kind of relationship Jaylin has with her, but
from what Shane tells me, it's nothing serious. I honestly think Jaylin just goes to her to get his rocks off. If
you expect for him to go without sex for months, I don't
think that's possible." She wiped her hands on a white
napkin. "Besides, why are you so worried about him,
anyway? If your relationship with him is a done deal,
as you say, why worry yourself?"

I folded my arms. "I'm just concerned about my children. LJ remembers Scorpio from the past, but I know
being around her will not sit well with Jaylene. Just
thinking about it drives me nuts."

"No offense, honey, but how do you think she felt
when you had her kids? She's probably got concerns
too, and you can't think one way without putting the
shoe on the other foot."

I threw my hand back at Tiffanie. She wasn't trying to hear me, so I changed the subject. "Okay. Now,

what are we planning for your wedding shower? Or are you planning to get wild and make me put together a memorable bachelorette party for you?"

"Believe it or not, Shane said he wanted to keep it simple. He doesn't know that I have my family coming from all over, but he asked Jaylin if we could use you guys' yacht for an out-of-this-world get-together the night before our wedding. I am *sooo* excited! I truly have found myself the best man in the universe. I owe you and Jaylin my life, and I am going to make Shane *sooo* happy. Especially," she added, touching her belly, "when I tell him I'm already two months pregnant!"

We clutched our hands together, shaking them in the air from excitement. "Congratulations!" I yelled. I was so happy for Shane and Tiffanie. I couldn't think of any other couple more deserving. Especially Shane. Being patient had definitely paid off for him. I couldn't help but think about Jaylin and me. As happy as I was for Shane and Tiffanie, I knew the upcoming weeks of watching them, and assisting with their wedding, would stir up my feelings. Watching them take the crucial steps forward would make me think about how Jaylin and I had taken so many steps backward. What a shame, I thought. How did we allow things to go so wrong for us?

Tiffanie and I had been running around like chickens with their heads cut off. The wedding planner had done a lot to help, but we didn't want to put every single responsibility on her. Besides, Tiffanie was a hands-on kind of person and she wanted to make sure everything flowed well. I understood why she wanted everything to turn out well, but we had truly exhausted ourselves. Even so, the day of the dinner celebration on the yacht, we still had plenty to do. We had to put up decorations and make sure the DJ had a space set aside for his music. We also had to direct the paid staff to set up a few tables for dinner. I really didn't think we'd be able to pull it off. After we finished, the setup was awesome. Tiffanie went with lavender and black. The bridesmaids' dresses were lavender like mine, and there were only three of us. Shane had Jaylin for his best man, and Tiffanie's two brothers were his groomsmen. Her siblings liked Shane a lot, but not as much as her father did. He knew he was getting himself a wonderful son-in-law. We all knew Shane would treat her with much love and respect.

After we finished decorating the yacht, I headed for home to get dressed. I wondered how Jaylin had been feeling about all of this. I knew he was anxious to see me tonight. I was kind of excited about seeing him too, as it had definitely been a while. Keeping it classy, I put on a hot pink strapless dress that had layers like a wrapped mummy. It was very pretty, and I jazzed it up with silver accessories. My hair was like the usual, and my nails and toes were polished with sparkling silver polish. I felt good about my appearance. Before I left my place, I sprayed on several dashes of my sweet-smelling perfume.

By the time I got to the yacht, it was almost eight at night. The sun was going down and the scenery was quite beautiful. The lights surrounding the yacht showed just how many people were already there, and there was plenty. I knew the yacht would sail at eight-thirty, so I made my way on, with a nicely wrapped gift with a big bow on it in my hand. As soon as I got on the yacht, I placed my gift on the gift table and started to mingle with everyone on board. Like always, everyone was so friendly. I spotted Shane's mother and Nanny B sitting in the parlor room, talking. I walked over to give both of them a hug.

"Hi, sweetie," Shane's mother said, giving me a kiss on my cheek. "You look so pretty."

"You do too," I said. "I know you're so happy for your son, aren't you? You did such a great job with him."

Shane's mother smiled. I sat with her and Nanny B for a while, talking about life and children. Mine were at home with Loretta, who had stepped in, in Nanny B's absence. According to her, all of the children were in good hands.

I wrapped up my conversation with the two ladies, and then found Tiffanie and Shane standing, hand in hand, talking to some of her relatives. Shane and Tiffanie introduced me to numerous people, and plenty of hugs and handshakes were exchanged. The waiters came by with filled champagne glasses, and all kinds of food were being served. I, myself, had already started to drink a lot of wine, and I was not alone.

Everybody was getting their drink on. When the yacht pulled away, we busted several champagne bottles on the side of it. Tiffanie's father gave a toast, and the party was on. Loud music played throughout the yacht. If you weren't up dancing, you were somewhere drinking or eating. I still had not spotted Jaylin, and I wasn't sure if he was there or not. The thought of Scorpio being with him crossed my mind, but he wouldn't dare go there, would he? It was just like Jaylin to avoid me, especially if he couldn't handle the pressure.

This was difficult for me too, but I forced myself to have a good time for the sake of Shane and Tiffanie. The caterers had made some Thai chili wings, which were off the chain. I kept piling my plate high with the wings, tearing them up. I had more glasses of wine; after I'd had enough of that, I started drinking Patrón with lime juice. I should have known better. I felt real tipsy. Knowing that I had to be there for Tiffanie and Shane on their wedding day tomorrow, I had to keep it cool. I chilled on the alcohol and sat next to Nanny B on the upper deck as we watched a soul train dance line forming. Everybody was clapping their hands, and Shane and Tiffanie boogied down the aisle first. No, Tiffanie could not dance, but Shane was doing his thing in his black suit. He removed his jacket and we all whistled and clapped louder. I reached down and whispered to Nanny B, asking where Jaylin was.

"A few hours ago, he told me he was going to the master stateroom to lie down for a while. Said his head was hurting a little bit."

I kept clapping and watching everybody doing their thing. I knew all too well what Jaylin's headache was about. As I watched the line of dancers getting longer and longer, I looked up; a smile grew on my face. Jaylin stood, leaning on the rail, with his dark black suit on. He looked so handsome, and the suit was cut perfectly to his muscular frame. It buttoned at his fitted waist, and a black silk shirt and tie were underneath. If he came to impress me, he did. He saw me look in his direction and nodded his head toward the dancers. He whispered from afar, asking if I wanted to get in line. I nodded and we both got in line to dance, waiting for our time to come. When it arrived, we did the bump, and everybody laughed.

The line dancing went on for quite some time. When my feet started killing me, I took off my shoes and sat on the cushioned seats next to the edge. Nanny B had taken my place in the dance line with Jaylin. The waiter passed me, so I hurried to reach for another flute glass of wine. I sipped from the champagne glass and crossed my legs. I put my shoes back on, and swung myself around to look out into the ocean. There were other yachts sailing. Each time we passed them, everyone waved. The sun had gone down, and the calming breeze, starlit sky and half-moon were breathtaking. I heard someone clear his throat. Without even turning around, by the smell of his addictive cologne, I knew it was Jaylin. He sat next to me, with a glass of wine in his hand too.

"Day one," he said. "Do you mind telling me your name?"

"It's Nokea. Nokea Brooks."

He chuckled and stroked his goatee. "So, uh, Ms. Brooks, are you married?"

"I was, but my husband tripped and blew it. I'm single right now."

"Shame on that fool. I'm sure he's suffering from his loss. If you were my wife, I would treat you like a queen. I would take care of you real good and make you the happiest woman in the world."

I gazed at the ocean. "Yeah, I've heard that before. I'm dealing with some trust issues now, and I don't know if I'll ever be ready to jump back into another relationship."

"No matter what, you can't give up on love, especially if it's so strong. No matter how much you fight it, it will never go away."

I moved my hair away from my eye and got a closer look at Jaylin. "That's what they say, but that's what you do when you're not sure. You fight those feelings because you're so afraid of putting your guard down and being hurt again. Besides, I'm all for taking it one day at a time. Who knows what the future holds? I thought I did, but I was so wrong."

"Forget the wrong, and make it right. Everyone deserves a second chance, and you can't hold the past against someone. If you'd let me, I'd love to take you on a date on the day after tomorrow. I gotta go to this crappy wedding tomorrow, and I'm sure it's going to tie me up all day. After that, I would love for you to wash your hands from that fucked-up husband you had, and give a brotha like me a chance. I'm different from him, and sometimes a man has to hit rock bottom before he eventually wakes up. I've been there. I never want to go there again, nor take the woman whom I love there again. One date, that's all I am asking. Will you go on one date with me?"

"Maybe. But you never told me your name."

"It's Jaylin. Jaylin 'My Heart Is So Broken' Rogers. I would love for you to help it heal, and I can help yours heal too."

I looked away again, thinking about going to get some more chicken wings. "Pick me up at seven o'clock for dinner. Don't be late, and I'll let you know what kind of restaurant I'd like to go to."

I stood to walk away, but he pulled my hand back to him. "Hey, is there any chance you give it up on the first date? Brotha kind of horny, and I can't even remember the last time I had sex."

"For the record, I'm not that easy. Sorry."

I walked away, blushing and excited about my date with Jaylin. Now I was more than ready to get my party on. Unfortunately, all of the wings were gone, but there were some awesome crab wraps, which filled my stomach. I got full from them, and the glass of Patrón with lime juice was back in my hand. The more I danced, the woozier I got. The music had gotten even louder. Before I knew it, I was being whisked away to another room. He had his arms around my waist, doing his best to keep me on my feet. We went up the spiral staircase.

When we reached the master stateroom, I dropped back on the bed, which was covered with silk sheets. Through my blurred vision, his stallion-like body looked sexy as hell! I reached for his pants, pulling him to me and unbuttoning them. I was hot all over. As I unbuttoned his suit jacket at his waist, his tight abs were in full effect. I rubbed his nicely carved chest, for

he had already unbuttoned his shirt. He dropped his
jacket and his shirt on the floor. He stepped out of his
pants and leaned toward me. Gentle kisses were being placed down my sweaty and salty neck. He rubbed
up and down my legs, taking squeezes on my thighs,
which truly turned me on. Next thing I knew, my dress
was being lifted up to my waist and my black lace panties were being removed. I saw them being tossed aside.
When his thick fingers entered my slit, I backed away
from the rotations that set me on fire.

"That feels *sooo* good," I whispered, taking pecks on
his cheeks and moving my mouth over to taste his lips.
The kisses were as wet and juicy as ever. Gobs of saliva
were being exchanged. When I looked into his loving
eyes, I squinted.

"Shane?" I asked, with a peculiar look on my face. He
paused, but I winked and smiled, just so Jaylin would
know I was joking. Smiling as well, he eased his fingers
out of my tunnel. He replaced his fingers with his dick,
and that's when I dropped back, smiling with relief.
"*Ahhh*, Jaylin. I know how this dick feels any day of the
week."

"The one and only," he whispered. He started to
gradually stroke inside me, causing my pussy to moisten
quickly.

I was so messed up, but I intended to take advantage
of this night. I needed him, and obviously he needed
me too. I rolled on top of Jaylin, straddling his lap.
I pulled my dress over my head, causing my perky
breasts to stare right at him. As I started to roll myself
around, my breasts were in motion. Jaylin reached out
to massage my tingling nipples and arousing me even
more. I dropped one of my legs to the floor, using it for
leverage. Like always, he was deep within me; but unable to take it all in, my wetness covered only part of his
shaft. I bounced up and down on him, while rubbing

his chest and leaning forward to place delicate kisses on it.

"Mmm," he said, rubbing my curvy backside and pulling my butt cheeks apart so I could feel more of his hard meat inside me. *"Ahhh, baby,"* he moaned. "You just don't know how this feels to me. You got some good-ass stuff, and I'm so glad to be in this pussy again. Thank you, damn, baby, thank you."

We rocked right along with the yacht, and Jaylin had turned on the music to calm down the intenseness of the mood. Chrisette Michele's "I'm Okay" was playing in the background and the bass was coming through the crystal clear speakers. Jaylin and I took in every word; and slowing down our pace, we stroked each other to the rhythm of the beat:

Time don't stop and wait for pain. Pain does fade away in time./ Guess it all was just a game, when you gave your heart and I gave mine./ I'm okay, I'm just fine. We'd fade away hardly crossed my mind.

I stood up, while Jaylin stood tall behind me. One of his hands was massaging and turning my breast in circles, and his other hand was cuffed over my pussy. He was switching his thick fingers in and out of my slit. Each time his long middle finger entered me, I whined, letting out deep sighs. The words from the song caused tears to roll from my eyes, the message was so powerful. My head was turned to the side, taking in as many kisses as I could from him. As we continued to tongue, he inched me forward close to the bed. I bent over, holding my hands out in front of me to grip the sheets. I separated my legs like an upside-down *V,* spreading them wide. Jaylin squatted, licking and tasting parts of my body where the sun didn't shine. I could barely keep still. As my legs weakened, his tongue became fiercer.

"Help me!" I cried out. "Why do I love you so much like this? God, I love you. Please, please don't ever hurt me again."

It wasn't long before I sprayed his lips with come and what was left started to flow down my legs. Jaylin wouldn't allow much to go to waste, and after he finished cleaning me, he stood up straight behind me. His hands roamed my hips and ass, touching places that he'd obviously missed.

"You have my word that I will never hurt you again. I swear just—just give us another chance."

Jaylin maneuvered his hard iron pipe into me and I tightened my teary eyes. My insides were so tight, making it almost unbearable for either of us to move. According to Jaylin, the feeling was too much for him to handle. He bent down over me, placing delicate kisses on my shoulders and back. "Give me a minute to calm myself, and don't move," he said, trying to slow his heartbeat. His passionate kisses had me on fire. When he started to stroke me slowly, the sounds of him stirring my juices filled the room. He remained bent down over me. When he saw a tear roll from the corner of my eye, he gently kissed it. So many emotions were going through me.

"Plea—please tell me you don't make *her* feel this good. Do you make her feel like this too?"

Jaylin halted his strokes and placed his lips on my ear. "I don't know how she feels," he whispered. "But no one makes me feel the way you do. No one, okay?"

I slowly nodded, trying hard to evade my thoughts of Jaylin being with Scorpio. His rubs and kisses helped. As he stood tall to stroke me slowly again, my mind was at ease. The lovemaking and the level of passion for each other had gone beyond anything I'd ever felt.

He forced me forward with each thrust, lightly slapping his body against mine. I pushed back, sucking in the wetness about to drip from my lips and thinking about how happy my slit was to feel all that he was giving.

Yeah, I was dizzy from all of the action, but that didn't stop me from enjoying the powerful forces that were taking every bit of the air out of my pussy. It wasn't long before I felt his warmness ooze in me, but we were both only down one orgasm—with plenty more to go. He set me on the very edge of the bed. While I was on my back, he held my legs apart with his hands. He aimed his hardness in the direction that he wanted it to go, opening me wide once again. We both had an opportunity to observe his insertions, attentively watching as his inches disappeared deep inside with each stroke. Pure lust, as well as undying love, was in our eyes. I started to rub myself, particularly playing peekaboo with my clit. Jaylin watched; then he closed his eyes, dropping his head back. He blew air out of his mouth, releasing a deep breath.

"It's time for you to bring this pussy back home to me. You've got to stop making me suffer without this. I'm so crazy about you, Nokea. I'll say it again, you are the only woman who makes me feel this way."

As well as he was working me over, all I could do was give him my word. "I don't want you to suffer anymore. This pussy belongs to you, and only you, I promise. Make me *commme,*" I strained. "Please make me come again."

All I had to do was ask, and Jaylin turned my insides like he was churning butter. His rotations were smooth as jazz; and the way he used his strength to hold my legs in place, while digging into me, was so impressive. I couldn't deny how much I'd missed this, even though my insides were killing me. It had been a long time since we had indulged ourselves to this magnitude, and my insides had tightened so much that I could barely endure the beating. I came in less than a minute after that, and we took a moment to regroup. He sat in a chair, while I sat on top, facing him. His arms were tightened around my waist, and my arms were resting on his broad shoulders.

"Have you sobered up?" he asked.

"No, I'm still on a major high. Help me come down."

"Nah, I don't want you to come down. Stay just like you are, as I have a feeling that I need to take advantage of this day."

"Please do. I'll do the same."

He stood, lifting me in his arms and kissing me. At least for ten minutes straight, we did not move. We enjoyed tasting each other's tongues, and all I did was tighten my legs around his waist so I could stay exactly where I wanted to be. A few minutes later, Jaylin went into our closet and put on a pair of swimming trunks. He covered my naked body with my sheer black robe, which I used to cover my swimsuits. He then took my hand and walked me out to the middle deck. We tiptoed to the deck underneath that one and stood close to the edge. The yacht was docked at a nearby island, and the party above us was still going on. Jaylin sat me on the rail; then he asked if I was ready to go for a swim. Before I could say anything, he tightened his arms around me and we both dived into the water.

The splash was loud, but Jaylin continued to hold on to me. We floated in the water, hugging each other, occasionally kissing and looking into the perfect moonlight. Deciding to chill, we made our way out of the water and to the sand. My sheer robe clung to my body, exposing every bit of my nakedness underneath. Jaylin seemed mesmerized as he laid me down in the sand, lying closely beside me. As he stared into my eyes, he used his finger to make wiggly lines down my chest. I felt the words "I love you" being scripted, and we both smiled as he expressed how happy I'd made him tonight.

"You just don't know what this means to me, Nokea. I know this will take some time, but I miss these kinds of nights between us. Don't you?"

All I did was nod. I was living in the moment, and I knew Jaylin was as well. Maybe this was the beginning of our putting our lives back together, or it could possibly be the end of that moment we never, ever got to have. At the moment, I wasn't sure, but being with him tonight was exactly where I wanted to be.

The wedding was beautiful and so darn emotional. Tiffanie's parents' eyes were overflowing with tears, and Shane's mother's sniffles were loud too. As the ceremony was in progress, I peeked over Shane's shoulder to look at Jaylin. He smiled and tapped his heart.

"I love you," he mouthed, and then winked at me.

Not wanting to make a scene, I nodded and momentarily placed my hand on my heart too.

While listening to Tiffanie and Shane take their vows, I only wished that mine had been taken more seriously. I regretted that they hadn't, and I was sure Jaylin was having some of these same regrets too.

Even so, I still wasn't sure where our lives were headed. I knew that one night of passionate lovemaking wasn't going to solve the issues we had. Because of Scorpio, those issues would forever remain. I wasn't sure if I could ever get to a point where I would completely trust Jaylin again, as that would be the most difficult thing I ever had to do. My answer to whether I would ever be Mrs. Nokea Rogers again, I simply did not know. Right now I doubted it, but I was a firm believer in you should *never, say never.*

JAYLIN

The wedding was over, Shane had moved out, and his mother was now a resident of Miami. I was really glad about that, for she, Nanny B and Loretta got along really well. I, myself, was getting ready for my first date with Nokea today. She told me to meet her at a steak restaurant that we went to on a regular basis, so I told her I'd meet her there at seven. I had no idea where these dates would lead us; but like I said before, it really didn't matter. Nokea would always be considered my wife, and that's all there was to it. Yeah, she still needed time to sort through some things and I was patient, as well as hopeful. I envisioned her living with me again; and whenever that day came, I would be ready.

As for Scorpio and me, I spoke the truth to her that day when I said that I loved her. My love, though, had limitations, and it could only go so far. The sexual connection we once had was fading by the day. I definitely knew why my dick had been acting funny, and so did she. Good sex would only last for so long, but Nokea had guaranteed love from me that would last a lifetime. Did that mean that another woman wasn't capable of ever making my dick hard? No. Did that mean that I would never look at another woman with lust in my eyes? No. Did that mean I would never converse with a woman who approached me? No. For me, I just knew that another woman would never have ownership of my heart. I reminded myself that what I wanted could never take the place of what I needed. I needed Nokea in my life, and that was a need that wouldn't go away.

The kids were in my closet with me, trying to help me find something to wear for my date. Justin was in my arms as Mackenzie, LJ and Jaylene picked through my clothes. They actually started pulling my things off the hangers, and that was a no-no for me.

"Find me one thing to wear. Everybody, pick out one piece of clothing for me. I really want to look spectacular on my date with Nokea."

LJ gave me a piece of clothing; Jaylene handed me some socks and shoes; Mackenzie gave me what she wanted me to wear too. Justin picked up one of my Rolexes, trying to put it on his wrist.

"Is this the one you want me to wear?" I asked.

He nodded; then he jumped down from my arms. They all ran out of the closet. After I showered and trimmed my goatee, I put on my clothes to go. The kids had gone to the lower level to watch a movie, and I stuck my head through the door, telling Nanny B that I was on my way out. She waved, telling me to have a good time. So did the kids. I thanked them for picking out my clothes for me.

As soon as I got to the restaurant, the waiter looked me over and stopped me at the door. "Will you be joining someone?" he asked.

"Yes, Nokea Rogers. I saw her truck parked outside, so I think she's already here."

The waiter motioned for me to follow him, but he stopped me when he looked down at my shoes. I had on a pair of brown leather sandals with black dress socks.

"Uh, sir, excuse me, but per our policy, I can't seat guests with those kinds of shoes on."

"Is the manager here? Let me speak to the manager."

"He's going to tell you the same thing. If you have some other shoes . . ."

"Man, silence yourself and go get the manager. My kids picked this outfit out for me and I intend to wear it."

The gentleman walked away, returning with a snobby-looking manager who already had "get out" on his face. I pulled him aside, explaining that my kids had picked out my outfit and wanted me to wear it.

He cleared his throat. "With part of your legs showing and the trench coat on, do you mind telling me what's underneath? I mean, we don't want the other guests to be . . ."

I opened my black trench coat, revealing my burgundy Calvin Klein boxers, a gray silk tie and my platinum Rolex watch on my wrist.

The man opened his mouth, as I guess my package poking through my shorts might have shocked him. "Sir, I'm sorry—"

I gripped his shoulder. "Listen. Like I said before, I'm here to have a nice dinner with my wife. The kids picked this out for me to wear, and I am anxious to see a smile on her face." I knew this wouldn't be easy, so I reached into my coat pocket. I pulled out ten $100 bills. "Here, take this and go buy yourself something nice. If anybody got a problem with me, see what you can do."

He put the money in his pocket and extended his hand. "Follow me, sir. I hope you and your wife have a lovely dinner, and I will send a complimentary bottle of wine to your table."

That's what I thought. The manager walked me toward the table, where I could see Nokea from a distance. She looked glamorous in her red pantsuit, as she had definitely gone all out for our date. She saw us coming and her eyes widened. People were no doubt checking out my socks and sandals, but I paid no mind to the whispers. I eased into the booth across from Nokea;

all she did was stare at me. The manager reminded me about the bottle of wine and left us in peace.

"Jaylin Rogers," she said, "what in the heck do you have on?"

I unbuttoned my coat and straightened the tie around my neck. "Do you like it?" She didn't respond, just sat in awe. "LJ picked out my boxers, Jaylene picked out the socks and sandals; Mackenzie picked out the coat." I raised my sleeve and tapped my watch. "Justin picked out the watch. Wouldn't you say that they have damn good taste?"

Nokea laughed, and that was my only intention.

"Good thing they didn't pick out a set of bra and panties. I guess you would have come in that too?"

I told Nokea that was taking things too far, and we both agreed. She couldn't believe that I sat through dinner dressed as I was. When another man in the restaurant asked where I'd gotten my sandals, I told him. His wife looked at him like he was crazy, and she hurried him out of the restaurant.

After Nokea and I shared an enjoyable dinner, we left. I had other plans, so I asked her to follow me in her truck. She did.

When I parked in front of a storefront location that was empty, she got out of her truck, inquiring about where we were.

I removed a key from my pocket to open the door. "Just come inside with me for a while."

When we got inside, the nearly 6,000-foot space was empty. The tall white walls were bare, and the marble flooring I'd recently had put down was perfect. In the middle of the floor sat a rug, two plush silk pillows, a bottle of wine and two champagne glasses. A huge box wrapped with a pink bow was nearby, and petals from pink and white roses circled the sitting area. I took Nokea's hand, but she looked skeptical.

"I don't understand. What's this all about?" she asked.

"Come over here with me and have a seat. Then I'll tell you."

We walked to the sitting area and sat back on the square pillows. "If you don't mind," I said, removing my coat. "It's getting hot in this coat and I want to get comfortable."

Nokea looked at me in my boxers, tie and socks. She smiled. "Maybe you should remove the tie too."

I took off the tie and, just for the hell of it, the socks too. I sat back on the pillow directly across from Nokea, looking in her direction.

"Are you comfortable?" I asked.

"Yes," she said, looking around at the huge open space. "But, what—"

"Just hear me out, okay?"

She nodded. I took a deep breath and began to tell Nokea about this place.

"About two months ago, I found this place and purchased it for you. I was surprised by how quickly you jumped back into work. I know you're taking this time away from me to gain your independence, but it bothers me to see you working to build a future for someone else. I know how much of a hard worker you are, and there's no doubt in my mind that with your ideas, you'll take the company you work for to new heights. If you're going to work, I'd rather see you working for yourself. Doing something that you enjoy and making as much money as you desire. Do you remember telling me, when we were growing up, about all that you wanted to do in life?"

Nokea nodded and looked down at her lap. "Yes, I remember. I wanted to design my own line of clothing and have fashion shows complete with runway models. I also wanted to come up with a perfume fragrance that would have women flocking to stores to get it, remember? I talked about having a dance studio and—and I also wanted to teach dance. There were so many things that I talked to you about; but then, life happened, and none of that seemed possible."

I moved over and sat next to Nokea. I took her hand, kissing the back of it. "It was all possible, but something happened."

"Something like what? What happened, Jaylin? Tell me."

"I can show you better than I can tell you."

Nokea looked puzzled as I moved behind her. My legs were straddling her and I put my arms around her waist.

"What are you doing?" she asked, smiling.

"Just pay attention. Hold your arms up like you're driving. Keep your hands tight on the steering wheel and I'm going to help you hold it."

Nokea lifted her arms, pretending that she was holding a steering wheel. I did the same, but my hands were on top of hers. I whispered in her ear, "Who's driving this car, me or you?"

"You are. Your grip on my hands . . . Well, the steering wheel is so tight and our hands are moving in your direction."

"That's right," I said, moving the steering wheel in the direction that I wanted it to go. "For so long, you've allowed me to drive this relationship. And guess what? I drove us into a ditch. When you let other people drive your life, that's what happens. Now I'm gon' let go of the steering wheel. But before I do, I'm gon' help you get out of the ditch. Most men ain't gon' do that, and they gon' leave you in that muthafucka until you figure a way out. However, I'm a nice . . . very nice and decent man. If I get you in a mess, I will do my best to get you

out. Afterward, I'ma let you drive. Do you think you
can handle it?"

Nokea blushed. "I know I can."

"Are you sure?"

"Positive."

I let go of the steering wheel and Nokea continued to
hold her arms up as if driving. She was cutting corners
and running over people in her way. "Damn, girl, look
at you do your thing. There you go. Now, go tackle all
of those things in life that you wanted to do, as each
and every one of them is possible. Hold on tight to that
wheel and never turn it over to another driver again.
Especially not me, because I can be reckless behind the
wheel."

She dropped her arms and laughed. "Oh, don't I
know it! Very reckless."

"I didn't ask for your two cents, but the truth is the
truth. I accept it. My point is . . . I know you had a
chance to talk to Nanny B, and she was so right. What
happened was, you stopped dreaming and you put me
in the driver's seat of your life. It became all about me,
and you spent years and years, trying to do right by me
and putting up with my bullshit. Instead of being the
kind of husband who motivated you, yet again, I managed to become a setback for you. I regret that, and I'm
never going to let you forget about your dreams again.
I thought about what you said at your condo the day
I confronted you about the baby. You gave me everything that you could, and yet I failed you.

"Now I have to suffer the consequences behind that,
but I don't want you to suffer anymore. I want you to
live out your life as you wish and bring your life full circle. Bring this place alive, you hear me. Whatever you
want to do, the sky is the limit. Come up with a business plan and incorporate Jaylene into your dreams.
Teach her how to become independent and strong. En-

courage her to follow her dreams, not someone else's.
If you lead, she will follow."

Nokea sat in silence for a while; then she turned
around to face me. "I agree. And what else can I say but
you're right. As for you failing me, I wouldn't necessarily say it like that, but you did disappoint me. I never
thought we'd be here and—"

I touched the side of Nokea's face. "Baby, I disappointed myself even more. And through all of this, I
learned more about me and you."

Nokea smiled. "Like what? What did you learn from
this?"

I got comfortable and laid my head on Nokea's lap.
She lay back on the pillow and started rubbing her
fingers through my hair. "I love it when you do that," I
said, referring to the way she touched my hair. "I realized some of the reasons behind my selfish and controlling ways. I think I figured out how to overcome, and it
starts with you."

"How so?"

"When I look back on my life, Nokea, I see myself as
an only child. Anything I wanted, my mother did her
best to get it for me. When she was killed, I had to fend
for myself. I was only nine years old. I had to think
of ways that I could make my life better. When my
grandfather's money came along, I jumped into this
all-about-me mode, and it worked well for me. I paid
for college; I bought my first house; I found the best job
ever. . . . I basically took care of everything. As far as I
was concerned, nobody could enhance my life, as I had
done it for myself. When the women started to come
along, I felt as if all they could give me was sex.

"With you, I had a lifelong friendship that I felt
would be with me forever, no matter what! As time
went on, sadly, I took advantage of that. I could never
get out of this all-about-me mode. For a man who has

had control over everything around him, it's been so
difficult to allow someone to come in and make decisions about my life. Married or not, I wanted my way,
because in the past, my way got me everything in life
that I needed. Now my selfish way of thinking has finally caught up with me. I've lost the most important
person in my life. For the first time, I have no control
over what will ultimately happen between us. You'll decide, and our future is in your hands. I feel good about
this, because I've gotten to the point where I can allow
myself to step back. I'm not going to pressure you, and
I want you to take as much time as you need to figure
out what is right for you. You know what I want. For
me to say what I want doesn't matter, that's a big step
for me."

"Huge step," Nokea added.

"Okay, huge step. But it's up to you, baby. And whatever you decide, if it's not in my best interest, I just
have to live with it."

"At this point, what is it that you want?"

"I want you to move back home and live out the rest
of your life with me. I want to cuddle and make love to
you every single day, and I want us to raise our children
together. I want you to have more of my babies, and for
us to someday move into an even bigger house than the
one we already have. I want us to be happy again, and I
want you to trust everything there is about me, feeling
as if I have your back and knowing that I will always
have your best interest at heart. I'm aware that you still
have issues with Scorpio, but I will give you the key to
her place, her address and her phone number. I have
nothing to hide anymore. If you ever think I'm doing
something behind your back, you can go see for yourself. Our recent connection has been more so about
Justin and Mackenzie. I need my children in my life,

and Scorpio just happens to be their mother. I know all of that may take some time to swallow, but those, indeed, are my wishes. What do you want?"

Nokea sat silently again. She looked up at the high, blank, vaulted ceiling and closed her eyes. "Right now, I want a friendship with you that can be respected, no matter what the future holds for us. I want to get my business off the ground, take care of my children and simply be happy. What you want will take some time. Even though I would love to give you everything that you want right now, I have to be realistic. You hurt me bad, Jaylin. More than you had ever done in your life, and I'm going through the healing process right now. I still do not trust you. Every time you mention Scorpio's name, I get uneasy. I don't like that feeling. Once things settle down, I can't predict where things will stand. I do still love you, though, and the true words from my heart are all that I can offer to you right now.

"As we both continue to deal with this, I would like for you to think about seeing a counselor. You know . . . someone you can talk to, other than me, Nanny B or Shane. It may help, and I think there are still some things about your past you're not dealing with. Like the loss of your mother, and then your father, as well as your daughter Jasmine and Stephon. You brush too much under the rug. I want you to start dealing with some of the hurt that is inside you. I know how you feel about counseling, but maybe it will help."

I listened and considered for a moment before answering. "I'll think about it. And pertaining to us, knowing that you still love me will have to be enough to get me through my difficult days ahead without you." I lifted my head to peck Nokea's lips. Afterward, I sat up and started to pour our wine so we could toast to new beginnings.

"What's in the box?" Nokea asked.

"Open it and see," I suggested.

She opened the box and pulled out the colored architectural designs Shane had sketched for her new clothing store. He hooked up the design with everything from the dressing rooms to the sitting areas. An oval counter was in the middle of the floor, and racks, as well as shelving spaces, were sketched out too. Even the two huge bay windows in the front were decked out with pink-and-green awnings, which had Nokea's name scripted on them. I had an awesome vision of what her place would look like, and I figured she'd choose something pertaining to fashion.

"So what do you think?" I asked, giving her a glass of wine.

She smiled. "Since you've been in control of this, I think your ideas were well thought out."

I pointed to my chest. "Who me? I won't be in control, you'll be. I was just trying to help. If you want to scrap the whole thing, you can. Come up with your own ideas, and you can do whatever you want to do with this place. Hell, open up a strip club, for all I care, as long as it's yours."

She chuckled. "No, I won't be doing that, but I—I do like—love—the design Shane created. Thank you so much. I already have a vision of what this place will look like in less than a year."

This time, Nokea leaned forward and kissed me. As the kiss intensified, I lay back and she rested her body on top of mine. "By any chance, are we visualizing the same thing right now?" I asked.

"We're always on the same page, aren't we?"

"I hope so. I know we're not married anymore, but I hope I can still get it at least once or twice a week. Is that possible?"

Nokea rubbed her nose against mine. "No way. Maybe once a month, but definitely not once or twice a week."

"Damn. You drive a hard bargain. And if you minimize me to once a month, all I can do is feel sorry for you. You are going to need an ice pack for that pussy, and our time together will be nothing pretty."

"Yes, it will. And just like tonight, I'm going to look forward to many interesting days ahead to come."

I eased up, reaching into the pocket of my trench coat. I gave Nokea a suede black box. She looked at it, already knowing what was inside. "I don't know what you've done with your wedding ring, but I suspect that it may be somewhere in the trash. I'm never going to take off my ring. Whenever you're ready, I want you to put this back on and wear it. Can you do that for me, please?"

Nokea opened the box and was hit with the sparkle from a 5.5-carat radiant-cut diamond ring, which was even bigger than the one she'd had before. I knew the size of the diamond never mattered much to her, but it did to me. She was so deserving.

"You know you didn't have to do this. And why would you waste your money on something like this when all I ever wanted was to—"

I placed my fingers on her lips. "I know what you're getting ready to say. I just want you to wear it. Every time you look at it, it will remind you of the many wonderful times we've had in the past, as well as what's coming in our future. We've come a long way, baby, and we still have a longer way to go together."

Nokea bit her bottom lip and sighed. "Again, I'm well aware of what you want, but don't forget about what I want. I will put this on *if* or *whenever* I'm ready. The last thing I want to do is hurt your feelings."

"I understand. Just keep it, and I know you'll take good care of it."

"I will," Nokea said, standing up. She reached for my hand. "Come on, let's go. I want to go somewhere and have some laugh-out-loud fun. What about you?"

"I thought we were getting ready to," I said, standing up. "What about—"

This time, Nokea put her fingers on my lips. "We'll get to that real soon. You being inside me makes me so emotional. Even though it's a good feeling, I don't want to express those kinds of emotions tonight."

"I know how that is, and I really meant what I said about this being your call. In the meantime, I know of an interesting place we can go. I may not be dressed for the occasion, but what the hell?"

After we gave a toast to new beginnings, we gathered our things and left. We went to a carnival that I had taken the kids to a while back. They had so much fun, and I figured that Nokea and I would too. We walked, arm in arm, licking an ice-cream cone and sharing cotton candy. I looked like a fool in 80-degree weather with my trench coat on, but I had my woman by my side and didn't care. I won two stuffed animals for her; and when we got on the Ferris wheel, Nokea laid her head on my shoulder. It really did feel like a first date for us, where I had a feeling that the woman I was with would one day become my wife.

"Are you enjoying our date so far?" I asked.

"Yep. And you really seem like a nice man."

"That's because I am. I meant to tell you that I already got five kids, but the fifth one I can't seem to find. I hate it too, but I guess it's something that I'll have to live with. Six . . . seven kids, I think, is my lucky number. I may decide to quit after that, and I hope you're interested in having some more babies with me."

"Well, this is only our first date, and I'm not trying to make a baby with someone I barely know. Let me get to know you for a while longer. After that, we'll see how it goes." Nokea paused and turned my face to hers. "I know your kids will give you everything you've always wanted, but I've been asking myself, 'Exactly where do I fit in?' It's so easy for you to say that you've forgiven me for what I did to our baby, but I know you, Jaylin. You'll hold it against me. Your children keep every breath in you, and they are the ones who make you whole. They basically have ownership of your heart. I have part of it, but not like they do. I have to decide if that will ever be enough for me."

In no way was I going to dispute what Nokea had said. Actually, Scorpio had said the same thing to me. My kids were my world. Now that I had them with me every single day of my life, I knew I couldn't go wrong. As the Ferris wheel spun around, I thought about how "day three" was already progressing.

Nokea spoke up about it before I did. "Day three, Mr. Rogers, and thus far, things are going pretty good. I would love for you to take me on another date, and I suspect it will be soon."

"You can bet it will be. But I hope I don't have to get you tipsy like you were the night before last. I wanted to choke you for thinking I was Shane. You'd better not be thinking about that fool like that, and I almost cut the action right then and there."

She laughed. "I knew exactly who you were. I was teasing you. I thought you'd get a kick out of what I'd said. Even if I were a bit confused, you quickly cleared that up for me."

"Go ahead and clean your shit up. That was pretty good, but I'll give you a pass on that, since you brought me back to life that night. I was like a kid in the candy store and I've been on a major high ever since."

Nokea laughed and put up two fingers. "Two kids in a candy store. It was definitely a night to remember."

We continued to go round and round on the Ferris wheel, laughing and talking as if our lives had not missed one beat. Afterward, I walked Nokea to her truck and put her stuffed animals in the backseat. She told me that she didn't want me to come to her place, but she agreed to go on another date soon. I was cool with that. After one last good-night kiss, I watched as she drove away.

The next morning, I was knocked out in my bed, resting peacefully. I'd been sleeping pretty well lately. In my sleep, I was thinking about my date with Nokea. I tossed and turned in my bed. When I felt someone lick my face, I smiled. I just knew it was her, telling me she was moving back in and trying to wake me from my sleep.

"Stop it, girl," I moaned. "Stop kissing on me like that." The licks continued, but they became a little annoying. "Baby, is that your breath smelling like that? Something ain't right with it."

When I heard a growl, I jumped from my sleep. I quickly sat up, only to see a dog in bed next to me. It was an enormous mastiff that was sitting with its tongue hanging out of its mouth, occasionally barking.

"Since when did we get a dog!" I yelled, and pounded my fist on the bed. "Who let this gotdamn dog in the house! Whoever did it, there will damn sure be repercussions!"

The dog jumped off my bed, and hiked up his leg to pee on the side of it. "Hell nah," I said, tossing off the covers. From the other side of my bed, I saw Jaylene ease her head up and peek over the bed.

"Are you the one responsible for this?" I asked in a higher pitch. "Where in the hell did you get that dog from?"

She climbed up onto the bed, lying next to me and batting her adorable eyes. "I found him outside, Daddy. Can we keep him, please? His name is Bo-Bo."

"How do you know what his name is?"

She shrugged and held out her hands. "It's what I named him. Can I keep him?"

I put my hand on my forehead and squeezed it. If the dog didn't have an owner, it was obvious that we would be adding him to our family soon. Damn, I really had to man up when it came to my kids. No doubt. I put Jaylene on my back and we headed out of the room to find Bo-Bo. I was hooked like I never thought I'd be. No matter what happened in Jaylin's World in the future, I had the loves of my life forever with me. My kids.

Eventually I took Nokea's advice about going to see a counselor. Maybe I did have some issues that I hadn't addressed, and they were affecting some of the unfortunate things about me: things that related to my feelings for women in general, how I really felt about the loss of my mother and how much I'd hated Simone for disappearing with my daughter. My time in the orphanage had affected me more than I was willing to admit, so I found a brotha to talk to who came highly recommended by Tiffanie. She said that she'd seen him before, and mentioned how easy he was to talk to. I got out of my new Aston Martin, dressed in a sheer button-down white shirt and dark jeans. My eyes were hidden behind my dark shades, and the expensive cologne I wore was a head turner. When I entered the counselor's office, the bubbly receptionist greeted me with a bright smile. I looked at my Rolex; it was almost three o'clock.

"I'm here to see Mr. Moore. My name, Jaylin Rogers."

"Have a seat, Mr. Rogers. I'll let him know you're here."

I took a seat in one of the three fancy black leather chairs, resting my elbows on my knees. I couldn't believe I was about to do this. Putting my business out there to someone I didn't know would be tough. Even I had to admit that I'd been holding in a lot of things that needed to come out. I would do whatever to make things right with Nokea, and this, indeed, was a start. I knew it would also help me too, so what the hell? Before I could pick up the sports magazine next to me, Mr. Moore came out to greet me. He was tall, almost like a basketball player. Had a bald head, with a dark complexion. He looked to be about my age, so I immediately felt at ease.

"Jaylin," he said, holding his hand out for me to shake it. I stood to shake his hand.

"Yes, Mr. Moore. I'm delighted to meet you."

He smiled. "Delvin. Feel free to call me Delvin."

I nodded and we headed back to his office. As soon as we entered, he took a seat behind his glass-topped square desk, neat as a pin. A wedding picture of him and his wife was on top of it, as well as a picture of a boy, who I assumed was his son. He asked me to have a seat on the leather burgundy chaise in front of his desk, so I did.

"Feel free to get comfortable," Delvin said. "And can I get you anything before we get started? Water, juice, tea?"

Feeling a little uneasy, I removed my shades and started to rub my goatee softly. "Nah, I'm good. Thanks, though."

Delvin first gave me at least a half-hour spill about who he was and how he could help me. We discussed his fees, along with more of his credentials. I was impressed, not only by him, but also by the numerous plaques hanging on his walls from accomplishments. I started to feel comfortable, so I sat back on the chaise with my arms resting on top of it.

"So," Delvin said, "let's talk and be as honest as you can about your answers. We'll start with your marriage, since you mentioned that a little bit on the phone. Are you still married?"

"I am; she's not."

He smiled. "Legally?"

"Legally I'm still married; in her mind, she's not."

"So, realistically, legally you're divorced; in your mind, you're not."

"Let's sum this up and move on. I'm still married to my wife, and will always be."

He paused for a moment, writing something on the paper in front of him. "Tell me how you feel about your control issues, Jaylin."

I shrugged. "What about them?"

"I mean, some men like you, with power and money, tend to feel as if they can control everyone and everything around them. Specifically, their women. And when they are the sole providers, these men often feel as if they have a right to do whatever they wish. Do you see where I'm going with this?"

"I see exactly where you're going, and I will admit that your statement applies to me. But let's just say I'm working on it, because having that mentality has caused me some setbacks."

"Well, at least you recognize it. And would you say your ways are more narcissistic too?"

"That will be for you to determine. For now, I'll just say that I control what I can, and it bothers me if I can't."

"So you're stuck on this 'your way or no way' mentality?"

"Exactly."

"What does that stem from?"

I shrugged again. "Don't know. That's why I'm here."

"Then let's see if we can get to the root of the problem. Tell me about your past. Mainly about your mother, father, siblings, et cetera."

"Mother was killed; father died a few years back. I have stepsiblings, and I don't know much about them."

"How did you feel when you lost your parents?"

"That's a stupid-ass question. How would one feel about losing their parents?"

He laid his pen down. "Not all people are saddened by the loss of a parent. My question is how did you deal with it?"

"I didn't. After my mother was killed, I had bigger fish to fry. Went into survival mode and had to man up at an early age. As for my father, after my mother was killed, he jetted. His death, however, was a disappointment."

"How was your mother killed and was her killer or killers ever found?"

"Found and convicted, but I don't wish to get into the details about what he did to her. Too painful."

"Talking about it may help, but when she was killed, whom did you live with? A family member?"

My mind traveled back to living in that orphanage. It was so lonely there, and I hated it. I had a hard time coping with the loss of my mother, but a lady named Nadine was so nice to me. Or so I thought. She was the first person who gave me oral sex and asked me to perform on her. Had to be at least in her late twenties and I had fallen head over heels for her. Next thing I knew, many of the other boys were saying things about her and she got fired. As the years went on, I felt guilty

about what I had done to her, and about what I allowed
her to do to me. I knew it was wrong, but I never said a
word to anyone.

"I lived in an orphanage for a while and disliked it.
Then I moved in with my aunt Betty."

"How was she?"

"She was a bitch. Didn't care much for her."

"Why not?"

"She was abusive and I don't do drug addicts."

He smirked. "I can understand that, but, uh, do me a
favor and go back to when you were in the orphanage.
I know you disliked it, but why?"

I sighed. "Because I preferred to be in a home with
my mother."

"Did you ever feel as if even though your mother was
killed, it was somehow her fault that you were sent to
an orphanage?"

"Sometimes. More so when I was a child."

"What about any mother figures at the orphanage?
Did you cling to anyone in particular that helped you
cope with your pain?"

"No. I did have sex with one of the staff members,
but she was fired."

"So, are you saying you were molested by—"

"Correction, it was consensual. I didn't mind at all.
The oral sex felt good, and what she did to me helped
me forget about some pain I was going through."

"But you were only a child, and she was an adult. You
were probably too young to understand—"

"I know where you're going with this, but nobody
did anything to me that I didn't want them to do. Let's
move on."

He wrote something on his paper; then he cleared
his throat. "How do you feel about women, Jaylin?
Then tell me about your ex-wife."

Delvin's referring to Nokea as my "ex-wife" was starting to upset me. I made it clear that she was in no way my *ex*. "I feel ecstatic about women, especially *my wife*. I guess the only woman I may currently have some anger toward is my oldest daughter's mother, Simone, who jetted years ago with my daughter. I haven't seen her since she was one. Other than that, I'm delighted that women can give me babies, and something about that just impresses the hell out of me."

"What if they can't give you a baby? Do you still find them useful?"

"Of course."

"Then let's talk infidelity issues. Did you have them in your *now* ex-marriage?"

Strike two, I thought. Throwing this *ex* thing up wasn't working for me. "Minimal infidelity issues. With an ex that I still had some feelings for. She had my baby, and the news shook up some things in my marriage."

"I'm sure it did. But why wasn't that child conceived with your wife? Can she have children?"

I paused, thinking about Nokea being unable to conceive a child. Yeah, it had been upsetting to me, but I never saw it as a reason to get back with Scorpio. "My wife and I have two beautiful children. She had an incident that prohibited her from having any more children, or so we thought. She's all good now, and I know she can conceive another child."

"So when you thought she couldn't have any more children, you strayed?"

"That's not the reason behind my infidelity issues."

"Are you sure about that? I mean, you said, and I quote, 'I'm delighted that women can give me babies.' Maybe you weren't excited about your marriage because you thought your wife couldn't conceive any more children."

I shrugged. "Maybe. Maybe not. Let's move on."

Delvin sighed. "Okay, Jaylin. You say you're ecstatic about women; yet for years, you felt as if your mother left you behind. You hated your aunt for being abusive, and you were molested by a woman who worked at an orphanage. Thoughts of Simone still upset you. Could it be possible that you've made the woman whom you say you love pay for what these other women have done to you? If so, you have to let all of that go, or else you will run her completely away, if you already haven't. Sometimes we hurt the ones we love the most, especially when we don't understand or recognize where the hurt inside us comes from. Do you get what I'm saying?"

I had no words, for everything he'd said to me was possible. Could I have made my loving wife pay for the hurt I had felt deep inside from others? The thought of it just tore me apart.

Delvin took a moment to jot some things on paper. I sat, thinking more about what he'd implied. The shit did make sense. In addition to that, I had given up too soon on Nokea having my baby, even though it was my fault that she couldn't. Damn . . . this was so fucked up.

"Jaylin, I'm going to pencil you in for next week. I think that's enough for today. When you come back, I'd like to talk more about your *ex*-wife and your mistress. We'll delve more into your background and . . ."

By this time, I was standing up. I put the palms of my hands on his desk, approaching him, man to half man. "For the record, I *won't* be coming back. And just as much as you can read me, I can read you too. As a client, who is adding to your wealth, if I tell you that my wife is no ex, then you need to accept what I say. If I tell you that it irks the hell out of me when a man does not look into my eyes and prefers to gaze between my legs, I mean it. . . . Your looks are disturbing to me and so are your greasy lips. And if I tell you that from a distance, I can see that you are only scribbling on your paper; then I'd have to also tell you to take your so-called evaluation and shove it up your loose ass. Now you've wasted enough of my time, and only because some of the shit you said made me think, please look forward to your check in the mail."

I snatched up my shades and covered my eyes with them. On my way to the door, Delvin called my name. I turned.

"Is there any way that we can do lunch? I used to feel the same way about men too, but you can't knock it if you haven't tried it. I'm just saying."

This motherfucker wasn't even worth my time. I cut my eyes, and kept it moving. By the time I reached my car, I had my cell phone in my hand.

"Hello," Nanny B answered.

"Say, we need to talk. I want to share some things with you and I need your advice."

"Sure. Where are you?"

"I'm on my way home."

"Okay. I just finished dinner, and it's your favorite."

I smiled. "Thank you. I love you, and I'll see you soon."

"With all of my heart, I love you too."

I shut my phone. Who in the hell thought I needed a counselor when I had Nanny B? I couldn't wait to tell Nokea about my visit today, and more than anything, I hoped that the explanation for some of my actions would be good enough for her. No . . . not good enough for anyone else, but definitely for her. After all, she was the only one who mattered.

Epilogue
NOKEA

A year ago, if someone had told me this is where my life would be, I wouldn't have believed them. If I was told I'd be able to heal from the hurt that was dealt to me, I would have suggested, "Never." Yesterday I cut the ribbon for the grand opening at Nokea's Place. The place was packed with people who wanted to come out and see my new clothing line I'd specifically designed for classy women.

While others browsed around, I stood by the dressing rooms, waiting for one of my customers to come out. She was trying on an after-five black silk dress I'd designed. It had a hint of lace around the neckline. I was anxious to see how it looked on her. She came out with her hands on her hips, smiling and looking spectacular as ever. Many people crowded around her, sharing how the dress made her look so fabulous.

"You have never looked that good," a friend of hers said, and laughed. "If you don't buy it, I'm buying it for you."

The lady turned around, while observing herself in the oval mirror in front of her. "Oh, I'm buying this, so you don't have to buy me anything. This is beautiful, and it is unlike any dress I've ever tried to squeeze these hips into."

I was overjoyed by the glee in the woman's eyes. I finally felt that my life was coming full circle. My assistant told the woman she would bring her some other items to try on. That's when I stepped behind one of the decorative tables that held an array of my fragrance line called Jaylene's.

"You have got to sample this," I said, spraying a dash of the perfume and applying lotion on the wrists of several of the ladies in front of me. The sweet fragrance lit up the air. Yet again, the women loved it!

"That smells awesome," one woman said. "I'm going to get the complete set for my sisters and my mother."

"Yay," Jaylene and Mackenzie said in unison, standing next to me and high-fiving each other.

The women laughed and congratulated us on our success. Jaylene had been such a big help to me; and surprisingly, so had Mackenzie. She and Jaylene had gotten so close, you would never see one of them without the other. They had this big/little sister thing going on that turned out to be a beautiful thing. Mackenzie was into the clothing thing like me, and instead of adding her name to the fragrance line, we were in the process of creating a girls clothing line just for her. I named it Kenzie Wear and she helped me come up with a dazzling line of clothes for girls from eight to twelve. We had a lot of outside help too, and the seven people whom I hired worked tirelessly to help me pull this off. They remained as my staff, and I couldn't have made it through this whole process without them.

Another person I couldn't have done this without was, of course, Jaylin. He was so supportive of my ideas. He sat in one of the leather chairs, staring at me, and the look in his eyes said it all. I strutted over to him and took a seat.

"Why are you watching my every move?" I asked, smiling.

"Because I'm so proud of you, baby. I knew you could do it. Life may have had some setbacks, but remember, setbacks are always setups for bigger and better things to come."

I couldn't have agreed with Jaylin more; he was so right. He'd given me all of the space I needed to get this done, and not once did he demand anything from me. He was ecstatic about my growing relationship with Mackenzie. When it came to Justin, as expected, I still had some work to do. The only way for me to get past all of the hurt that I had built up inside me was to forgive Jaylin. I'd made myself miserable by being so bitter and unforgiving. Being that way was so out of character for me; but at the time, I didn't see how it was affecting me. My healing began right after I sat down with Jaylin at dinner one day, pouring my heart out to him about how I truly felt about his betrayal.

He continued to apologize, and he tried to explain how being constantly approached by women was challenging. According to him, he had done his best to remain faithful, and loving me had helped, or so he'd thought. I reminded him how challenging being his wife was as well. It was so hard loving a man who was desired by many. Even though I felt confident about myself, I knew there were plenty of women who would do anything for him.

That day, I told Jaylin the truth. I didn't trust his relationship with Scorpio, and I could never handle being Nokea Rogers again. Those shoes were, and had always been, too big to fill. He was so worried about me being with someone else, or seeking revenge; but running to another man, as I had done with Collins, had never crossed my mind. I had done that before and had hurt a man who in no way deserved it. Maybe it was Karma finding its way back to me? Either way, this time, I realized that I didn't need another man to help clean up my mess, nor did I need one during my downtime to make me feel whole. I was surprised that I could go many

months without being with Jaylin, and it was obvious
that he needed me way more than I needed him.

Still, I kept thinking . . . if God could forgive Jaylin, why couldn't I? Besides, we had been through too
much for me to have any kind of hate for him inside
me. As I looked back on what had happened to us, I
felt grateful for our challenges. They had made me
stronger and wiser. They had made me realize that no
matter how perfect our lives might have looked on the
outside, our lives weren't exempt from challenges. Just
like a woman who lived in the ghetto, a woman with
a master's degree, or an athlete's wife with all of the
money she could spend . . . we could all find ourselves
in the same predicament. I tackled mine as best as I
could. For me, I now have no regrets.

Basically, I had to give up some things, in order to
gain a lot. I do believe that everything happens for a
reason. Had it not been for this last incident with Jaylin, I wasn't sure if I'd be in the position that I was in today. Now I felt free, and the only person's hands on the
steering wheel were mine! I was living my dream, and
my daughter had a mother she could look up to and be
proud of. I didn't have to live in Jaylin's World, unless
I wanted, and I had definitely created a world of my
own. For so long, I'd focused too much on what Jaylin
was doing, and should or could have been focused on
what I needed to do with my own life. My solution was
simple. . . . I had to remove him from the driver's seat,
find myself and live out my biggest dream. That kept
me busy and away from unnecessary foolishness.

I wasn't even sure about Jaylin's current status with
Scorpio; but to be honest with you, I didn't even care.
He'd made it his business to tell me that nothing was
going on. Also, the few times that I had spoken to Scorpio while Mackenzie was with me, Scorpio said that she
had gotten back to playwriting, something that she had

done aside from stripping, when she first met Jaylin. She was preparing herself to put some of her plays in production. According to her, she and Jaylin were only dealing with each other because of the children. She said that she'd been dating again, and spoke about how much she enjoyed living in Miami Beach, Florida. I rarely had much to say to her, but I always wished her well.

I had no clue how the dating thing had gone over with Jaylin, but he knew better than to say anything to me about it. I was in a different place in my life, and he was aware that none of that mattered to me anymore. He seemed pretty upbeat, and most of his time was dedicated to his children, especially his sons. They went everywhere with Jaylin, and so did Shane and his son. They were all about making money, and I had never seen a team of men who were so ambitious. That was a good thing, and I don't think people gave enough credit to the black men of the world like them, who took care of their children and provided for their families. That's what I loved about Jaylin the most, and it was that side of him that I would love forever.

As for our relationship, well . . . I was still living apart from him. I wasn't wearing my wedding ring and, for now, that's what I wanted. Forgiving him didn't mean that I had to forget. Trust was something that had to be earned, and it didn't come by someone just saying that you could trust them. I was well aware that Jaylin had some issues from his past that he had failed to deal with; he needed to correct those more for himself and not so much for me.

He seemed to be on a path to recovery and I was glad about that. Jaylin's recognizing his own faults made it easier to be around him; and because of our children, we continued to spend an enormous amount of time together. There was never a chance that we'd go one

day without seeing or talking to each other. I was still
so deeply in love with Jaylin. Whenever I needed a
laugh, a friend or a shoulder to cry on, he was there.
If I had a sexual urge, I could always count on him to
satisfy my needs. Yeah, it was going down whenever I
wanted it to, and making love to him was something I
didn't want to depart with.

Right after the opening celebration and evening ceremony was over last night, Jaylin and I went back to
my condo and celebrated alone. Our evening together
was so perfect; in the morning, I stood looking out the
picture window, thinking about us slow dancing last
night in pure darkness. It was as if the earth had stood
still. One slow jam after another, we embraced each
other in silence. We didn't even get a chance to make
love, but that was fine by me.

Thoughts of our long lives together consumed our
minds and we both accepted that this was ultimately
where our journey together had led us. As I continued
in thought, Jaylin came up from behind, dressed in
his black silk pajama pants that tied at his waist. He
wrapped his arms around me, kissing my cheek.

"What's for breakfast?" he asked. "Or do we even
care right now?"

I turned, placing my arms on his shoulders and looking into his eyes. We hadn't had sex in almost a month,
but I always looked forward to being intimate with the
love of my life. "I'm a little hungry too," I said. "Do you
have any suggestions?"

"Plenty."

We smiled, backing up to the bed and laughing as
we plopped down on it. Many things in our lives had
changed. At the end of the day, however, the love that

we carried in our hearts for each other would always remain the same.

Jaylin halted our kisses and got up from the bed. I sat up on my elbows, watching him close the door. Not only the door to my bedroom, but the door to *his* world as well. Finally he was willing to step into *our* world, a world that was pieced back together as best as we both could do it!

Epilogue
JAYLIN

Yeah, yeah, I know. A book ain't supposed to have two epilogues, but that was Nokea's take on things, here's mine. You ever hear the saying "You never miss a good thing until it's gone"?

Well, many of us can say that, and I'm sure there are those who look back at their past relationships, wishing they had done things differently. That's the case with me. If I could turn back the hands of time, yes, I would have made better choices. At this point, Nokea wasn't gone completely, but in no way was I 100 percent satisfied with where things stood between us.

Simply put, I want my wife back; in no way was I giving up! At this point, I felt as if I was ready to be everything that she needed me to be. I had learned some important things over time; but the one thing that I know for sure is, I could not profess love for two women and make both of them happy. Someone had to lose, and it was only fair that it was me. Scorpio was busy doing her thing. Even though she claimed to be content with the way things were, I knew that she deserved better. I didn't know if she would ever find it, because it was pretty damn hard to top me. Either way, the door was opened for her to go after it, and I'd always given the ones I'd loved options.

Nokea seemed to be moving on as well. For now, I was learning to cope with her being away from me. I was lucky—damn lucky—that she was willing to give me any of her time at all. Bottom line is, I'd made my bed, and I had to be man enough to lie in it. Most of the time, alone, but I was still hopeful that my wife would one day come home, where she belonged.

I want some more of those babies too; I have to stay optimistic. With that, just wanted to thank readers for all of the love and I'm delighted to have gotten to know many of you on Facebook and through e-mails. The entire Naughty Series was based on many of my experiences, as well as the author's own life. Better than most, Brenda Hampton knows that sometimes life can be good . . . great, but it can also deal you a fucked-up hand.

When you throw a brotha like me in the mix, ain't no telling what can happen. Stay up, as your today doesn't dictate what your tomorrow will bring. Ask yourself, who is in the driver's seat of your life? Make sure it's you, and no one else!

I've enjoyed my part in all of this, but it's time for me to shut it down and move on to bigger and better things. I won't say good-bye, only say I'll someday see you at the movies, in a television series, play or on DVD.

Sounds good? Then make some noise with me; as I will tell you, the story goes on. Share the Naughty Series with everyone you know, and let's show the directors in Hollywood what's really up! Tell BET, Bounce TV, VH1, Bravo, OWN . . . all of the cable networks to get on it! I'm definitely up for the challenge. But when you think about it, haven't I always been?

My Naughty Angels in Jaylin's World on Facebook, y'all know we have shown our asses over the years. People have laughed at us, pointed fingers and even shook their heads with disgust. Many have joined us, though, and I couldn't have made it through my more challenging days without you ladies in my corner. I'm sure I have healed some aching and troubled hearts too. So what Facebook has joined together, let no one put asunder. With two fingers in the air, peace and, yes, All Love . . . Jay Baby.

Notes